W9-AMM-567

DARK OMENS

A perplexing new mystery for Libertus set amongst the backdrop of a Roman Britain in turmoil at the death of the Emperor...

Libertus accepts a contract to install a pavement for Genialis, a self-important citizen from a nearby town, in the house of the customer's intended but unwilling and young bride, Silvia. However, the winter is exceptionally severe, and although the mosaic is laid in time to earn the promised bonus, Genialis goes missing in the snow before payment can be made.

Meanwhile, at an important feast, the sacrifice is spoiled as an aged priest lets go of the sacrificial ram – and when news arrives that the Emperor is dead, it seems that these dark omens are being realised. The subsequent discovery of not one, but two mutilated corpses only adds to this. Who holds the answer to the mysteries? Everyone had motive; Libertus attempts to solve the mystery against a backdrop of superstitious fear of auguries, and public riots following the confirmation of the Emperor's death.

DARK OMENS

Rosemary Rowe

Severn House Large Print
London & New Year

This first large print edition published 2014
in Great Britain and the USA by
SEVERN HOUSE PUBLISHERS LTD of
19 Cedar Road, Sutton, Surrey, England, SM2 5DA.
First world regular print edition published 2013 by
Severn House Publishers Ltd., London and New York.

British Library Cataloguing in Publication Data

Rowe, Rosemary, 1942- author.
  Dark omens. -- Large print edition. -- (A Libertus mystery
  of Roman Britain ; 14)
  1. Libertus (Fictitious character : Rowe)--Fiction.
  2. Romans--Great Britain--Fiction. 3. Slaves--Fiction.
  4. Great Britain--History--Roman period, 55 B.C.-449
  A.D.--Fiction. 5. Detective and mystery stories. 6. Large
  type books.
  I. Title II. Series
  823.9'2-dc23

  ISBN-13: 9780727896889

Printed digitally in the USA

To Owen and Beryl

FOREWORD

The story begins in Glevum (Roman Glouces-
ter, a prosperous 'republic' and a colonia for
retired soldiery) on New Year's Day AD193.
The Kalends of January was perceived as a time
of new beginnings and – as today – an occasion
for good resolutions and wishes for good luck,
as well as little offerings to the two-headed god
Janus, for whom the month is named. Everyone
did an hour or two of token 'work', thus inviting fortune in the year ahead, and visited neighbours (as the tale suggests) for the exchange of
good wishes and symbolic sweetened gifts.

This particular Kalends, however, was a new
beginning in more ways than the citizens of
Britannia could have realized. Their province
was, as it had been for two centuries by now,
the most far-flung and northerly outpost of the
Roman Empire: occupied by Roman legions,
criss-crossed by Roman roads, subject to
Roman laws and administered by a provincial
governor answerable directly to Rome – and
thus ultimately to the Emperor himself. The
man who had worn the imperial purple for the
last twelve years was (to give him the full list of
titles he'd bestowed upon himself) Lucius

7

Aelius Aurelius Commodus Augustus Herculeus Romanus Exsuperatorius Amazonius Invictus Felix Pius, a megalomaniac who was by this time increasingly deranged, and whose lascivious lifestyle and capricious cruelties were infamous. Hated by many, he was fearful of his life, imagining conspiracies on every hand, in consequence of which he was popularly said to have 'spies in every house'.

However there was obviously cause for his mistrust since he was assassinated just around the time the story starts. There are many versions of exactly how and when he met his death – a popular myth (on which the film *Gladiator* was based) suggests that he was murdered at the New Year Games, in which he had certainly intended to take part, as he prided himself on his gladiatorial prowess, and exaggerated claims as to the numbers he had killed and the variety of animals that he had put to death – though detractors claim that his human opponents had been armed with wooden swords against his metal one, and the creatures had been helpfully dosed with opium.

Another account suggests that he was wounded by a poisoned blade, at a rehearsal bout the day before the games.

Most experts, however, are now agreed that he was murdered at his home on New Year's Eve – though (rather like Rasputin) he proved difficult to kill. It is likely that his sister had already ineffectually attempted to poison him that night, which he survived by vomiting his dinner up again, and he was finally strangled by an athlete-slave, with whom he used to practise wrestling, though even then there is dispute about whether this happened in his bed or at his bath. (Think Roman baths here, with plunge-pools, steam-rooms and a scrape-down afterwards, not a modern tub of soapy suds.)

It seems that differing rumours were circulating from the start, though all shared the central fact that Commodus was dead. The strength of his unpopularity can be gauged from the fact that the senate instantly declared that he was a public enemy (*damnatio*), denied him funeral, and tried to expunge his name from monuments. The ex-governor of Britannia, Pertinax – patron and friend of the fictional Marcus in this story – was nominated as successor and acclaimed within hours.

News spread like wildfire, as such things always do, and one ancient writer makes the boastful claim that 'news had spread to all parts of the Empire before the Agonalia' – the major festival of Janus and Fortuna on the ninth. Given the time of year and the condition of the roads, this frankly seems unlikely, but for the purposes of the story it is taken to be true – though even here it is assumed that later (written) confirmation would have been required, and it is the arrival of this which sparks the riot in the book. There is no evidence that there were actually disturbances of this kind in Glevum and though fragments of an outsized stone figure were unearthed during excavations in the mid-twentieth century, there is nothing to suggest that it depicted Commodus or that it was deliberately destroyed. However, public demonstrations are attested in several places elsewhere in the Empire, including the pulling down of statues of the fallen Emperor.

Nor is there any evidence that the weather at the time was especially severe, in the way depicted in the book, although the effects described are based on genuine accounts of other bitter winters experienced elsewhere. Travel on icy roads was difficult. Dorn, a town which is mentioned in the text, was a small but significant settlement at the time, a centre for the gathering of tax, but is now a mere hamlet, scarcely mentioned on the map, a mile or two from Moreton-on-the-Marsh. Glevum was a much more important town: its historic status as a 'colonia' for retired legionaries gave it special privileges, and all freemen born within its walls were citizens by right. However, this coveted status, though it conferred prestige and legal rights, was no guarantee of wealth, and those who gained the rank merely by this accident of birth might well be struggling – like the farmer Cantalarius in the tale.

Most inhabitants of Glevum, however, were not citizens at all. Many were freemen, born outside the walls, scratching a more or less precarious living from a trade. Lucius, in the story, is a successful example of this type of man, with a flourishing import-export business at the docks, but others – like the tanner – led less salubrious lives. Hundreds more were slaves – what Aristotle once described as 'vocal tools' – mere chattels of their masters, to be bought and sold, with no more rights or status than any other domestic animal. Some slaves led pitiable lives, but others were highly regarded by their owners, and might be treated well. A slave in a kindly household, with a comfortable home, might have a more enviable lot than many a poor freeman struggling to eke out an existence in a squalid hut.

Power, of course, was vested almost entirely in men. Although individual women might inherit large estates, and many wielded considerable influence within the house, daughters were not much valued, except as potential wives and mothers, whereas sons were the source of pride. Indeed, a widow of a rich man who produced no surviving male might well be seen as a lucrative speculation for a prospective groom, who would then have rights to use the profits from her dowry (and inheritance) as his own, though she was entitled to the capital if he divorced her later on. A woman (of any age) was deemed a child in law, and lacking a father or male relative, would need a guardian. (Marriage and motherhood were the only realistic goals for well-bred women, although tradesmen's wives and daughters often worked beside their men and in the poorest households everybody toiled.)

People of both sexes and from all walks of life were much concerned with omens at this time –

though, as the story suggests, women were viewed as the more superstitious sex. Roman gods had temples in every major town and public attendance at some rituals – including the Imperial Birthday feast – was compulsory. Curse and prayer tablets were regularly offered at the shrines, as surviving examples indicate, and there were special officials at the temple whose function was to consult the auguries, or read the entrails, and ensure that sacrifices met the approval of the gods. The slightest deviation from proper ritual could mean that the offering was void and the entire ritual must be begun again, for fear of offending the Roman deities.

Most townspeople had recognized the Roman gods by now, but all the same a number of local gods survived, and were openly worshipped by their followers, often in conjunction with the Roman ones. In fact, the authorities officially declared quite a number of these Celtic deities to be manifestations of some member of the Roman pantheon – often Mars Lenis, as in this narrative – and the sacred places and shrines were recognized and adopted accordingly. Of course, a few rebellious souls still clung to ancient ways and followed Druid customs, though only secretly: the sect had been formally outlawed by the state because of its practice of human sacrifice, and the hanging of the severed heads of enemies (including Romans) as a grisly offering in the sacred groves of oak. (This was the 'forbidden religion' at this period: the few Christians – and it appears there were some in Glevum at the time – were regarded with a mixture of contempt and tolerance.)

The rest of the Romano-British background to this book has been derived from a variety of (sometimes contradictory) pictorial and written sources, as well as artefacts. However, although I have done my best to create an accurate picture, this remains a work of fiction, and there is no claim to total academic authenticity. Commodus and Pertinax are historically attested, as is the existence and basic geography of Glevum. The rest is the product of my imagination.

Relata refero. Ne Iupiter quidem omnibus placet. I only tell you what I heard. Jove himself can't please everybody.

ONE

I spent the first part of the Kalends of Januarius in my mosaic workshop in the town – just as everyone in any kind of business always did. After all, the dual-faced deity is the first to be called upon in any invocation of the gods and anything you wish to have his blessing on should – according to custom – be conducted a little for his benefit on the first day of the year.

Not that I was really doing any work. My adopted son and I were wearing togas, for one thing, in honour of the day – and that is not a garment which allows much in the way of physical exertion, as any unconsidered move is likely to bring it snaking down in unfolded coils around your feet, quite apart from needing laundering at the slightest smudge. So we two were simply making a pretence at sorting out the stocks of coloured stone while my two young red-headed slaves swept down the floor and tended to the fire.

'Happy Kalends!' That was the surly candle-maker from next door, popping his head around the inner door with a traditional gift of honeyed figs. Even he had managed to fix a smile upon his face today. 'I shan't say "of Januarius" – in case one of your servants is an Imperial spy.'

That was unlikely, as he full well knew. The boys had been a gift to me from my patron, Marcus Septimus, one of the wealthiest and most important magistrates in all Britannia, who had bought them several years ago to be a matching pair. However, they had grown at vastly different rates, which rather spoiled the visual effect, and Marcus had been happy to pass them on to me in return for a service I had done for him.

My neighbour knew that, and he spoke in jest – and I replied in kind. I got to my feet to greet him, saying cheerfully, 'I can never remember what we're supposed to call the months, these days! So go on calling it Januarius, after the god of doors and new beginnings, by all means. Everybody does. After all, Janus is unlikely to be flattered by the change, and to offend him might be just as dangerous as to offend the Emperor!'

My neighbour shook his head. 'I'm not so sure of that! Gods can be propitiated with a sacrifice, but Commodus...' He tailed off, uneasily. 'Be careful, citizen. A spy in every household – that is what they say. I wouldn't take the risk.' He took the New Year honey cake my slave held out for him, looked furtively around him and scurried from the shop.

Junio laughed. 'He always was suspicious! But you can hardly blame him, can you? Have you heard the latest tales? They say that Commodus ordered the execution of a whole town

15

because he thought that someone in it looked at him askance! And you know that he served up a roasted dwarf to entertain his friends...' He broke off as there was a tapping at the outer door. 'Another visitor!'

It was not altogether a surprise. We'd had a dozen people making calls on us today. Welcome ones, of course. The feast of new beginnings is a traditional time for wives to plan improvements to their homes – such as fresh pavements for the dining room – and many a husband will send his steward round that day with seasonal gifts of sweet-tasting food or small-denomination coins, and a casual request for me to call. (Not that every such enquiry will guarantee a customer, but it is a rare year when I do not get one profitable contract out of New Year's Day.)

So it was easy enough for me to wear a hearty smile and be very careful that all my words were 'sweet' today, as tradition demanded. This, of course, is supposed to ensure a full twelve months of sweetness afterwards, just as the little gifts are said to do. I am a Celt, and not a follower of Roman gods myself, but I had already collected several honey cakes and figs, and dispensed a few small tokens in return.

So when this new caller came into the outer shop, this time dressed in a magisterial toga with a purple stripe, I hurried round the partition to greet him with my broadest smile. It is rare that people of quality come out here to this muddy northern suburb outside the city walls

16

(generally they send their servants to bring us New Year tokens and messages to call) so I was especially hearty as I greeted him.

'Janus's blessings for the Kalends, citizen,' I cried, extending both hands in welcome, although I did not recognize the face.

He ignored the gesture and stared stonily at me. He was clearly not a young man – perhaps only a few years younger than I was myself – but he wore the decades easily, as only a man of private wealth can do. He was well-fed, with a polished look, his hair close-cropped and unnaturally black – the shiny colour that only comes from using dyes of leech and vinegar – and his face was pink and scraped from barbering.

'Blessings indeed! We shall have need of blessings if this threatened snow sets in.'

'Snow?' I was startled. This was serious. The top floor of the workshop had burned out years ago, and my new home was at least an hour's trudge away – built on a piece of land my patron had granted to me, a tiny fraction of his out-of-town estate.

It was miles through the forest to the round-house where I lived, and the ancient path was treacherous and steep: not a track to follow when it was slippery and the rocks disguised by snow. There was another route, along the military road, but that was half as long again and far more exposed to bitter winds – quite enough for a pedestrian to die of cold; indeed several people did so every year. If it was threatening a blizzard it was time to leave at once.

My visitor assumed that my concern was for him. He nodded. 'It's come up suddenly. It's most unfortunate. And here am I, more than two-score miles from home!' He looked me up and down, clearly contemptuous of what he saw, though I was wearing my best toga and it was newly cleaned. Up to that moment I had felt well-dressed and smart, but the scrutiny was making me aware of the worn places on the hem and my own unfashionably greying beard and hair as he added curtly, 'Are you this Libertus that I have heard about?'

This would have been regarded as impolite, even on an ordinary day. Today it was particularly marked – no careful Kalends courtesy to be expected here – but I contrived to keep the New Year smile on my face. I have no special faith in Roman deities, but there is no point in courting their disfavour – just in case.

'I am. Longinus Flavius Libertus at your service, citizen,' I agreed, in my most silky tone. 'Whom do I have the honour of addressing in my turn?' I had deliberately used my full three Latin names to stress the fact that I was a citizen as well, and I'd adopted the most formal turn of speech – both things which I very rarely did. Behind me I could almost see my two slaves boggling.

The newcomer made a short, impatient noise. 'My name is Gaius Mommius Genialis,' he said, portentously. 'I am a town magistrate from

Dorn.' He spoke as if this were a major town, instead of an insignificant small tax-collection centre further to the north.

As for his name, it was so incongruous it almost made me laugh. Genialis might be his given cognomen, but – since the word means 'joyful, zestful and lustful' – it manifestly did not describe him in the least. However, I recalled the conventions of the day and managed to ask, politely, 'So what brings you to me?'

There was a silence while he turned the heavy ring-seal on his hand, as if he were deciding how he should reply, but after a long moment he deigned to answer me. 'I have come to Glevum to claim myself a wife.'

It was hardly an answer to my question, but I was about to mutter something congratulatory when he held up a warning hand.

'That is not a cause for special celebration, citizen. She is my elder brother's widow, that is all. However, she is very young and has no surviving family of her own, and the courts have decreed that – for the time, at least – she should pass into my *potestas*. She would no doubt have other suitors, given time – although she is as ugly and wilful as a mule – but I have decided that I'll marry her myself.'

I heard my son, behind me, make a strangled noise and I swallowed hard myself. The Roman attitude to young widows is not a pleasant one – a woman without children has no rights in law. Legally she is herself a child, and – if she lacks a father, who is more likely to consult her tastes – her guardian has the right to give her in marriage to anyone he likes, usually the highest bidder. Or, if he is single, he might marry her himself and so keep the dowry. This is regarded as good business, and even boasted of. The lady could, of course, decline to speak the vows – but then she is likely to be classified as mad and locked up for the remainder of her natural life. I did not envy this poor woman, whoever she might be. 'But I thought you found her un-attractive, citizen?' I said.

He gave me a look that would have frozen fire. 'I daresay I shall manage to do my duty by her, all the same – although once she is with child I shall not greatly trouble her.' At the prospect he managed a bleak smile. 'There are practical considerations, citizen. My brother was besotted with his Silvia, poor deluded fool, and has left her everything he owned to be a marriage portion if she wed again. By his will it will pass in time to any child of hers, but of course a husband would have the usufruct, meanwhile.'

The interest and profit on the capital, he meant. Of course! He was demonstrating his good Roman common sense. I wondered what this Silvia thought about these plans, though obviously – since Genialis was her legal guard-ian – she would have no choice at all. However, I made the conventional remark: 'Then may good fortune smile upon you both.'

He gave what might have been taken for a smile. 'Good fortune. Ah, indeed. That is ex-

20

actly what has brought me here. The house that Silvia lives in – which is part of the dowry she brings with her, and which I hope to move into soon myself – contains a mosaic pavement in the entrance-way, which was commissioned by my brother when they wed. Unfortunately it depicts a boat, since that was the way he earned his wealth.'

'I think we know the place.' That was my adopted son, Junio, stepping forward to take up position at my side. 'The house of Ulpius! I believe my father and I laid the original design.'

As he said it, I remembered too: a fine town-house on the other side of town, and the excited Ulpius boasting of the lively dark-haired girl that was to be his wife. More contrast to this soulless brother it would be hard to find. 'Of course we did!' I said.

Genialis ignored this interruption totally. 'But since her husband died by falling overboard she feels that it's an evil omen now, and keeping it would be an invitation to ill luck. She won't consent to marry anyone until it has been changed. Of course a widow's sensibilities in such a matter are permissible – if only in con-sideration of her grief. Therefore I need some-one to lay a different floor and fast – and you were recommended. I presume that you are equal to the task?'

Some instinct made me hesitate. 'I already have a number of commissions to fulfil.' It was an overstatement. All I had at present were mere enquiries, but my sympathies were all with Silvia. I judged that the lady was a most reluctant bride – and intelligent as well. Even her guardian could not force her into marrying if she could convincingly plead ill-omens before the temple priests. I mentally saluted her ingenuity.

Genialis's dark eyes had narrowed with surprise at my reply. 'I am prepared to pay you very handsomely, provided that the work is done on time. A gold piece, perhaps. A sacrifice to new beginnings, you might say – since that seems appropriate to the day. I want it finished well before the wedding date – which will be before the beginning of next moon.'

I found that I was nodding. No Roman – let alone a superstitious girl – would ever marry in Februarius, which is considered the most ill-starred of all the months. 'Could it not wait until the month of Mars?' That would buy Silvia an extra month or two, and perhaps I could find extra reasons for delay. 'With these other contracts, it would be difficult...'

He interrupted me. 'Citizen, I warn you, I intend to stand as an *aedile* in this town, as soon as I legally qualify for nomination to the post. You will find it in your interest to assist me in my plan.'

Meaning that I would regret it, otherwise. The aediles are elected officers with considerable powers, especially in relation to trades and market-stalls. But it made sense of course – the post is generally accepted as a route to nomination to the council later on – and explained why he was in such haste to wed the girl. Elections to public office still generally take place in March, on what was New Year's Day on the ancient Roman calendar, before the Emperor Julius readjusted it. Candidates are required to have a dwelling of a certain size within the confines of the town and obviously this house of Silvia's would satisfy the rule, but to achieve it he had to marry her. Besides, he would need a little time to build a reputation with the electorate – mostly by promising to pay for public works – and he would also have to find a serving councillor to stand as referee, though presumably that could be arranged, given a sufficient 'fee', or bribe.

I did not have the property requirement to vote, although today I almost wished I did – so I could cast my marble for anyone except my visitor. However, I kept my January face. 'I do not think that in the time available...'

This time it was Junio who interrupted me. 'We do have pattern-pieces, father, which we could install. Reasonably quickly if the price was right. It is only a small entrance lobby after all. Providing only that the customer could find a design that he was happy with. Shall I drag out the patterns and let him have a look?' He led me over to the corner of the shop where all my pattern-pieces were stored upon a rack, and as we went he whispered in my ear. 'I've just remembered something. He could be dangerous. I'm sure I heard that there was something strange about the way that Ulpius died. If we get into the house we might find out if that was true. And even if there's nothing to be learned, an *aureus* is a lot of money after all. Better that we should have the work than it should go elsewhere.'

He had a point, of course. I could hardly help poor Silvia by turning down the job – there are several other people who would take it on at once, and more than likely make a far worse job of it. All I would do is lose a valuable fee. And Junio was right. If we managed to discover anything, we might yet put a stop to this marriage after all. I nodded. 'Bring the slaves and take the patterns out there in the light, where our client can have a better look at them,' I said aloud.

Genialis made a dismissive gesture as we hurried back to him. 'That will not be necessary, pavement-maker,' he said airily. 'Anything that has not got ships in it will do. Something neutral – birds or flowers perhaps? If you can get it finished by the Ides, I will pay you that gold piece – double if you can get it done before Agonalia.'

That took my breath away. A single *aureus* was a substantial fee. Two of them would keep my family for months. But the feast he had mentioned was just nine days away – the Festival of Janus proper, when a ram was sacrificed, not just the votive crackers which were offered up today. That would not offer poor Silvia much respite – nor give me much time for my enquiries. 'I do not know if it is

24

possible, so quickly,' I demurred.

Genialis gave another of his unpleasant smiles. 'Take it or leave it, citizen. That is the contract I am offering. Until the Ides to get the pavement changed and earn the basic fee. If you do not finish it in time, I do not pay at all. Do it before the Agonalia and I pay you twice as much. If you are willing, come out to the street – I have a pair of other citizens ready and waiting to witness the affair. If not, I will look for someone else.'

'There is hardly time for anyone to take a pavement up, make good the foundation and lay another in its place!' I retorted, rather piqued in my professional pride.

He raised an eyebrow. 'Laying pavements is your business, citizen, and I would not presume to offer you advice. But I don't see why you need to take up what is there. The current pavement is well-laid and absolutely flat – thanks to your own excellent craftsmanship, I understand. Could you not simply lay the other one on top?'

Of course it is common practice, where the base is good enough. 'But the lady Silvia?' I protested. 'Will she not feel the curse has not been moved?'

He looked pityingly at me. 'And who will tell her? She will not be there – I propose to take her back to Dorn with me today. I am selling all her slaves and replacing them with mine – leaving just a guardian doorkeeper, while we are away. I shall most certainly not mention her anxiety to him and you won't either, if you have any sense. All he needs to know is that you're coming in to work and do not wish to be disturbed. Tomorrow, if you are minded to begin. Now do you accept the terms or not? Otherwise, as I said before, I'll find someone who will. And I warn you, I am not a man who easily forgives people who thwart him. Make up your mind. I cannot linger here – the carriage will be waiting with Silvia at the city gates. I want her under my protection until our wedding day and we must set off very soon for Dorn. It will be two days' journey at the best, and – as I say – it is already promising to snow. Fortunately it is a military road and the army doubtless will be sending out fatigues to keep it clear.'

So he was making sure that his bride could not escape. And nor could I. The promise of a mystery, and such a fee as well! I looked at Junio and he raised his brows at me. I turned to Genialis.

'Then I accept the contract. Lead me to your witnesses,' I said.

TWO

Genialis was right about the snow, as I saw when I went out into the street. The sky, which had been merely overcast when we came into town, had turned to leaden grey and as I shook hands with my customer, and we exchanged the legal formula in front of the pair of worthy citizens whom he had brought – and doubtless paid – to act as witnesses, I saw the first flakes start to settle on the rooftops opposite.

One of the men, Alfredus Allius, a minor official on the council whom I slightly recognized, was clearly anxious to be safe at home. 'This weather is coming from the south,' he said. 'If you hurry, Genialis, you might beat it yet – and I can get home with my toga dry.'

The other – stouter – councillor agreed. 'My villa is a dozen miles away.' He turned to Genialis. 'I'm not going there myself this afternoon – but of course, citizen, it lies upon your way and you and your lady are welcome to my hospitality if you should find the road to Dorn is blocked. I'll send my slave boy with you, to explain that to the house.'

Genialis acknowledged this as no more than his right. 'Thank you, Bernadus. Though I hope

27

it will not come to that. Adonisius! Have you got the traveller's offering for the altar in the arch?'

A handsome muscled youth with olive skin detached himself from the group of waiting servants lounging by the wall, looked at his master with sullen almond eyes and mutely showed the votive biscuits in his hand.

Bernadus said, 'Then you can be on your way. As I say, treat my villa as your own. My slave will show your driver where it is. I shall ride out there myself within a day or two, if the roads permit. But you will be lucky to get that far this evening with a cart if you do not make haste.' And he hustled my visitor away.

I glanced towards the sky. The councillor was right! This snow was coming quickly, and from the south as well – the very direction where my round-house lay. I ought to think of closing up and setting off before it was too late.

I was about to turn into the house when some-one called my name. It was another Kalends well-wisher (this time the steward of a frequent customer) and there was a dusting of white flakes upon his cloak. He was bearing coins and figs. I could not in politeness refuse to let him in but I rushed through the civilities as fast as courtesy allowed, inwardly fretting because the man was garrulous and always wanted to pass on all the gossip of the town.

I had a sudden inspiration. 'I've just won a contract at Ulpius's house – putting in new pavement for his lady wife. The old one apparently reminds her of her loss. Poor fellow, did I understand he drowned?' I winked at Junio.

The steward sipped the remnants of his New Year wine. He shook his head. 'Most unfortunate. They say that the ship had just set off for Gaul, and he went to see the helmsman as he always did – but lost his footing and fell overboard. The rumour is he'd had too much to drink, but I don't know if that's the truth of it. Tell you who might know more about it – that's the man next door. I understand that Ulpius had a cargo of his skins.'

I nodded. My workshop was between the candle-maker's and a tannery. 'It's rather difficult for me to ask him anything,' I hinted, cautiously. 'I had an altercation with the tanner's wife over an old slave she lost a year or so ago – she's always thought I was responsible for that.'

He put down the cup and rose slowly to his feet. 'Well, I can hardly call there – I'm on my master's business and he's never had dealings with the man. However, I'm to tell you he'd be glad if you would call. Something about a new mosaic for the atrium.'

I thanked him heartily and showed him out, but the moment he was through the door again we hurried round the workshop putting things away.

'I'm already wishing that I hadn't taken on this work for Genialis,' I grumbled to Junio as we tied thick rags around our feet and wrapped our bodies in our warmest cloaks, ready for the long trudge back to our respective round-houses and wives. 'Though if that ship was really setting off for Gaul, it doesn't seem possible that Genialis was involved – he could not have been on it when it left the dock. But I wish I hadn't taken on this contract all the same, though I suppose we're stuck with it. In this weather it will be hard for us to come and go to town, and if we don't complete it we shall not be paid at all. Besides, if there is no one living in Ulpius's house it will be cold and damp, and then – no doubt – the mortar will not set.'

Junio stood up and pulled his cloak-hood round his ears. 'Perhaps I should not have been so eager to talk you into it,' he admitted ruefully. 'But I did think that we could help the lady if we took the work. Moreover, I didn't want that lovely pavement to be utterly destroyed and replaced by something second-rate. I hoped we could have lifted some of it intact and used it somewhere else – though I realize that it won't be possible, in the short time we've got.'

'It will be shorter still if we get snowed in on the road.' I got to my feet and gestured to the slaves. 'So, if you two are ready, we can start for home.'

Minimus leapt up and scurried to the outer door. But when he opened it, he stopped, appalled. 'Great Janus! Look at that!'

I was already looking, in horror and surprise, though there wasn't much to see. Even the little shops across the lane were hardly visible. The air between was thick with swirling flakes and

30

a deepening white carpet covered everything.

Minimus looked doubtfully at me. 'What do you think, master?'

I shook my head. 'We can't go home today!'

'Thank Mercury!' The boy looked quite relieved. 'I hate the forest at this time of the year. I am afraid of wolves.'

I understood his feelings. Walking the ancient unfrequented woodland track was treacherous in winter, anyway – rain always turned it slippery with mud – but cold increased the danger of marauding animals, driven by hunger nearer to the towns. To go that way in this would be inviting accidents.

'We'll simply have to sleep here overnight,' I said. 'If this has gone tomorrow, we will try to go home then. Though it looks as if we might be stuck here for a day or two.' I glanced at Junio. 'We might make a start on that pavement, I suppose. I must say I feel rather sorry for our wives.'

He nodded. 'They'll obviously be worried, because they won't know where we are. But there's no help for it. There's no way of sending word. And they would not want us to set off in this. We'll just have to stay here until the weather clears.'

Maximus – who, despite his name was the smaller of my slaves – edged up to me and cleared his throat, as a signal that he wished to speak. I did not insist on such formality, but after the recent pranks at Saturnalia – when slaves and owners change roles for a day – he was being specially careful to show me due respect.

I nodded my permission. 'What is it, Maximus?'

'I'm sorry, master, but I'm a bit concerned. I don't know how we're going to make a fire. We've just thrown water on the embers to make sure that they were out and there isn't any flint or tinder left. And there won't be anything to eat, unless we go out to the thermopolium. We've finished all the bread and cheese we brought, and there are no pie-sellers likely to be out in this.' He shook his head. 'Even the hot-soup stalls are likely to be closed. No one who can help it will go out on the streets – one slip and you could break an arm or leg and end up maimed for life.'

'He's right,' my son agreed. 'Though perhaps it's no great loss. The stuff they sell is disgusting anyway: turnips and nasty bits of bone and hoof.' He looked enquiringly at me. 'But if they are open, it would at least be warm – if you think the chance of that is worth a struggle through the snow. The workshop will be very cold without a fire.' He brightened. 'Although I see there's wood and kindling on the pile. I've seen that servant, Brianus, that you gave to me last year, using a sort of bow and string to bore into a stick and make a flame. I've watched him do it – I could try my hand at that.'

I grinned. 'I've thought of a better strategy,' I said. 'Let's pay a New Year's visit to the tanner after all. He keeps a furnace burning all the

32

time, brewing up the cutch to tan the skins – I'm sure he could be persuaded to let us have some fire, if only in honour of the day.'

Junio laughed, though rather doubtfully. 'Father, are you sure? His wife has not forgiven you for costing her that slave.'

I grinned. 'And isn't this the day for healing rifts?' I asked. 'In any case, we've much to gain and nothing much to lose. So let's untie these ugly rags from round our feet and try to look like the Roman citizens we are. We'll make a formal visit, with the slaves escorting us – that way I'm sure the man will let us in and Minimus and Maximus will be admitted too, to wait where it is warm. Just bring those sugared figs the steward brought to us and keep a Kalends smile fixed on your face.'

So away we trooped to knock upon the gate. The tanner himself came grumbling out to open it, holding a lighted taper to peer into the snow. But when he realized who it was, his manner changed at once. Perhaps it was the togas, but we were welcomed in at once, and plied with heated wine. Even the hard-faced wife contrived a smile, though she left us men to it and went back to her tasks.

I managed to bring the talk around to Ulpius, but the tanner had no real information to impart – except that he was not inclined to blame the wine. 'Ulpius was never one to drink too much, especially at sea. More likely it was just the movement of the deck. The weather in autumn can be terrible. And it wouldn't have been carelessness; he knew the job too well. Freak accident, that's all. The ship turned back of course, but it was far too late, and Ulpius had disappeared beneath the waves. They thought the body might be washed up in the end – so it could be given proper burial – but it never did. Eaten by the fishes I suppose. But the trading has gone on – they sold all my skins, and I've been paid for them. Ulpius's junior partner saw to that.'

'There is a partner?' I hadn't heard of this.

'Oh, indeed. A pleasant man, though not a citizen. Started life as a freeman-forester and dealt with Ulpius over timber and the like, but he always had a natural aptitude for trade, and Ulpius took him on. Lucius proved to have a splendid eye for general goods, and they formed a partnership. Now, of course, he's running things alone. I got this wine from him, for instance. It is very good. Can I offer you another drink of it?'

A half-hour later, when we went back to the shop – fighting our way now through a rising blizzard on the street – we brought away not only a hearty New Year gift of honey cake, but a heap of hot embers burning in a pail.

The two young slave boys set to with a will and soon had a cheerful blaze alight again and a couple of tapers burning to give a welcome light – the afternoon was dark though it was not long past midday. With the warmth, however, I felt my spirits lift. We had a pan, and my favourite spiced mead that we could heat in it, and now we had the honey cake to ward off hunger pangs, so with our cloaks to sleep on we would do well enough – at least until the morning when the street-hawkers began and we could purchase bread and milk again.

I looked at Junio. 'Well, it seems that after all there is no mystery to solve, but shall we have a quick look through those patterns while we're waiting here, and try to find something suitable for that entrance hall? I can't recall exactly the dimensions we require, but we could estimate within a hand's breadth either way.'

Junio nodded. 'Best err on the slightly smaller side,' he said. 'Then it would be easy to fit a border round.' He picked up a lighted taper. 'Let's go and have a look.'

The half-dozen premade 'patterns' which I kept to advertise my skills were versions of my most popular designs, stuck to a linen backing and placed on wooden boards, so they could be moved intact and shown to customers. Most clients used them simply as a guide and ordered something individual – but it was possible to install the samples exactly as they were.

Junio held up the candle to illuminate the rack while I pulled out my favourites, but he shook his head. 'Remember, we're being paid a fixed amount for this, and we'll have to make another version to replace the one we use. If there is nothing to be learned by lingering at the house, it's obviously sensible to choose the simplest piece – something that will be quick and easy to repeat.'

35

He was right of course and it did not take us long to settle on an appropriate design: a pattern of triangles around a central square, in which was depicted an inoffensive flower.

'There we are!' I said triumphantly. 'Put a border round this and you could lay it anywhere. Starting tomorrow, if this weather clears a bit and it still isn't possible for us to get back home. Though it will be quite a tramp to Ulpius's house – or Silvia's house, as I suppose that I should call it now. If I recall correctly, it's over by the river on the other side of town.'

Junio looked doubtful. 'I expect the streets are clearer once you're inside the wall.'

I nodded thoughtfully. Genialis was right about the army sending out fatigues: they would try to keep the military routes available, at least to horsemen, and so allow free passage to the imperial post. And that included the road through Glevum to the garrison. So if we could struggle to the northern gate we should get through town all right – even if the country tracks were still impassable.

'We wouldn't need the hand-cart to start with, anyway,' I said. 'We don't want the pattern-piece until we've got the site prepared and measured up. So we'll try tomorrow, if the snow has eased,' I said. 'Now let's get back and sit beside the fire. The boys have already heated up the mead.'

The warm drink was welcome though we saved the food until we estimated it was supper time. By then we were so hungry that even

Junio, who had been raised in Roman ways, was content to have me offer only a token sacrifice – the merest crumb or two – to appease the household gods. Then we huddled near the fire and did our best to sleep.

The morning found me stiff and chilled but I must have slept, because I woke dreaming of Ulpius floating in the tide, covered with seaweed and the hides of goats. I could almost smell the smoke that had been used to cure the skin. When my eyelids opened and I looked around it was to find Minimus already kneeling by the fire, adding fresh firewood from the pile and using the leather bellows to improve the blaze. Of my other two companions there was no sign at all.

I grimaced as I eased my aching bones. 'I see you managed to keep the fire alight?'

'Maximus and I have taken it in turns to tend it overnight,' he told me with some pride. 'He's gone out now with the young master to see if there are any street-vendors about, although it is still snowing ... Ah, but here they are!'

He broke off as the front door opened and the other two returned, shaking the snowflakes off their capes and stamping cold slush from their rag-wrapped feet.

Junio put a package on the bench and shook a rattling water-pail at me. 'Only stale cakes this morning, I am afraid, and we found an urchin selling clean ice that we can melt to drink. The pumps are frozen and there's no water to be had. But the town gates are open and pedes-

37

trians are able to get through. Word is that the authorities are going to open the emergency grain-store in the town, so there might be someone selling fresh bread later on. In the meantime, this is all we have.'

Even stale cakes are welcome to a hungry man – better still when they are toasted at the fire – and our little party scoffed them with a will, though it did occur to me to wonder what we were going to do if this freeze continued. Food would get expensive and credit hard to find – and I had only a small sum in my purse. I said as much to Junio.

'Fortunately, we have a contract for a profitable job – and witnesses to prove it – so if we really need to we can venture out and borrow something from the money-lenders in the forum,' he replied.

I countered his enthusiasm with reality. 'I suppose that's possible – but the interest they charge is quite extortionate – sometimes as much as twenty-four per cent.'

He made a grimace. 'Better make sure we get that pavement finished, then. Otherwise we won't earn anything at all – and still have the wretched loan to pay. But it may come to borrowing. There's obviously no prospect of getting home for days.'

That was self-evidently true. 'As soon as we have eaten, we'll try to get to Silvia's house and make a start,' I agreed. 'We'll take you, Maximus. We'd better leave Minimus to keep the fire alight.' I turned to the slave in question, who was looking rather glum. 'I'll leave you a *sestericius* from my purse, so you can watch out for street-vendors while we're gone, and we will do the same in town. There might be some cheese on offer, I suppose, though I doubt that there'll be fresh milk or vegetables today. No one will be able to come in from the farms.'

So we left him to it, leaving our bedraggled togas to dry off before the fire – all three of us wrapped up like swaddled babes against the snow. Progress was difficult and slow and treacherous, but Junio was right, it was a little easier once we were through the gates. A few brave shops were open, with half their shutters down, and some tradesmen had even tried to clear the space outside their doors, but most establishments were firmly shut and barred. The unswept pavements were piled knee-high with snow and we saw several gangs of soldiers as we passed, continually shovelling yet more from the roads – which were very slippery, but had become the only place to walk.

We battled on until we reached the riverside. The troops had been especially busy here so it was relatively easy to approach the house – a fine one in a little court that opened to the street – but we had to thunder on the door for quite a time before we could persuade the slave to open it. When he came, he was a surly-looking man, with a mop of curly hair, clutching a heavy cudgel in one hand and in other holding a grubby blanket round him like a cloak.

He glared at us suspiciously. 'And who in Dis

are you?'

I explained our errand. 'Genialis told you to expect us, I believe! And we must make a start. I have contracted to complete it in nine days or less.'

'Oh, I see – the pavement! I wasn't expecting anyone today!' But reluctantly, he did allow us in to eye up the passageway – though he kept a careful watch on us throughout, from his little guard-cell by the door where he had a tiny brazier and a bed.

Preparing the site would not be difficult. We had done a good job with the ship mosaic – although I say so myself – and it was flat enough for us to use it as a base without disturbing it. All that it required was wet mortar spread on top so that the new pattern-piece could be lowered on to it and plastered into place. A row or two of border would complete the job. I left Junio and Maximus to measure up with string, so that we could judge the quantities required, while I accosted the suspicious doorman in his cell.

I was going to need him as an ally – and not only if I hoped to find out what he knew about the fate of the former master of the house. In this weather I could not be sure that Genialis would return from Dorn in time to verify that the contract had been fulfilled on the date specified – and the would-be aedile was just the sort of man to try to wriggle out of paying me, on some such legal technicality. I might need the doorman as a witness by and by. He was

40

clearly not a friendly sort of chap – men in that position rarely are – but I thought I knew a way to win him round.

'You'll have to keep an extra brazier in this entrance overnight,' I said, knowing – as he did – that he would benefit, but careful to phrase this as a professional demand. 'We'll never get the mortar to harden otherwise. Do you have a larger brazier in the house?'

He pretended to consider this. 'There is one in the kitchen building you might use, I think – though I am not supposed to go out there myself. My master left me bread and cheese and apples when he went, and money to buy something from the street vendors as well – though I haven't seen one since the snow began. The house is usually heated by a hypercaust, but I don't have the slaves to keep the furnace lit and he told me not to hire any until the day of his return. But if you need a brazier, that's another thing.'

I nodded. 'I'll take full responsibility. Besides, in this weather who knows when he'll return? You can't be sure he even got to Dorn. There was talk that he would lodge with Bernadus midway. He could return at any moment.'

'Or not return for weeks.' He gave me a mirthless grin. 'You'd better hope he does. Or – I know my master – he will try to find a way of claiming that your contract was annulled, because you couldn't prove you'd done the work in time. He's very short of money for his election schemes.'

Exactly what I'd thought myself! I gave him a cheerful smile. 'But you could witness that I'd finished it.'

He looked at me blankly. 'More than my life's worth, citizen, to testify against my master's interests. Besides, who takes any notice of a slave? Much better you find a citizen to speak for you – didn't you have witnesses when you agreed the work? He generally insists on things like that.'

'Indeed we did.' I frowned. 'He brought them with him. Alfredus and Bernadus. I know them both by sight. They are councillors, of course, so they must have accommodation in the town – but I don't know where they live and the curia won't be sitting in this weather, I'm sure. How could I be sure of finding them before the Ides?'

'You could go to the Festival of Janus, citizen, the Agonalia – in eight days' time. That is if you've done the work by then. They're certain to be there.'

That was a sensible suggestion. I should have thought of it myself. The Festival is always a very big affair, with a senior priest to make the sacrifice. This year the celebrant was particularly grand – a Flamen of Juno, all the way from Rome. I knew that, because he was due to stay with my patron overnight. 'A good idea,' I told the doorkeeper. 'Anyone who is anyone is likely to be there. No doubt Genialis will want to get there if he can – though who knows if the roads will be passable by then.'

The doorkeeper permitted himself a wry grin. 'We had better hope so, pavement-maker! He'll be furious if he can't attend the ritual after all. He was boasting that he'd be there with all the councillors, making sure that he was seen by the electorate. He even offered to provide the sacrificial ram – hoping to make a public show of that – but some citizen from the outskirts had already promised one, and could not be persuaded to withdraw. My master had to be content with offering barley cakes and wine. He wasn't very pleased – he told me that everyone influential would be there. So wait outside the temple, you should find your councillors.'

'I'll do more than that,' I chuckled. 'I'll attend the feast myself.' I saw his startled look. 'Oh don't worry, I'm entitled – I'm a Roman citizen and I can wear a toga with the best of them. Then, even if your master isn't back himself, it would be courteous to invite the witnesses back here to see the pavement in its finished state.'

'And Genialis could not deny the contract then.' The doorkeeper gave me a conspiratorial wink. 'Just don't let him know that I suggested it! He'd have me flogged within an inch of death for costing him the fee. He's manic about money.' He dropped his voice. 'I pity that poor lady – and there's the truth of it. In fact ... I shouldn't say this, citizen, but I have sometimes wondered if the death of Ulpius...' He broke off as my son and slave appeared at the entrance to his guard-cell.

I waved them off and turned to him again.

'What did you wonder about Ulpius's death?'

But he had already thought better of his unguarded words. He shook his head. 'Nothing, citizen.'

'That it was convenient for your master, possibly?' I tried to win his confidence again. It was frustrating to have come so close to what was clearly his suspicion of the truth.

However, he was not to be cajoled. He looked at me coldly. 'Of course not, citizen. I would not dare to speak about my owner in that way. I merely wondered if the death was quick and merciful. Now, if you have finished, shall I show you out? I'll attend to the brazier before you come again.'

And that was all that he could be prevailed upon to say, either that day or the five days following as Junio and I – after struggling with the hand-cart through the icy streets – laid the new pavement in the entrance hall.

THREE

We made a good job of the pavement, and with a day to spare. The fact that the base was water-proof helped, making it possible to simply put a mortar-bed on top and lower the backing-layer on to it, instead of installing the mosaic upside down and soaking off the linen as we'd have had to do outdoors.

There was nothing to be got out of the door-keeper again, but at least the extra brazier made the entrance hall a pleasant place to work, and the mortar set more quickly that I'd dared to hope. So by the sixth day there was little left to do, except clean up the surface and collect our tools – though it seemed more and more certain that we'd need our witnesses, for Genialis was unlikely to be back in time himself.

The snow had stopped by now, but it was freezing hard instead, and even the main roads were still closed to carriages and very hazard-ous for pedestrians. The country tracks were blocked entirely, which meant that my son and I were stranded in the town – and there still was no way I could think of to get word to our wives. It would be inhuman to send a slave the long way round on foot – and we could find no mounted messenger who would agree to go.

So I was startled, after our last day working at the house, when we were struggling through Glevum with a handcart full of tools, to chance upon a neighbour in the market place – a free-born Celt called Cantalarius, whose round-house-property lay not far from my own. Like myself he was a Roman citizen – in his case by right, because he was born within the walls of the colonia – but the rank had not brought him any special privilege; he still struggled for a living on his muddy fields.

He was an ugly fellow with a twisted arm, and famed for grumbling, but I was fascinated to discover how he had got to town. I left Junio and the slave to watch the hand-cart and slithered over to the pavement on the far side of the street, where he'd set up a makeshift stall – and found that he was selling cabbages and turnip-tops from the panniers of a pair of mules.

Judging by the sample he was holding up, his wares were rather limp and blighted by the frost, but there were people clustering round to buy them all the same. Food had been very difficult to get these last few days, though some enterprising farmers on the river-bank had acquired a raft and brought things in by water every day – milk and chickens and a slaughter-ed sheep or two. There was a rush to buy them as soon as they arrived, though the price was very high: but Ulpius's house was fortunately placed and we'd managed to acquire a scrawny hen or two, which Minimus had turned into a warming meal. The public granaries were open, so there was bread on sale and one day we'd also paid a fortune for some fish – which had been very scarce, because the water in the forum fish pool was inclined to freeze, until some prisoners from the jail were sent to stand in it and work with poles to stop the ice from forming on the top. Another team was doing the same thing by the docks, in case a large ship came up the river to unload supplies – though with the recent weather none had managed it.

So vegetables would be a welcome treat. The mules had solved the puzzle of how he'd got to town, but I joined the crush of customers surrounding him and in a little while he spotted me. 'Citizen Libertus! What are you doing here?'

'I might ask you the same!'

He shrugged his humped shoulders. 'I struggled into Glevum with this pair of mules. Had to come here to fulfil a vow, and thought that I'd improve the day by selling something too.'

'A vow?' I was puzzled.

He dropped his voice. 'I promised to provide an animal for the Janus offering...'

'*You* did?' I interrupted in astonishment. Perhaps my reaction was not polite, but it was quite a compliment to be permitted to donate a sacrifice for any ritual at all. To provide one for a major festival was an honour generally reserved for rich and influential citizens – like Genialis – who wished to make a public show. 'I heard that a "citizen from the outskirts" was offering a ram, but I never supposed that it was you.'

Cantalarius misunderstood my evident surprise. 'It was at my new wife's insistence, citizen. We are not usually driven to such Roman practices, but we have had a dreadful run of luck ever since the moment that she married me. Half my crops are rotting in the fields, my barns burned down last summer so we've no feed for the sheep and now a spotted fever has brought low all my slaves – and none of the Celtic rituals have helped. My wife consulted a soothsayer in the end, and he told her that it was obvious that she'd upset the gods by marrying a hunchback like myself – and that only a significant blood sacrifice would lift the curse.'

I nodded. 'So you thought of the feast?'

'My wife insisted on my pleading with the temple priests and – perhaps because she made me promise what little gold we had, the remnant of her dowry, as an additional donation to the gods – I managed to convince them that I could send a ram, and now I can't supply one from my flock. It has to be a spotless one, of course, delivered to the temple in advance, and I had picked out my best – but it's proving quite impossible to get it here alive. The poor thing's half-dying of starvation anyway, since we've run out of feed, so it would likely have been rejected by the augurers.'

No wonder he was worried. This was a serious matter – quite apart from the humiliation of it all – failing to fulfil a public vow was an offence in law. 'And the temple can't provide one for you?' I enquired. Generally they keep a few creatures in reserve, in case there is some problem with the entrails of a sacrificial animal in which event a second offering would be required.

He shook his head. 'It's been the same for them – nobody can get their animals to town. I did contrive to get one from the army in the end: they've cleared the road out to the *territorium* – the military farm – so that they can bring supplies in for the garrison and they've managed to find one that was acceptable.' He dropped his voice so only I could hear. 'A yearling ram. It's not as good as mine was, but at least it means that I am not publically disgraced. Though the army wanted such a price for it, I'm going to be obliged to borrow money from the usurers, I think.'

I made a sympathetic noise. 'I have been forced to the money-lenders too. With the rising price of food, they've done a roaring trade. They're probably the only people in the town to benefit from snow.'

He made a helpless gesture with his hands. 'But how am I to pay them back? That's what I cannot see. I can't even afford to provide another ram to ensure a substitute – though I gather that someone else has seen to that. Ironic, isn't it? That sheep-offering was intended to improve my luck! And what was the result? The priests have all my money and I'll be deep in debt, while this–' he waved a withered leek towards the mules – 'is all that's left for us to sell – unless we sell ourselves to slavery.'

'Well, I'll take one of these.' I selected the least damaged of his cabbages – Minimus could boil it later with some herbs – and offered him a coin, far more than the wretched thing was worth. He took it, with a sigh. 'Thank you, citizen, every quadrans helps.'

'Then perhaps I can assist you further, Cantalarius!' I said. 'I see you've brought your mules. When your panniers are empty they could take a different load. Can you take a slave back with you, when you've finished here?' I gestured towards Maximus who was standing by the cart. 'Get my servant home and I'll pay you handsomely!'

He looked at me distrustfully. 'And find you holding me liable for his slave price if he should freeze to death before I got him there? And that's just what would happen, the way Fortune's treating me. I think not, citizen. Why do you want to send the boy back anyway? You seem to be managing quite comfortably here.'

'I want him to take a message to my wife – she has not seen or heard from us since New Year's Day.' A thought occurred to me. 'Or perhaps you could consent to take her word yourself?'

He brightened suddenly. 'I'm sure that could be managed, citizen. After all, I'm passing quite close to your door. Though it will cost, of course. The military route is passable with care

50

– they're putting salty sand on it to melt the ice – but the minor roads are still extremely treacherous, even for a mule. And no doubt it will soon come on to freeze again. I've nearly finished here. How long will it take you to get a note to me?'

I made a swift decision. 'Forget about the note.' I knew I had a wax-tablet in the shop, but fetching it would take a little time. 'Just call in at the house. Tell my wife you've seen me and we are all safe and well. We have had a commission for a pavement, which we have fulfilled, so we've enough to eat–' no need to worry Gwellia with news that I'd been borrowing – 'and we'll come home as soon as ever we can walk the track. Or at least, the others will. I may have to stay here till after the Janus festival.'

He bowed his comprehension. 'I think you suggested that I would get a fee?'

'My wife will see to that.' It was usual for the recipient to pay – a guarantee that the message would arrive. 'Shall we say two sesterces?' It was more than generous, but I was desperate.

He gave me a doubtful look. 'A half denarius? Oh, come on, citizen. She won't believe me if I tell her you've agreed to that.'

'Tell her I said to give you the money from the onion-pot.' There were a couple of sestertius coins in there the last time that I looked – saving for a pair of sandals for the household slaves. 'That way she'll know that your request is genuine – and if she won't produce it, I'll pay another time.' I gestured to the little clutch of

51

waiting customers. 'I'm prepared to swear to that before these witnesses.'

Cantalarius allowed himself a rueful smile. 'Then I'll trust you, citizen. But don't blame me if something happens on the way and the message doesn't get there. It would be typical. I'm beginning to believe that I am genuinely cursed. Otherwise I'll see you at the Festival – supposing that I manage to get back here with the mules.'

I nodded. As donor of the sacrifice he would be invited to the rostrum with the priests. 'Then I'll look out for you at the Agonalia,' I said. 'Let's just trust that the soothsayer was right and that your blood-offering brings you better luck.'

'Great Mars, I hope so!' he replied. 'Things cannot well get worse. Enjoy your cabbage!' And he turned away to sell his other wares.

I went back to where Junio and Maximus were waiting with the cart: blowing on their fingers and stamping their feet to drive away the chill. I explained what I'd been doing for so long. 'At least I've managed to arrange to get a message home,' I said. 'And we have got some cabbage for the pot. So now all that remains for us to do is to go back to the workshop and keep warm – until it's time to go to the temple and find our witnesses.'

The day of the Janus Agonalia dawned damp and wet – always a bad omen for an outdoor festival – but it least it brought the promise of reopened roads as the rain began to turn the frozen snow to slush. I was beginning to wonder if Genialis would manage to return and witness the completion of the pavement after all, but when I reached the sanctuary there was no sign of him.

In Rome there is a famous temple to the dual-faced deity, but in Glevum Janus has no building of his own and the annual Festival was held at the Capitoline shrine, where there was a little altar set up near the *cella* of the goddess Juno. Of course there were niches in the gate-ways to the town where travellers could make small personal offerings and prayers, but for the big occasion the large temple was required – and this year it was packed to near-capacity. Perhaps it was because the weather had been so severe since New Year's Day, and the citizens were anxious to propitiate the god and obtain a better outlook for the remainder of the year.

Whatever the reason, it was hard to get a place and after we had left the slaves to wait outside, Juno and I found ourselves standing almost at the rear. This made it rather difficult to hear, but potentially easier to scan the crowd for our two witnesses. Everyone was huddled up in woollen cloaks against the cold, of course, but only the sacrificing priest would wear a hood, so our men's faces would be clearly visible.

However, I could not see them for the press of citizens and after a few moments Junio – with the advantages of youth – climbed up on a column-base to get a better view. He earned himself some disapproving stares but he ignored them and looked steadily around.

After a moment he climbed down again and came to stand demurely at my side. 'There they are,' he murmuring, gesturing. 'Right down at the front, with all the other councillors, close to the altar where the sacrifice will be. Your neighbour Cantalarius is there as well.'

I stood on tiptoe to see the area that he was pointing at and made out the pair, resplendent in their togas and their coloured cloaks, standing in the area which had the closest view, along with a lot of other local dignitaries. Even the commander of the garrison was there.

I grinned at Junio. 'We'll catch them afterwards. We'll never fight our way down there before the ritual. But we're going to need them, by the look of it. There's no sign of Genialis anywhere. Or of my patron either, which is rather strange. If Cantalarius can get here on a mule, you'd think that Marcus would manage on a horse – he is a splendid horseman and he does not lack for mounts.'

'Unless he is in the cella of Juno with the priests?' Junio nodded towards the inner sanctum of the temple, where the public could not go. 'I can hear the flutes, so the ritual must be almost ready to begin – and they would not start without him, would they? He's the most important guest and wasn't he bringing the officiating priest?'

I nodded. 'I believe that was the plan. The man was travelling from Aqua Sulis to attend and was due to lodge with Marcus overnight.' I looked at Junio. 'You don't suppose ... Ah, but here's my patron now! And he wasn't in the temple. He's just come from the street!'

The clamour of voices had faded to a breathless murmuring and Marcus Septimus Aurelius was striding down the central aisle in the direction of the altar at the front, flanked by a pair of slaves. They were impressive in their crimson uniforms but he himself was quite magnificent. His patrician toga, with its broad purple stripe, had never looked more dazzling, and round his shoulders he had draped a white cape of finest fur, which swung open at every step he took to reveal the scarlet lining underneath.

The spectators who had crammed into the courtyard for the feast, so tightly that – a moment since – there seemed barely room to breathe, somehow contrived to melt away to either side to let him through.

A bevy of priests came out of the inner room as he approached, all robed and hooded for the sacrifice, and there was a hasty conference at the rostrum steps. The crowd was silent, suddenly – all whispering had ceased and even the flautists and recorders had stopped their tootling.

Then Marcus strode up the steps on to the central dais, accompanied by a temple slave on either side. It hardly needed the lituus-player to herald his address: attentive silence had already fallen before the crooked horn rang out.

Marcus turned directly to the crowd. 'Citizens of Glevum, Romans, friends. I am the bearer of disappointing news. The high priest of Juno from Rome, whom we had hoped to welcome here today, has not been able to reach us in the snow. As you may have known he was supposed to stay with me last night, but we received a messenger from him only yesterday, to tell us that his carriage had been unable to proceed – and indeed had only with difficulty managed to take refuge in an inn.'

There was a murmur at this. There are strict observances required of a priest, which would not be easy in a common hostelry.

Marcus was still speaking. 'Even the messenger on horseback had trouble getting through. So our hoped-for celebrant will not be with us for today.'

There was a louder murmur. People were muttering about ill omens getting worse, but Marcus held his hand up and uneasy silence fell.

'Fortunately there is no problem with the Janus sacrifice,' he went on. 'You will know that the duty by tradition falls to the most senior priest available, so we are lucky in having another venerable celebrant, the former High Priest of Diana, and of Luna and Fortuna too – to act as our "rex sacerdotum" and perform the sacrifice. He has agreed to do so, and as soon as he has performed the ritual ablutions and prepared himself, the ceremonial procession will begin. In the meantime, the flautists and singers will perform for us.'

There was sporadic clapping in some sections of the crowd but most people were looking at each other in dismay. The 'venerable' priest of whom my patron spoke was very old and frail and had ceased to officiate at public gatherings. This was officially because of failing health, but there had been an incident a year or two before when he almost forgot a portion of the ritual – which would of course have meant that the sacrifice was void – so if he had not been prompted (just in time) by a judicious cough from a watchful acolyte, the whole ceremony would have had to start again.

Today, however, he seemed in better form. When, a short time later – after the musicians had performed a song – he emerged from the inner cellum, duly washed and anointed with the sacred oil, he looked almost sprightly. He had buckled on a brazen belt over his long under-tunic, his fresh toga was of sparkling white, and when the pipes and flutes struck up again and he joined the procession towards the altar steps, he almost seemed to march along in time. Behind him came a pair of temple servants with the ram which, by contrast – perhaps perturbed by the golden collar and the wreath of leaves around its head – seemed most reluctant and was having to be tugged along by the gilded halter-rope. Last of all came the assistant priests, the *victimarius* who would wield the sacred knife, and the augurers to read the entrails afterwards. As they approached the altar steps Cantalarius stepped up to join them, as was now his due.

One of the temple officials swaggered to the dais and gave the exhortation, 'Still your tongues,' while the old priest pulled up his toga-folds to form a hood and stepped forward for the *adoratio*, reverently touching the altar with one hand. The opening prayer is an elaborate recital, beginning with Janus and working through the whole pantheon of gods, but he managed perfectly – although I noted that an acolyte was standing by, with the proper formula written clearly on a scroll.

Then it was time for the sacrifice itself. Sacred breadcrumbs, mixed with perfumed herbs, were duly sprinkled on the ram, and the sacerdos lifted up a cup of wine for all to see, took a symbolic sip himself and scattered the remainder on the animal. This is of course the prelude to the central act: the waiting victimarius had already raised his knife and the old priest's attendant was stepping forward with the sacred golden vessel to collect the blood. But as the pipes and flutes began again, as loudly as possible to drown out any unpropitious sound, the sheep – presumably startled by the unexpected noise – panicked and decided to make a run for it.

It was a young, strong animal and if it had indeed been dosed with poppy-juice – as rumour says that sacrificial creatures are – then it was not enough. The sudden violent movement caught the old priest unprepared: he let go of the rope. The ram eluded the victimarius, leapt off the dais like a mountain goat and went charging off into the crowd – causing consternation as it went. Worse, the old man made a futile grab for it, lost his balance and went tumbling down the steps.

There could hardly have been a more dreadful augury. There were shouts and cries of anger, some against my patron ('this is what comes of using a substitute as priest!') and for a few minutes there was pandemonium. But the ram was captured finally and dragged outside the court (there would be no question of using that one now) and I saw Marcus and the priest in solemn conference, together with the commander of the garrison. Then the soldier left the sanctum with a temple slave while the old priest brushed his toga down and climbed the steps to speak to us. His voice was trembling.

'It is clear the gods have chosen to reject the sacrifice. The augurers assure me that it is for the best, as the omens would be inauspicious if we'd killed that beast. It is not the result of any change of priest. No doubt the fates are angry with the donor of the ram. So there's no cause for alarm. Keep your places. We will offer up a pig – as is required to propitiate the gods and cleanse the altar – and then we will attempt the sacrifice again. We are fortunate to have another ram available, personally donated for the festival by the commander of the garrison.'

There were some sullen mutterings and the pipes began again. I felt sorry for Cantalarius, who had been publicly humiliated now and was obliged to leave the temple in disgrace. Poor fellow, matters had gone from bad to worse for him and as he left the rostrum things took a nasty turn. Members of the crowd began to jostle him, and soon he was being buffeted and kicked and cursed and spat upon – though the incident had really been no fault of his. In the end a temple slave was sent to clear a way for him and he was able to make his way outside, followed by a chorus of angry jeers and threats.

The hubbub subdued into a muttering, supplanted by a cheer as the commander of the garrison returned. However, he was not followed by the attendant with the pig and ram – but by a dishevelled rider from the imperial post and a legionary soldier with his sword unsheathed. This was such an unusual event, inside the temple precinct, that there was a sudden hush. I felt a little tingle down my spine.

The men strode to the front and spoke to Marcus and the priests, but it was my patron who climbed on to the rostrum steps. It was clear that he was shaken. However, he was a skilful orator. His voice rang out with dreadful clarity. 'Citizens, I have historic tidings to impart. We have just received a verbal message that the Emperor is dead. The details are not absolutely clear, and we are awaiting written confirmation which is following. When we have fuller information it will be announced.'

There was a general tumult – though nobody knew whether it was safe to cheer. Commodus had long been hated by the populace: not only for his overweening pride – renaming Rome and all the months in honour of himself – but for his lascivious lifestyle and capricious cruelty. But no one ever dared to say so openly; the man was also famous for his spies, and Commodus was said to have amused himself by inventing more and more ingenious techniques for the execution of his so-called 'enemies'.

However, there are generally certain protocols which have to be observed following the death of any Emperor. No doubt there were still paid ears and eyes amongst us even now, so all the crowd could safely do was indistinctly roar.

Marcus raised his hand for silence, and went on again. 'In the meantime, there is to be no public mourning of his death, no wearing of dark togas or rubbing ashes in your hair, and private feasting may take place as usual: the senate has issued a *damnatio memoriae*, a statement that the dead man does not deserve your tears. The name of the successor had not been formally ratified by the Senate when the original messenger left Rome, but it is likely that the Empire will be safely in the hands of Pertinax, the one-time Governor of Britannia.'

This time there was no mistaking the crowd's shouts of joy.

Marcus let them celebrate a bit before he spoke again. 'In the circumstances, this festival will have to be adjourned. The priests will perform the cleansing sacrifice but the rest of the ceremony is herewith postponed...'

He was interrupted by a general gasp and cries of 'Dreadful omens!' 'We shall offend the gods!'

He raised his hand again. 'Citizens of Glevum. Do not fear! The auguries are good. It was as if this news was blessed by Jupiter – it travelled so swiftly through the empire. It is the height of winter, but every pass was open, every wind was fair and every rider reached his goal with speed. There will be a special offering here this afternoon, praying fortune on the succession of our new Emperor – amalgamated with the ritual that should have taken place just now. However, this will necessitate a change of celebrant. The sacrifices – and there will be several, at that time – will obviously include an offering to Jove and all the major deities, and must therefore be conducted by the Capitoline priests, aided by the Servir of the Imperial cult who will naturally perform the Imperial offering. I shall be providing the animals myself.'

He stepped down to a smattering of applause and the garrison commander took his place. 'There will be a formal announcement of all this from the steps of the basilica after the sounding of the midday trumpet and any further details will be announced. In the meantime, you should all go to your homes.'

He turned away. The crowd had been dismissed.

I turned to Junio, having to raise my voice above the hoots and cheers. 'You realize what this means? No wonder that Marcus was looking shocked just now. Pertinax is his bene-factor and his special friend. That means that my patron is likely to become not just the most powerful magistrate for miles, but one of the half-dozen most influential people in the world!'

But I was talking to myself. My son was being borne away, swept along in the crush of people rushing to the gate.

FOUR

Once outside the temple I could not see my son nor, for that matter, the two councillors I had come to find: indeed it would have been hard to find anyone in the milling crowd. The whole forum was in pandemonium. People were already jostling for position near the basilica, and if it had not been for the presence of armed members of the watch the shoving and shouting might have turned into a riot. As I pushed my way through to the fountain at the end (which – in default of other arrangements – was our usual meeting place) I was elbowed and glared at by several of my fellow citizens, though others turned eagerly to babble of the news. It was obvious that rumours were flying everywhere. A complete stranger grabbed me by the arm to tell me that the Emperor had been wounded in the New Year Games.

'You know he always liked to boast of taking part himself, especially in gladiatorial contests,' my informant said, raising his voice to be heard above the hubbub. 'Well he did it once too often; his opponent this time had a proper sword – instead of the wooden one he was supposed to use!'

I shook my head. 'That isn't possible. The New Year Games. That's just eight days ago. No one could possibly have got the news to us by now.'

I spoke so loudly that the man in front turned round.

'I don't know so much. I heard the story from a member of the watch, just now. As soon as Commodus was dead, dozens of messengers were sent out with the news, and every army post along the way sent out relays of its own, until there were hundreds of the fastest horsemen, travelling day and night, changing mounts at every opportunity and requisitioning the fastest ships and ferry boats. My informant said exactly what his Excellence Marcus Septimus told us at the shrine: it was as if the gods had given the message wings. The slowest part was getting word from Dubris to here, apparently. And he confirmed that the Emperor was stabbed, though he said that there was poison on the blade...'

A ragged street-hawker had been sidling up nearby, attempting to peddle his unappealing wares – a brace of dead pigeons dangling from a string. It was a measure of the strange nature of the day that he dared to interrupt a group of citizens. 'Poisoned, was he? And on the Kalends? Is that the truth of it? I had it from the sentry at the gate that Commodus was strangled at the plunge-pool in his bath the night before, by a slave he used to practise wrestling with.'

All eyes turned to stare at him, but no one

took offence. After a moment someone even laughed. 'Perhaps all three stories have an element of truth – the Emperor was said to be in league with the powers of the underworld so it wouldn't be surprising if he proved difficult to kill. But even if he somehow managed to survive for hours, it seems that Justice got him in the end.'

'You citizens had better be careful what you say!' Another newcomer tugged at my toga urgently. 'Someone just told me that he isn't dead at all, and this is just a rumour that he put about himself, to see what people do – and woe betide you if you show disrespect.'

I left them arguing and went to find my son. I found him standing by the fountain with the slaves. He made a rueful face at me as I approached. 'I am sorry, Father, we've lost your witnesses. They had litters waiting for them on the street. I saw them getting in and moving off, but we couldn't get across the crowd in time to speak to them.'

I patted his shoulder. 'Never mind. I doubt that they would have agreed to come with us just now in any case – I imagine all the members of the curia have gone somewhere private to discuss the news. I'll simply have to find out what their town addresses are, so I can call there later on. If I can find Marcus, he might be able to tell me where to look for them: he's on dining terms with everyone official in the area. Though I imagine he'll have left by now as well.'

Junio made a little gesture with his hand. 'On the contrary. Your patron is just coming from the temple now. I can see him on the steps – though he's got that priest with him and the commander of the garrison. Perhaps the moment is not convenient.'

I turned and saw what he had seen, but I shook my head. 'I think I'll take my chance. As his protégé I owe him my congratulations anyway, since Fate has made him a favourite of the potential Emperor – and he may be feeling especially cheerful and cooperative today. Wait here a moment, while I try to catch his eye.'

It wasn't easy forcing my way back to the temple steps, and I might have missed my patron even then, but fortunately I was not the only one to seek an audience. Cantalarius had already interposed himself between Marcus's little party and the crowd below. There was clearly some kind of argument going on and when I got there I found my farmer-neighbour confronting the old priest, much to the amusement of the spectators.

'Call yourself an experienced celebrant!' He was so angry he was shaking both his fists. 'You let that creature go! Don't try to fob me off with talk of auguries. This wasn't a judgement from the gods at all! It would not have happened if you'd simply held the rope. Well, I'm not satisfied. I paid good money to make that sacrifice, to lift a curse that has been placed on me, as you are well aware. Don't try to turn away. The least that you could do is come out to

67

the farm and make an offering at the household shrine to put things right!'

He had a point, of course, and the crowd – elated by the news from Rome – was clearly on his side. There were even some whistles of support and shouts of, 'What do you say to that?'

It was causing a commotion and the commander of the garrison was already making signals to the guard to have my neighbour dragged away. Even Cantalarius could see that it was dangerous to stay and he allowed his new supporters to take him by the arms and hustle him back down into the throng – but at the bottom of the temple steps he turned, and shouted over his shoulder, 'You haven't heard the last of me, I'm warning you! I want an assurance that something will be done within a day or two.'

More shouts and hollers. The crowd was restive now. The old priest raised his hand. 'Very well,' he murmured, smiling vaguely at the seething populace. 'For a little fee, I'm sure that some kind of arrangement can be made.'

There were whoops of joy at this victory and people turned away. Cantalarius – though clearly none too happy at the mention of a fee – was obliged to pretend to be content. 'Very well. Then I accept your promise.' He shook himself free from the restraining hands and disappeared into the crowd. No doubt he was wise. The mob was satisfied and he'd lost their sympathy. Any further protest would have led to his arrest.

The little breach of public order, however, made me think again. Marcus was not looking very pleased and was tapping his baton against his leg in a way that I knew of old. Obviously his patience was wearing very thin. I decided that discretion was the better path, and was about to melt away into the crowd when I heard my patron calling after me.

'Libertus! My old friend!' I turned. He had parted company with his companions now and was walking down the steps towards me with his slaves. 'Had you come to look for me? Do not fear to interrupt, I have finished all my current business here.' He paused and extended a ringed hand for me to kiss. 'What think you of the news?'

There was no escaping now. I went down on one knee at once to make obeisance. It wasn't easy, on a flight of narrow steps, and I was glad when he permitted me to rise – saying as I did so, 'Patron! Hearty congratulations on your likely rise to power. What a blessing for the Empire if Pertinax succeeds.'

He flicked his baton hard against his leg. 'Libertus, you are no doubt a very clever man – indeed I have often relied upon your intellect. But if you really think that I find this welcome news, it shows that you know nothing of Roman politics.'

'But Pertinax will make a splendid Emperor!' I said. I spoke with feeling. I had met the man myself and had a high opinion of his intelligence.

Marcus shook his head. 'Of course he would, if all he had to do was rule.' He looked around and pulled me to one side, murmuring softly so that only I could hear. 'The trouble is, he's far too honest for the role. If he's confirmed as Emperor – as he no doubt he will be, as he's highly regarded in the capital – he'll refuse to bribe the soldiers of the Pretorian Guard, and they will turn against him in no time at all; they are used to having handsome bonuses from the Imperial purse.'

I stared at him. 'But surely they are the Emperor's private guard?' I said.

'Exactly! Which is why it's so important to ensure their loyalty. But Pertinax would never dream of offering them cash – for him a soldier's duty is unquestioning. He would not think additional inducements were required.' He sighed. 'So there is nothing for it. I shall have to go to Rome – assuming that I get there soon enough. I have to make him listen to rational advice.'

'But surely a letter – if there is such haste? Nothing moves faster than the Imperial Post.'

He shook his head. 'It's too dangerous to write – someone is almost certain to intercept the messenger. A man who becomes Emperor has enemies at once – though Pertinax will take some time to understand that truth. I shall have to go and warn him. I only hope I can persuade him to do what's sensible. He's upright but he's stubborn and will do his duty – as he sees it – come what may! Even Commodus came to realize that. That's why he raised him to the Prefecture of Rome.'

'Of course,' I said sagely, to show I understood. 'Though at one time...' I was about to add that Pertinax had once been exiled in disgrace, but it occurred to me that – now that he was likely to be Emperor – it might be more prudent not to mention that. '...His father was a slave,' I finished unconvincingly.

Marcus looked at me as if he'd just remembered I was there. 'Forgive me, Libertus. I had forgotten how little you knew of politics. And this is really no concern of yours – except insofar as the Emperor is everyone's concern.'

'My patron's safety is of some concern to me, especially on a long and hazardous journey such as you propose,' I ventured, earning a reluctant smile for my flattery. 'The weather has been dreadful and the roads are treacherous. When do you hope to leave?'

He waved an airy hand. 'As soon as possible – once the news is definite – though arrangements will obviously take a little time. A half a moon or so at most: though no doubt my wife will argue otherwise and say that, since our son is very young, we should wait until the weather turns more fair. However, this is urgent and it cannot wait. I shall simply have to persuade her of the fact tonight. In the meantime you can escort me to a carrying-chair. Come!' He strode off down the remainder of the temple steps and into the crowded forum area. People fell back on either side as he strode through the crush, and I was obliged to potter after him.

As slave boys hurried off to find a chair for

71

him, he turned to me and smiled. Marcus could be very charming when he chose. 'I'll have to get your wife to come and talk to mine – I know your Gwellia has a persuasive tongue. Of course, the women will not know about the Emperor's death as yet but I will send word to your house as soon as I get back, though – since I am providing the sacrifice myself – I can't leave town until the offering is made.'

I seized the moment. 'Then, before you go, perhaps you could tell me where I can find two officials of the curia: Alfredus Allius and Bernadus?' I explained the circumstance. 'I have fulfilled the contract, but Genialis isn't here and they would be the obvious ones to witness that the work's been done. If you are able to tell me where they live, I can go and find them and request that they should come – supposing that they find it possible today.'

Marcus surprised me. 'I'll do more than that. I will come and see the work myself – I don't suppose your Genialis is going to question my word on the affair?' He saw that I was ready to protest, and added with a smile, 'There's an hour or two to fill before the feast begins and though I shall have to pay for the sacrificial beasts, I can't do that until the garrison has found me some appropriate animals. That will take a little time. I don't want to be drawn into local politics meanwhile.'

Of course, my patron's word was better than a raft of councillors. I stammered out my thanks. 'But if you're going abroad in half a moon or so...' I ventured. 'Perhaps, if Genialis is delayed by snow, you will not be able to tell him what you've seen?'

Once Marcus had decided on a scheme, he was not easy to dissuade. 'Oh, I'm sure he'll be here in a day or two. If not, I'll report my findings to the market police,' he said. 'Under my seal, should the need arise. I trust that will suffice? Now, my slaves will be here with that litter very soon. Where exactly is this pavement?'

I gave him directions. 'I will meet you there. I have my son and servants with me,' I said, before he could suggest that I should take a litter too (which I could ill afford) or – worse – expect me to accompany his own. I am far too old to run along, keeping up with bearers and his fit young slaves, so I added hastily, 'There is a doorkeeper in residence; he'll let you in and show you where the pavement is, I'm sure. I won't be long behind you.'

'Ulpius's house! I think I know the place.' His slaves had found a litter by this time (not difficult when you represent His Excellence) and the bearers were already waiting at his side. He climbed on to the cushions and drew the curtains closed, and I saw the carriers hoist him shoulder-high and go loping off with him, his scarlet-suited servants trotting after them.

I struggled through the crowd again, rounded up my little party and we set off ourselves. Away from the forum the streets were very quiet – everyone was at the basilica by now –

and now that the worst of the snow had slightly thawed, it did not take us long to reach the house. So I was astonished to discover a brace of slaves outside of it, each of them holding a handsome horse. There was no sign of any litter and these were not my patron's slaves – though they seemed to be guarding the entrance to the house.

They looked up as we approached. 'Do you have business here?' The sulky one with acne was quite belligerent.

'I was expecting to find Marcus Septimus Aurelius,' I said.

'Why, it's the pavement-maker, isn't it?' The younger slave flashed a languid smile at me, and I recognized him as the handsome Syrian I had seen attending Genialis when he called on me.

'Ah, Adonisius, I see that it is you!' That rather altered things. 'Has your master managed to return himself?' That would be even better for my purposes, of course, though Marcus would be irritated by a wasted trip.

The slave was flattered that I'd called him by his name. 'So you remember me? But you'll be disappointed, citizen, I fear. We presumed that my master had returned to town – he set off with that intention several days ago – and we came in to meet him as arranged. But it seems he isn't here.' He saw me glance towards the horses and explained, 'These are the animals that we two used ourselves. Bernadus lent them to us.'

'You two?' I nodded at the other waiting slave, surprised to find mere servants charged with such splendid mounts.

He shook his head and laughed. 'Of course not, citizen. Myself and my new mistress: that is what I meant. This slave, Pistis, and his master came over here on foot.'

I was hardly listening. 'You mean the lady Silvia has come?' I was even more surprised. It is not unknown for well-born females to learn to ride, but since they do so sideways it is not usual for them to venture very far. Yet it seemed that plucky Silvia had been brave enough to ride a dozen miles, on roads still difficult with snow – and with only her guardian's slave attending her. 'It's a long way for a lady of her rank to ride, especially with so little bodyguard. Though I suppose there was no real alternative. I remember Genialis telling me that he had sold off all her slaves when they were setting off for Dorn.'

Adonisius made a little face. 'I am officially assigned to her while my master is away, and we did have extra escort in Bernadus and his page. He came out to the villa the day after New Year – I think he felt obliged to, since we were staying there – but he always intended coming here today.'

'To attend the Janus festival! Of course!' I should have thought of that. 'I'm sure the lady was grateful for the protection on the road. No doubt that's why this day was chosen for her to return?'

The Syrian nodded. 'Though in fact her coming here was rather a mistake. The place is cold and empty, and the only servant here – a wretched doorkeeper – declares that he was not expecting us and he hasn't heard from Genialis since the day he left. It's quite a mystery: he should have been here several days ago. Always supposing that this doorman's story is the truth. Ulpius's business partner is questioning him now – and fortunately there's some hugely important magistrate who's just arrived and who could order more rigorous interrogation if...' He broke off suddenly. 'That wouldn't be this Marcus you were looking for?'

'That's right. My patron,' I explained. I saw a new respect dawn on the slave boy's face, and some wicked instinct made me add, 'Rumoured to be related to the last Imperial house and certainly a favourite of the incoming Emperor. He came here at my request. I had better go inside and talk to him. But there's no need to order any torturers. The doorkeeper is right. There's been no sign of Genialis. I can testify to that. You said he should have been here several days ago. Well, I have been working in this house from dawn to dusk – laying the pavement that I contracted for – right up to the morning before yesterday. In all that time there has not even been a messenger.'

The two servants exchanged a glance at this.

'Dear Mercury!' the pimply one exclaimed. 'He must have changed his mind and gone to Dorn instead. Whatever is my master going to do?'

'Your master? You belong to this partner of Ulpius's, I presume?'

He looked at me as if I ought to know. 'That's right, citizen. Lucius Tertius he's called, and of course he half-owned everything with Ulpius. There are already problems over the estate. Of course, as Silvia's legal guardian Genialis has the running of her share. He wants to close the business down – sell the ships and rent the warehouse out. Says it is a way of making money without risk.'

I nodded. 'But Lucius isn't happy?'

'He wants to buy him out and purchase Sylvia's share – he's even found a sponsor who might come in with him, but the man will only do so if it gives a quick return. The would-be partner has no other source of funds at all – he's dependent on the income from his capital – and there's something else he might invest in if this business takes too long.'

'But does Genialis have the right to sell off Silvia's share, in any case? I thought he only got the profits on her capital?'

Lucius's servant gave a knowing smile. 'Only after they are married, citizen. Until then he can dispose of it if she agrees in front of witnesses, and – though I'm certain that she would fight him all the way – in the end he could compel her to do that. Though she'd gladly give consent for him to sell to my master, I am sure; she's fond of him and knows that Ulpius trusted him.'

'How do you know all this?' I asked, but I knew the answer as I spoke. 'You were there when the matter was discussed and you could not help but overhear, I suppose?' I've been a slave myself and understand these things – owners think that servants have no eyes or ears.

'That's right, citizen.' He was unaware of any irony. 'And this arrangement would be the answer for everyone, I'm sure. The trouble is, I don't think Genialis knows about it yet – Lucius was hoping to talk him into it – and if he's gone back to Dorn instead of coming here, it is almost certain that the arrangement will fall through.'

'I wonder.' It occurred to me, from what I knew of Genialis, that he might well have known – and gone to Dorn on purpose, to put pressure on Lucius and so increase the price he could demand. I turned to Junio. 'I think we'd better go inside and see. Maximus and Minimus can come as well – they don't have horses to look after, like you two, and I presume that Marcus has taken his attendants in.'

The allusion to my patron seemed to do the trick. Adonisius and his friend had been standing right outside the entrance way – taking the place of the doorkeeper I suppose – but now they moved aside to let us pass. 'You will be unannounced,' Adonisius muttered, doubtfully. 'Unless you would like one of us to go ahead of you and tell them you are here?'

I shook my head. 'We'll take our chances, thank you very much. After all this is not a social call and the household is not currently equipped for visitors. You stay here with the horses.' And so saying, I led the way into the house.

FIVE

I found them gathered in the atrium. When I was there before it was devoid of furniture, but someone – perhaps the doorkeeper – had produced a pair of folding stools, and Marcus and the lady were sitting either side of a little table which was set up on the far side of the room, near the altar to the domestic gods, and which held three goblets and an empty jug. Obviously a minimal refreshment had been found. The third cup had evidently been used by a cheerful-looking fellow whom I didn't recognize, who stood beside the table at the rear. This must be Lucius Tertius, I thought.

He must have been twenty-five or thirty years of age and was obviously used to working out of doors. His face was tanned, his arms were muscular and (though clearly prosperous) he did not appear to be a citizen. A freeman, probably, because he sported a very un-Roman beard and side-whiskers – particularly striking in this environment because they were the same amber colour as his embroidered tunic and his hair. He looked up to greet us as our little group appeared.

So did the rest of them. Marcus's two scarlet-uniformed pages were ranged against the wall, and they came hasting forward to take our capes and cloaks – though only to add them to the armfuls they already held. Standing alone in the middle of the room, evidently the centre of a recent storm of questioning, even my gloomy friend the doorkeeper turned around to stare.

'Longinus Flavius Libertus,' I announced myself, before my slaves could say a word. 'His Excellence is expecting me, I think.'

Marcus nodded. 'So I was.' He flapped a hand at me. 'Do you know Lucius Tertius?'

I bowed towards my fellow beard-wearer. 'Ulpius's partner? We have not met, but I have heard of him.' I turned to Silvia. 'And this must be the lady of the house – as beautiful as Ulpius always said she was.'

Indeed, only a man who had a preference for Syrian slave boys could possibly have called her 'ugly as a mule' – though she might be wilful, I could imagine that. She was still in mourning for her husband, naturally, and her *stola* and undertunic were of sombre black, but she wore a lustrous girdle made of plaited silk arranged in the becoming Grecian style, so that it came round her shoulders, crossed over in the front, then looped around her body to be tied off in a knot – thus emphasizing both her waist and her other attributes. She was a shapely woman and was aware of it – as were all the adult males in the room. Her veil, which should strictly have obscured her face, was thrown back to form a sort of lacy frame from which a tangle of

81

dark curls had half-escaped and the sparkling dark eyes which looked boldly into mine seemed more amused than grieved.

Her voice, however, was decorous and low. 'Libertus!' She half-rose in greeting and held out a plump, well-manicured white hand. 'I, in turn, have heard of you. My late husband spoke most highly of your work.' There was no offer of refreshment for me or Junio. Of course we were here as pavement-makers rather than as guests, so perhaps I should not have been expecting it. Silvia rather underlined the thought. She turned to Lucius. 'This is the man who laid the entrance pavement with the ship.'

'And the one which has replaced it,' I pointed out, taking the hand and bowing over it. 'Completed before the Agonalia, as I contracted with your guardian.'

'And thereby meriting the double fee. That fact has been noted!' Marcus murmured, with a nod.

Lucius said bluffly, 'Then it is to be hoped that there's enough to pay for it. Genialis has been spending money as some men pour out grain, and who knows what will be left in his estate?'

Silvia rounded on him, looking shocked. 'What makes you say that? You speak as you think that my guardian is dead. I know the weather has been terrible, but I don't think you need to worry about that. He's a splendid horseman. He is known for it. Anyway he had borrowed Bernadus's horse, branded with a most distinctive mark, so if anything had happened to him on the way we'd certainly have heard. Surely – as I pointed out before – it's more likely that he's simply gone to Dorn?'

Lucius looked doubtful. 'I suppose you're right. Under the circumstances, perhaps, it's just what he would do! If only to disoblige us.'

'Hoping to panic you a bit, so that you would agree to pay any price at all for the part of Ulpius's business that was left to Silvia?'

If I had hoped to startle him by saying this, I failed. Lucius simply threw back his auburn head and laughed. 'I see you have the measure of him, citizen. I would no doubt have paid him, too – like an idiot – if he had turned up just in time and made a high demand. Anything to make sure the deal went through.' Then realization must have come to him. He frowned. 'But how did you come to hear about this, citizen? I didn't tell you, and I'm sure my potential partner has not mentioned it to anyone. I didn't think that even Genialis knew what I had hoped to do, though – since on reflection I agree it's likely that he has gone to Dorn – perhaps I was mistaken in supposing that. If you've heard about it, citizen, perhaps all Glevum has!'

This time it was Marcus laughing. 'Oh, Libertus has a way of knowing everything! That is why I often call on him to find things out for me.' He cocked an eyebrow at me. 'Though I don't suppose that even you can deduce what's happened to our host? It seems he left Bernadus's villa several days ago, and at the time he said that he would come directly here.'

'And there was no message for him which may have changed his mind?' I said, thinking aloud rather than expecting a response.

Silvia, however, gave a sudden startled squeak. 'But of course there was a message. I'd forgotten that.' She dimpled at me. 'The rider reached me at the villa shortly after Genialis left, and I told him where I thought my guardian had gone and he set off after him. Something about provision for a sacrifice, he said. I had supposed that the message was from Glevum, but on reflection...'

I turned to Silvia. 'You think it came from Dorn?'

The lady coloured, rather prettily. 'Otherwise, surely, the courier would have passed him on the road before he reached the villa? I didn't think of that. Of course, I can't be absolutely sure. I should have asked the messenger, I suppose, but I was more concerned to send him riding straight off in pursuit. He'd only missed Genialis by an hour or so. But now I think of it, he must have come from Dorn. Some kind of emergency, I suppose – something connected with the weather possibly. It's the obvious explanation of why my guardian isn't here. How clever of you, pavement-maker, to have worked it out.' She turned to Lucius. 'So it seems the doorkeeper was telling us the truth.'

'I could have testified to that, in any case,' I said, earning myself a grateful smile from the slave in question. 'I have been here myself, laying the new pavements in the entrance hall, for days. Unless Genialis turned up yesterday, after I had gone – which seems unlikely, since he wasn't at the feast today which he was so anxious to attend – he has not been back to Glevum since you saw him last. And there's been no word from him. I suggest you send to Dorn – and while you are about it, ask at every public inn between.'

Lucius nodded. 'You are quite right, of course. I will despatch a messenger at once. Excuse me, Excellence – citizens – I will go and see to it.' He bowed himself away.

She flashed a smile at his retreating form. 'How helpful Lucius is. He has been very good. He has even offered me accommodation over-night, since it is obvious that I can't stay here alone: there is nothing civilized to eat and not even a female servant to be had – the slave market does not operate today. So lacking my guardian, and in the absence of a deciding court...'

Marcus had put on his imperious face. 'Mad-am, forgive me, but that would not be proper, in my view. You are an attractive lady–' he looked appreciatively at her – 'and you are a mourning widow, after all. You cannot with propriety accompany a man who – by what you told me when I first arrived – is not in possession of a wife or even of any female relatives. Besides – forgive me – Lucius may be a freeman, and a wealthy one, but he is not a citizen. Genialis is still your official guardian and he would be affronted by the mere suggestion if he knew.'

'What suggestion, Excellence?' Lucius, having obviously despatched his slave, was reappearing just in time to hear the words.

Marcus had risen to his feet. He could look imposing when he tried. 'The suggestion that you should accommodate the lady Silvia at your house. Much more appropriate that she should come with me. I have a large apartment in the town and there are servants there – including female ones – who can attend her overnight. Tomorrow or the next day we may have word from Dorn, and then we can establish how we should proceed. In the meantime – in my role as magistrate – I am assuming temporary potestas.' He paused and looked at Silvia – obviously waiting for her to express her gratitude.

After the briefest of hesitations she provided it. 'Excellence, your kindness is more than I could have looked for.' She held out a jewelled hand to Lucius. 'And your kindness, naturally, as well. Two offers of protection in a single day – and such protection too! I'm a lucky woman. But His Excellence is right to think of my good name. And he has the authority of law should Genialis decide to make a fuss.'

I could only mentally applaud her tactfulness. She had managed to produce a gracious form of words – almost suggesting that she had a choice, and had opted for Marcus with fluttering regret – though of course in practice she had no choice at all. Marcus had pronounced himself her legal guardian and he had too much authority to be argued with.

Both men, however, were looking gratified – though there was a touch of disappointment in Lucius's tone, as he bowed over the extended fingers and murmured, 'Of course. His Excellence is more than generous. You will be safe with him.'

Marcus looked self-satisfied at this. 'Unfortunately, for a moment, it will not be with me. I shall have to go and arrange this sacrifice and I can't afford a page at present to accompany you. Libertus, you have visited my apartment, haven't you? You can escort the lady to the place. My slaves know who you are.'

Behind me I heard Junio give a muffled laugh. I had almost forgotten that he was listening in: he had once been my slave, till I adopted him, and – like my red-haired servants – he knew how to stand by and make himself completely inconspicuous. But I knew what had amused him. My most recent visit to Marcus's apartment had been undignified – I was effectively under house arrest and had climbed out of the window to escape.

However, I did not allude to that. 'I'm certain they will recognize me instantly,' I said – and almost provoked another snigger from my son.

Marcus ignored it; if indeed he heard. 'Then you can escort the lady there. Tell them I sent you and I'll call there later on. They are to provide a meal and wait on her meanwhile. It should not be difficult. There is a room prepared and there will already be provision in the house – made ready for the priest from Aqua Sulis when he came, in case he decided that he wished to stay with me tonight, rather than at the temple. But then he didn't come at all.'

'And what about the horses?' I asked, with real concern. I used to be an avid horseman in my youth – I was a Celtic nobleman with stables of my own before I was captured into slavery – but it was many years since I had ridden properly. 'There are two of them outside and there's nowhere to keep them at your apartment block. Do you wish me to arrange to have them stabled somewhere else?'

Marcus looked lofty. 'I will take the horses with me to my villa when I go. You wouldn't like to ride one back for me, I suppose? Or perhaps you, Junio? Silvia's attendant can ride the other one. Though I suppose that they belong to Bernadus anyway. He ought to be consulted.' He turned to Silvia. 'He'll be at the curial meeting I suppose. With your permission, I'll send your Syrian along to his town house speak to him. Unless...?' He looked questioningly at Lucius.

Lucius shook his head. 'I had no hand in that arrangement. Let the Syrian go.'

Silvia was rising to her feet. She shook her head. 'Though remember, Bernadus only came to Glevum for the sacrifice, and intends to go back to his country villa afterwards. Better send your messenger out there.'

'That will get one of the horses back, at least,'

Lucius agreed. 'Adonisius can walk back if he needs, I suppose. In the meantime I should go and meet the man from whom I hoped to raise the money – and try to persuade him to wait another day.' He nodded towards the scarlet-suited pageboys by the wall, who came hurrying forward with the cloaks.

Silvia smiled. 'From what I hear of Alfredus Allius, he'll agree to a delay. This deal would make an easy living for him, after all.'

'Alfredus Allius?' I murmured in surprise. 'He was the other witness to my contract with your guardian. A friend of Genialis, isn't he?' Somehow, whoever the investor was, I had not expected that.

Silvia turned to me, as Marcus's young page – having helped his master fasten on his cape – assisted her with hers. 'You are astonished? I am not surprised. He knows nothing of shipping, as I'm sure you know. But as a friend of Genialis – if you can call him that – he must have seen that the opportunity was there. He was the one who came to us, in fact. Promised to provide the cash to buy my portion of the firm – intending to leave the management to Lucius alone, while taking half the profits. Not a bad return.'

'And you are sure that you can trust him?' I said, doubtfully.

Lucius gave his characteristic hearty laugh. 'I'm sure that I cannot. That's why the contract stipulates that I can buy him out again, as soon as I can raise the capital. Of course that isn't likely to be for several years, unless I'm very lucky with some commodity. But one never knows.' He gave me a wink which told me that he knew very well, and already had a particular commodity in mind. 'But it gives a man a goal to work for, doesn't it?' He took his cloak and – spurning pageboys – put it on himself.

Marcus had been standing by, as if impatient of all this talk of trade. 'Well, that concludes our business in this household, I suppose,' he said testily. 'I have seen your pavement – it is very nicely done, and I'll say so to Genialis when I see him next. I shall want a word with him in any case.'

'To chide him for dereliction of his duty, I suppose. Leaving his ward to travel all alone and failing to prepare her house for her?' I said.

Marcus shook his head and, seeing that Lucius and Silvia were making their farewells, he leant across and murmured in my ear. 'It's about this shipping business. If this Alfredus deal falls through, I've half a mind to see if I can buy Silvia's share myself.'

I said nothing. I could not believe my ears. My patron was not the sort of man to sink his gold in trade.

Marcus saw my look of disbelief. 'It would oblige the lady!' he murmured softly, so that only I could hear. 'Besides, if Alfredus Allius thinks there is a profit in the deal...' Then he raised his voice. 'Now if everyone is ready, I think we've finished here. Libertus, would you like to lead the way outside?'

SIX

Once we were outside in the frosty air again, Lucius took his leave – looking a little discomfited, I thought. Perhaps it was because his servant had set off for Dorn and he was now obliged to walk the streets unattended, but I suspected it was more to do with disappointment over Silvia. Marcus, though, seemed oblivious of any discontent and was happily issuing orders to the various slaves: sending his own pages off to find a pair of carrying chairs and despatching the Syrian to find Bernadus.

'If you can't find him in Glevum before the sacrifice, you'll have to go and find him at his country house. At least, I suppose, you know the way by now,' my patron said. He turned towards the doorkeeper. 'I shall leave the other horse in your care meanwhile.'

The man did not seem happy with the task, judging by the doubtful look he gave the beast and the timid way in which he took the reins, but he was trained in obedience. 'As you say, Excellence!'

'When Adonisius comes back, and we hear from Bernadus what he wants done with the horse, you can send and let me know – since I am now responsible on Silvia's behalf,' Marcus said with a pretence at innocence, though of course was certain what the reply would be.

Bernadus would offer my patron use of it till he returned to town – that is, if he didn't make an outright gift of it – otherwise he might seem to be discourteous and could never hope to make further progress in the town.

Marcus knew it, too, which was doubtless why he was smiling as he said, 'I shall be at the garrison *praetorium* till noon – I'm invited to have a little refreshment with the commander there, to look over the animals for potential sacrifice this afternoon. After the rites, you may enquire for me at home. In the meantime you can tether this creature somewhere here.'

The doorman nodded gloomily, and plodded off with it, obviously hoping to find a hitching point in the alleyway nearby.

That left my little party standing in the street alone with Marcus and the Lady Silvia. My patron turned to me. 'Shall I see you at the temple later on?'

It would be expected of me, but I glanced up at the sky. The chilly wind had blown away the clouds and a pale sun glittered wanly from an expanse of palest blue. I made a swift decision. 'I don't think so, Excellence. With this clear sky, it promises to freeze again tonight, and if we two hope to reach our wives and houses today we should set off soon, before the roads become impassable again. We are – after all – on foot.'

I feared I would offend him, but he simply waved a hand. 'Then I will say farewell for now. But be good enough to call in at the villa on your way and tell my wife that I shall be detained in town tonight. My duty keeps me here...' He frowned. 'On second thoughts, perhaps I'll ask the commander of garrison if he can spare a horseman to act as messenger. It will be almost dark before you get there, walking, I suppose.'

I bowed. I was relieved to have been spared the need to call myself. For one thing, the villa was not really 'on my way' – in fact it was almost a Roman mile further down the lane – and for another I have never been good at hiding things from Julia, his wife. If she had asked me what the nature of this 'duty' was, she would soon have deduced that Silvia had undoubted charms. However there was no need to tell my patron this.

I murmured meekly, 'I would have been honoured to be of service to you, Excellence, of course.'

He gave me a brisk nod. 'Of course. And later on I shall have need of you. I'll be home tomorrow and I want to talk to you. I'll send a slave for you as soon as I arrive.' He gestured towards Silvia and shook his head, as if to indicate that he did not wish to spell things out while she was listening. I must have looked surprised because he added, with a smile, 'That little venture that I spoke to you about – I think that I would value your advice.'

I understood his meaning all too clearly now. No doubt he'd want me to look into Lucius's affairs, to find out what the prospects of a profit were and what kind of men were his associates! I gave an inward groan.

I'd encountered Ulpius's contacts when he was alive and I was laying that previous floor for him. He'd brought them to admire it: traders and foreign merchants to a man, for many of whom their only home in Glevum was a ship. I could see that this affair of Marcus's was likely to entail a visit to the docks, and that I would have to go aboard these vessels for myself. It was not a prospect that delighted me. When I was first kidnapped by the pirates in the south and they dragged me from my home, they had forced me to their ship and flung me in the hold, where I'd spent days of terror chained up in the pitching, stinking dark before I was hauled out and sold to slavery. I have hated boats and water ever since.

However, Marcus was my patron and I could only say, 'At your command, as ever, Excellence.'

'Very well. I'll send for you tomorrow,' he said cheerfully. 'Now, I see, my pages have summoned me a chair.' He gestured towards a pair of litters which had just arrived. He turned away and climbed nimbly into the nearest one, with the assistance of his scarlet-suited slaves. 'The other chair's for Silvia, of course!' he called, pulling the curtains closed, and before I could ask him who was to pay for this, the bearers were already trotting off with him, with his attendants scampering along on either side.

I turned around. Silvia was already being assisted up into the second chair by Minimus and Maximus. There was nothing for it! I gave instructions to the litter bearers: 'To the wine shop opposite the baths. Payment on arrival!' I winked at Junio and he winked back at me.

'Very prudent, Father – but we'd better follow them!' He pointed to the bearers who had already started off and were almost disappearing round the corner of the street. Of course they were strong lads, accustomed to the task, and they moved very fast, so I left Junio to hurry after them, while I – accompanied by my slave boys – puffed along behind.

Perhaps it was fortunate for me that just around the corner, the street was shadowy. The wintry sun had not yet done its work and the pavements were still slippery with slush and heaps of piled-up snow – to the joy of groups of urchins who were using them as slides. More sober pedestrians had therefore taken to the road, and nearer the forum there was still a pressing crowd so I soon caught up with Juno and the litter in the crush. But the litter bearers were happily adept at jostling, using their elbows and their poles to clear a path, so that by following as close behind them as we could, we soon reached the building where the apartment was.

'You want us to stop at the doorway to the upstairs, citizen?' the nearer bearer said.

I nodded, still too breathless to reply. The wine shop occupied the lower floor, but there was another entrance way a little further on, which gave on to the stairs. It was, as usual, swarming with people of every age and rank – most of whom were craning to look as we appeared.

'Take no notice,' I said to Silvia, helping her to get down from the chair. 'They are just the people who live in flats upstairs.'

She nodded. 'From the top floors, mostly, from the look of it,' she murmured nervously.

She was right of course. There are always several storeys of apartments in a place like this, and the size and status of these establishments decreases dramatically the further up you climb. So elegant apartments, such as Marcus's, might take up the whole first floor, but the attics are a warren of squalid little rooms crammed to bursting with the free-born poor. There is never any means of heating, in these topmost floors – even braziers are forbidden, lest they cause a fire – but people very often improvize, dragging illicit firewood up flights and flights of stairs, and there are smells of cooking cabbage and telltale wisps of smoke. All this would mean an instant punishment, of course, if the aediles – the market policemen – caught you in the act, so there are often idlers on the landings, or people playing dice, watching all comers with suspicious eyes.

Today was no exception and Silvia drew back a little, obviously alarmed.

I took her by the arm. 'They are simply curious,' I told her, hoping I was right. 'There's no need to be frightened.'

Junio stepped forwards. 'Why don't you wait down here with lady Silvia?' he said. 'The slaves and I can go upstairs and tell them we are here – and bring back the money to pay the litter men. That will save you being stared at while they open up the door and they will be waiting for you when you do arrive.'

'An excellent arrangement,' I agreed. 'Tell them to send someone to attend the lady up, as well. I think she would be grateful for a female slave.' Junio nodded and he started up the stairs, with my slave boys ready to lead the way for him. But they were not required to force a path, in fact – people here were doubtless used to Marcus's visitors and they stood back quite respectfully to let the toga past.

Silvia watched them and her fingers tightened slightly on my sleeve. 'Forgive me, citizen. I see that you were right. There isn't any danger. I always fear the worst. Ulpius used to say it was my greatest fault.'

I still held her elbow and I turned her round until I was looking full into her eyes. 'And yet, forgive me, it does not apply – it seems – in matters that affect your guardian,' I said.

She coloured prettily. 'I'm not sure I understand you, citizen.'

'Oh, I think you do. Genialis sets off on his own, rides through the bitterest of snow, does not arrive at his destination as arranged – and yet you seem convinced that he is safe. Indeed, you chided Lucius for suggesting otherwise. Yet I think you should prepare yourself for the possibility that your guardian has met an accident.'

She shook her head with vigour. The pretty cheeks were bright vermilion now. 'Oh, Genialis will turn up safe and sound – people of his type always do.' She laughed and drew me a little further from the bottom of the stairs, as though she feared she might be overheard. 'Citizen, may I be completely frank with you? You say I do not fear the worst where he's concerned. I do! I fear that he is safe. I dare not allow myself to hope that he is dead – though perhaps you find that hard to understand?'

I shook my head. 'Not as difficult as you might suppose. I imagine that Genialis is not an easy man.'

'Easy! He is well-nigh impossible! Pompous, vain and selfish – and a spendthrift gambler too. A man more different from my Ulpius it would be hard to find.'

'Yet they were brothers?'

She made a deprecating gesture with her hand. 'Half-blood, that is all. They shared a father, certainly, but Ulpius was the offspring of a different wife and was always favoured – even as a child. I think that Genialis hated him for that.'

'But did his family duty, anyway, by applying to be your guardian?' I said.

She gave a bitter laugh. 'Not because he cared

for me a jot – he much prefers his pretty Syrian slave, though Adonisius hates the sight of him – and certainly not out of any family duty towards poor Ulpius. He wanted the use of my inheritance, that's all – and I, poor fool, had no one else to speak for me. Lucius might have done it; he was always good to me, but he is not even a proper citizen – what hope would he have had? Genialis had the stronger case in law...' She broke off as Junio came clattering down the stairs, accompanied by my servants and – bringing up the rear – a plump and moon-faced female slave of Julia's.

I faintly knew the woman; she had been a nurse to Marcus's young son when he was small. I gazed at her, attempting to recall her name.

Junio supplied it for me. 'This is Nutricia, Father. I believe you've met before. I'll leave her with you while I go and pay the chair.' And he suited the action to the words.

The slave woman waddled over – it was the only word for it – and bobbed a clumsy curtsy. 'Why, citizen Libertus! I know your face, of course. I've seen you at the villa. Don't you remember me?'

'Nutricia! Of course!' The name derives from 'wet-nurse' and I should have known. 'I did not know that you were still...' I tailed off.

'Oh, they keep me out of kindness – or the lady Julia does. I help the household here with general chores and attend on my mistress – and that dear child of course – on the rare occasions when they come to town. But now I am to have another charge, I hear.' She turned to Silvia, her fat face wreathed in smiles. 'Though I see you are in mourning, my pretty little lamb.'

Silvia said nothing; she just glanced at me so I answered for her. 'She is a widow, though she is betrothed again.' I saw the look of scandal on the nurse's face and added quickly, 'Her husband's brother is her guardian and he should be here, but he has somehow been delayed by snow, so Marcus has taken temporary potestas of her.'

Silvia smiled prettily at this, looking so attractive that she positively glowed and – since the nurse was clearly fond of Julia – I wondered if my explanation had simply made things worse. Nutricia, however, seemed entirely satisfied. 'How like the master to be kind like that,' she said. 'Well now, my lambkin, you come along with me. Nutricia will see that you're looked after properly. I've got the kitchen slaves to warm some water through, and I've got some rose petals that I've been keeping by, so you can have a nice warm scented wash for your poor feet. Citizen Junio tells me you've been travelling for miles!' She went to lead my charge away from me.

'I will accompany the lady to the apartment door,' I said, rather nettled at having to insist, but I was glad enough when Silvia was safely in the flat, out of range of prying eyes and under the protection of the household slaves, so I could hasten back to Junio and the boys.

I found them waiting for me in the street. We hastened to the workshop, my son and I took off our togas while the two slaves doused the fire, and then – wrapped in the warmest cloaks and clothing we could find – set off at last towards our houses and our wives.

SEVEN

The journey home was every bit as demanding as I'd feared. The forest track – steep and treacherous at the best of times – was made even more challenging than usual by slush and standing snow: indeed it was still slippery with frozen ice in parts, so progress was difficult and slow, in spite of the impromptu walking staves we picked up on the way. Moreover, the sight of recent wolf tracks in several places near the path was an inducement to hasten where we could. We met no marauding animals, I am glad to say, and my young companions managed well enough, but I took several tumbles at steep points on the path, which left me bruised and shaken – not to mention soaked in icy water to the waist.

But we were all shivering and weary to our very bones by the time we reached the inter-section with the better road and the adjoining clearing where our enclosures were. It was growing dark by now, so only the silhouettes of palisades and buildings could be seen, but I turned to Junio. 'Isn't that the most welcome sight that you have ever seen?'

He grinned wearily at me. 'Your roundhouse

in particular! I can see the glimmering of candles at the door – and isn't that the smell of cooking in the air?'

I sniffed and realized that he was right. Mingled with the wood-smoke from the central chimney hole, a delicious hint of stewing chicken came wafting out to us.

This promise of warm comfort would have given us new heart to hurry on in any case, but before we'd taken another pace towards the house my outer gate flew open and Kurso, my little kitchen slave, was rushing out to greet me with a lighted brand.

'Master! We thought we heard the sound of voices on the road. We have been watching and listening for you half the day. Thank all the gods you're safe! And you too, Master Junio – and my fellow slaves, of course. The mistress says to tell you all to come in here.'

My son shook his head with obvious regret. 'My own family and slave will be expecting me...'

But Kurso went on, opening the gate: 'Master Junio, they are here awaiting you and we've been keeping a pot of stew warm on a trivet by the fire.'

We followed him into the roundhouse where the smoky warmth enveloped us at once. Our wives rose to greet us from their stools beside the fire, though Junio's wife, Cilla, held a finger to her lips to warn us against making too much noise, because the infant was asleep nearby. All the same she flung herself into her husband's arms, while my Gwellia made her embraces with her eyes.

'I am glad to see you, husband!' That was all she said, but her expression told me how worried she had been. Then her dear face softened to a smile. 'But don't just stand there in those freezing clothes, or we shall have you dying of a chill.' As she spoke she came forward with a towel.

There were clean woollen tunics and warm cloaks laid ready upon the bed, and Gwellia herself assisted me to dry and change my clothes while Junio's slave boy did the same for him. (Normally this was a servant's job, of course, but the unusual arrangement suited everyone tonight. It not only allowed my wife to show her care for me but also freed Kurso to help his fellow slaves.)

'Now,' Gwellia said, when we travellers were all fully dried and clad. She spoke in a hushed voice so as not to wake the child. 'You can tell us what you have been doing since we met. I had a garbled message which put my mind at rest, saying you had some sort of contract in the town. I did not know that you had any work in hand.'

'Neither did we,' I whispered, with one eye on the babe. I squatted on the stool beside the cooking fire and warmed my hands and feet while Gwellia stirred the pot. Junio stretched out close by me on the sleeping bench, and together we explained how the unexpected commission came about. 'He agreed a splendid price, provided that I finished it by the Agonalia,' I finished. 'I managed to do it, but he was not there to see that for himself, though fortunately I have witnesses to the fact.'

Gwellia nodded. 'Well, that is a good omen for the new year,' she murmured, as Cilla passed her a pile of wooden bowls and she began to ladle out the meal. 'The money will be useful, certainly, after all this snow. Things in the garden plot are wilting with the frost.'

I shook my head. 'It is to be hoped the fellow pays me, that is all. He was expected back in Glevum a day or two ago, but he has not arrived – though it is possible that he has gone to Dorn instead. Marcus knows about it. We are awaiting news.'

Gwellia shrugged. 'This man is wealthy, from what you say of him, and a member of the curia – or he wants to be. People like him don't perish in the snow, as poorer folks might do. He will have found some sort of shelter in an inn, or foisted himself upon some private house by boasting of his rank. Well, let's hope he turns up with his payment soon. In the meantime, eat your food before it spoils.'

I didn't persist in saying any more. I did not want to spoil either my dinner or the mood. For now it was time to pull more stools around the fire and enjoy the luxury of huge bowls of steaming stew. Maximus and Minimus, who had been given bowlfuls too, and were sitting on straw pillows a little further back, were almost tearful in their gratitude at not being required to wait until their master had consumed his own.

The Romans talk about ambrosia, but give me Gwellia's chicken stew, with turnips, leeks and barley – and flour dumplings on the top! From the first tasty morsel I could feel the warmth suffusing my whole body like a magic charm, and with every mouthful strength came seeping back.

'Wonderful!' I murmured to my wife – and everyone agreed, with such enthusiasm that the infant stirred. After that we were content with smiles and nods, but they expressed our satisfaction as well as any words. In companionable silence we finished off the stew and followed it with cups of steaming mead.

Then Cilla said to Junio, 'Husband, I think that we should leave. You and your father are in need of rest.'

I would have protested, on my wife's account – Gwellia dotes on our adoptive grandson as if he were her own – but she caught my eye and shook her head, so I commanded Kurso to reignite the brand and light the young family and their slave boy up the short path to their home. 'And when you have finished bring the torch back here!'

Delighted by his new importance – everyone agreed it was not his normal role – Kurso took the torch, held it to the fire and brandished it with such gusto that I feared briefly for the thatch.

The child half-woke when his father lifted

him and wrapped him gently in a corner of his cloak, but an instant later he closed his eyes again and there was scarcely a whimper as he was carried out into the dark and cold. The little party set off up the rise and I gave my red-haired slaves permission to retire in turn, to their own little sleeping house beside the outer door. Then I reached out a lazy hand towards the pan and poured myself the remnants of the hot spiced mead.

'I don't know if you heard about the sacrifice today...' I began, ready to share the scandal with my wife.

'Not now, husband!' she murmured at my side. 'This is no time for telling tales and drinking mead. You are very tired and you forget that you are old. You should go to bed. Kurso and I will finish the last chores and then I'll come myself.'

I would cheerfully have helped to rake out the fire and set tomorrow's bread and cakes to bake, but Gwellia would brook no argument. I took off my outer tunic and lay down sleepily on the mattress of fresh reeds, under the woollen blanket and the furs.

'I'm sorry you were worried,' I murmured drowsily. 'I hoped to spare you that. But at least you got the message, saying I was safe?'

She nodded, pausing in the act of kneading dough. 'Several days ago. That farmer, Cantalarius, came here with his mules. He was full of grumbles, as he always is, boasting about some sacrifice he'd promised to the gods. I didn't take it in. But I was glad to hear from him. I could not be sure you had not set off on the Kalends and been caught out in the cold – but once I knew that you were safe in town I was reassured.'

'I'm not like Genialis,' I said sleepily. 'If I set off, I generally arrive.'

'Husband, you know it's not an idle fear,' she said, not smiling at my teasing. 'I've already heard of two people who have died. Poor old Lotta, who used to come round selling herbs, was found up at the spring – slipped in the ice and broke her leg and hip, and died of cold before they discovered her. Kurso saw the body when he went up with the pail. And you know that bit of marshy pond down in the woods?'

I did. There was a place in the forest where the land had once been ground, but the land was too waterlogged to support a crop and the effort was abandoned, leaving an area of swampy pools. It was a little distance from the track and in the summer it was screened by leafy trees, but it was easily visible at this time of year. 'Of course,' I said. 'We passed it just today.'

'There was a tragedy down there the other day as well. When that Cantalarius was here, he told me that he'd seen it from the road. Half a dozen people trying to retrieve a body from the lake. He almost stopped to help them, but it was getting dark. Some poor man who'd slipped and fallen in head first – either drowned or knocked his head and froze to death. The ice had formed around him and they were having to break it up to get the corpse.' She shuddered. 'What an awful way to go. And that's just the two fatalities that we have heard about.'

I made a sympathetic noise. Of course she had been worried. Every winter there are several deaths like that – and this winter had been particularly cruel. 'Never mind,' I said. 'It has begun to thaw.'

She gave a rueful laugh. 'As soon as I saw that I was concerned again. I knew that you would try to come as soon as possible, but the paths are terrible and I've heard wolves howling in the forest on several nights. And Cantalarius said that something had been gnawing at that corpse.' She shook her head at me. 'Time we bought a mule, ourselves, so you don't have to walk – it would make your life a great deal easier. It would save me nightmares, too.'

'But what about poor Junio and the slaves?' I said. 'Or are you suggesting we buy mules for them as well? And what should I do with the animals while I'm in the shop? Leave them with a hiring stables and pay fees for them?'

She didn't answer – usually a sign that she knows I am right.

I pressed my advantage. 'Besides, how many times since we've been living here have you known the roads to be impassable with snow – let alone for them to stay that way for days?'

'Cantalarius seems to manage to afford a mule,' she said, shifting the subject in that way she has. 'And he's much worse off than us.'

'You managed to pay him, I suppose?' I said.

'I know that two sesterces is a lot to give for simply bringing you a message, when he was coming this way in any case – but I felt it was worth it to stop you worrying.'

She rolled the dough into a ball and slapped it down on to the baking iron. 'You'd squander money on a thing like that, but you will not think of purchasing a mule. But I paid him, certainly – I gave him the money from the sandal fund, as you sent word to do – but it wasn't two sesterces, I'm afraid. I'd already spent the larger part of that, laying in some extra oil and kindling.'

I sat up in surprise. 'How did you manage that? Surely you didn't go walking into town?' It was a foolish question – I knew the forest tracks had been impassable on foot – but Glevum was the only local marketplace for oil.

She shook her head and laughed. 'Of course not, husband! Would I come without alerting you? But when the snow began I feared that we would soon run out of heat and light, so I went to Marcus's villa and talked to Julia. She let me have some from the household store, and a mobius measureful of flour as well. I insisted that I'd pay her – I don't like to beg – but she'd only take a fraction of the proper price.' She grinned at me. 'But it still left only a few brass coins in the onion-pot. I gave them to Cantalarius. He seemed to think you'd promised him much more.'

'I did. Poor Cantalarius. I'll have to go and see him sometime soon and give him what is due. Supposing that Genialis ever does turn up. You know, wife, I'm not convinced he has sheltered in an inn. There's more to his disappearance than you know about.' I was about to try to tell her everything, all about Silvia and the messenger – leaving out my visit to the money-lenders, of course – but again she shook her head.

'Tell me in the morning. You've finished your contract, so you can stay at home now for a day or two – especially as you say your client isn't there to pay you yet. So there isn't any rush. And you need to rest – you are exhausted, I can see.'

I thought of protesting but I closed my eyes, and there can be no doubt that she was right, because a moment later – as I thought – when I opened them again, there she was still fully dressed and leaning over me.

'Have you not come to bed yet?' I said stupidly.

She smiled indulgently. 'Husband, it is very nearly noon. The slaves and I have all been up for hours, although we slept through till dawn. I was content to let you sleep – you clearly needed rest – and I am sorry to have to wake you now. But there is someone here. A page of Marcus's – he wants you to accompany him as soon as possible.'

EIGHT

Already close to noon and Marcus's impatient page awaiting me! I sat up, groaning, and flung the furs and blankets back. Of course my patron had warned me that he'd want to see me soon. Obviously he'd already come back from the town today, and that fact – more than anything – persuaded me how long I must have slept. 'Dear gods,' I murmured, rolling out of bed. 'And I left my toga in the workshop yesterday.'

Gwellia nodded briskly. 'Never mind. You've got your old one here. I've sent the boys to hang it in the sun while you have some food. That will freshen it, at least. It's frayed and mended, but it will have to do. Better than attending Marcus in a tunic, anyway. And you'll have to wear a cloak in any case – it's fine this morning but it is very cold. The water bucket had a full thumb's breadth of ice on it, and when Kurso went up to the spring to get the day's supply, he had to break the surface with a stick and wait a little while for it to thaw enough to flow.'

'I trust that he was careful?' I said, recalling the fate of the poor herb-seller.

'It took him twice as long as usual. But he brought it back and there is some here ready for

112

you in the jug. Wait and I'll call Minimus to help you wash and dress.'

'No time, if I'm wanted at the villa instantly.' I had poured a little of the water out into the bowl, dipped my face and hands in it – though it was so cold it almost took my breath away – and was pulling on a cleaner tunic by this time. 'Where is this toga?'

Gwellia shook her head. 'You have your oatcakes first.' She gave a knowing wink. 'Don't worry. You have sufficient time. Marcus's page is in the servants' roundhouse now, eating one that I had Kurso serve to him – and a cup of watered mead as well. Just as well you left some, when you went to bed!'

'My clever wife!' I laughed approvingly. Offering the messenger refreshment in this way would be regarded by my patron as a courtesy – honouring the slave is an established way of honouring the slave owner as well – but it also gave me the opportunity to rise and eat and dress without keeping Marcus's servant waiting idly at the door.

Gwellia grinned and produced two still-warm oatcakes from a cloth beside the fire, and I ate them greedily, together with a little of the strong and crumbled cheese made from the summer milkings of the goats. A cup of fresh water and my meal was done. By this time my two red-haired servants had appeared and I was ready to be dressed in the sorry toga which they'd brought in with them. I rose and held my arms up while they draped it on. Maximus was

113

especially dexterous at the task, but even he could not arrange the folds in such a way as wholly to disguise the patched and mended hems. All the same it was the best that could be done. I nodded my approval.

'Very well. Minimus, you can go and tell the page that I am ready to accompany him.'

Minimus scurried off to do as he was told, while Maximus looked doubtfully at me. 'Master, will you be wanting us to go with you as well?'

I stole a glance at Gwellia. 'Just one of you, perhaps. I can hardly pay a visit unescorted by a slave. Marcus would not think it fitting for a citizen, especially not a favoured client like myself.'

'You can go with him, Maximus,' my wife agreed. 'Minimus can stay and help me in the house – the bed needs changing soon, and I haven't got the reeds. It's been too cold to cut them since the year began – do it when they're frozen and they simply spoil.'

'The page awaits you, Master,' said Minimus, who had reappeared and now was standing glumly at the door, obviously disappointed to be left behind – not so much because he longed to come with me, I guessed, as because he faced the prospect of a cold, unpleasant chore.

I grinned at him. 'Never mind. I'll take you with me next time, and Maximus will get his turn at cutting reeds: he can take over from you as soon as we get back.'

But when we set off for my patron's villa it

was clear that very little reed-cutting would in fact be done today. The day was crisp and bright enough; a pale sun shone wanly in a clear blue sky, but there was no warmth in it at all and it had clearly been freezing overnight. Pools of melt water stood beside the path – and sometimes on it – with a crust of ice on top and despite our cloaks the chill bit to our bones.

So I was not surprised – when we encountered someone coming towards us on a skinny mule, leading another with a frame across its back, on which some heavy load was covered with a cloth – to find that the rider was muffled in a cape and had the hood pulled forward to protect his face. I muttered the conventional 'Greetings!' as we passed, expecting simply to be answered by a grunt.

To my surprise the traveller brought the creatures to a halt and pushed his hood back to reveal his face. 'Libertus! I see that you are home again.' It was Cantalarius, a look of grim dissatisfaction on his face.

'Indeed, citizen neighbour,' I replied at once, before he had time to utter a reproach. 'I got here late last night and I was intending to call on you sometime. I understand you didn't get the fee I promised you for delivering that message to my wife – thank you for doing so. It saved her – as I hoped – from much anxiety. She did not have the money, and nor – just now – have I. But I have not forgotten, and I gave my word. I am owed money for that pavement that I told you of, and as soon as I get it you shall have your fee.' I gave him what I hoped was a placating smile.

His grim expression did not change a jot. 'That couple of sesterces might assist, I suppose. But it hardly seems to matter any more. My wife is right – there is some kind of curse. You know what happened to my sacrifice, I think?'

I nodded. 'It was most unfortunate.'

'Unfortunate? It was an insult to the gods. And all the fault of that confounded priest. How many hundreds of offerings take place without the slightest hitch in ritual? And then – when it is vital for me to placate the deities and I have already spent a fortune to provide the sacrifice – he doesn't simply put the wrong foot forwards first, or make an error in the ritual, which might have been recovered with a prayer or two – no, he has to let the animal escape so that it is useless for anything at all!' It was a long speech for Cantalarius.

I raised an eyebrow. 'You might have eaten the mutton, I suppose?'

He shook a mournful head. 'Even to eat it would be unlucky now. My wife would not have considered doing so – she's very superstitious where omens are concerned – and everyone in town had witnessed what occurred so I could not sell it to the butchers' stalls. The army would not take it back again, because they said it would be folly to try to breed from it. In the end I had to sell it to the gluemakers for only a fraction of what I had paid for it – and even they

116

weren't very keen, in case the carcass brought bad luck while they were boiling it.' He stopped and glowered at me.

He was obviously distressed. I said, sympathetically, 'But didn't you ask the priest responsible to come and try to lift the curse? I heard you in the forum and I thought that he'd agreed to do it, for a fee.'

He shook his head. 'Why do you think I'm setting off to town today? I mean to see him and persuade the wretch to come as soon as possible. Tomorrow, preferably. I've still got my ram at home – the one I meant to offer to the gods before the weather changed, though that will starve to death, as well, if there's much more delay from that confounded priest. It's the only pure white sheep that I possess – all the rest are speckled – so let's hope he comes in time. If it helps, I'll even send a mule to bring him there and back.'

'You know where to find him?' I asked in some surprise. There is accommodation at the temple site – in the sacred grove behind the Capitoline shrine, near where the Imperial temple stands – but mostly that is for temple slaves and duty celebrants, though it is also sometimes used for visitors. Of course the Imperial Servirs have a room there for the year in which they serve, and the senior Priest of Jupiter and his wife have an official residence next door, but most of the other priests have private homes – and often families – elsewhere. 'Does the priest of Diana not have an apartment in the town?' I enquired.

My neighbour shook his head. 'He has no family left and he's too old and frail to live alone, even if he had a household full of slaves – which he does not. I understand the temple's given him a private cell these days, within the dormitory for the temple acolytes. I'm sure I'll find him there. I want him to come and make this sacrifice, though no doubt he'll ask for an enormous bribe – he'll call it a "donation" but it comes to the same thing – and how we are to find that I simply cannot see. I've collected almost everything that we can't do without – mostly the remnants of my poor wife's dowry, I'm afraid.'

'You've obviously found something,' I murmured doubtfully, gesturing to the large, wrapped-up object on the mule. I had supposed that there was nothing left he could sell.

He made a little face. 'That! It's a most dreadful statue of some ancestral god. A river deity or something of the kind. Her great-great uncle was armourer for the Romans once, but he was not a great craftsman at the best of times, and he contrived to drop some molten metal on his leg – he carved this as a thanks offering for healing, I believe.'

'And your wife permitted you to you take it?' I exclaimed in some surprise. 'I thought you said that she was superstitious?'

He gave me a grim smile. 'She wasn't keen to let me bring it – said it was certain to bring still more ill-luck – but as I pointed out, it hasn't brought us much protection up to now. It didn't even help her ancestor – he died a little later by falling in the fire. He was no better at wood-carving than at working bronze, and it's an ugly thing – but it's inset with bronze and gold and amethyst and that will have some value I expect. Enough – I hope – for the priest to accept it as a gift.'

'Although it represents a Celtic river god?'

'There is no problem about that. This deity's a version of Mars Lenis, the Romans have declared. They've taken over his local temple on those grounds. And if it's Mars – at least officially – there's no problem with the priest accepting it.'

I nodded. The chief temple – where the ill-fated rite had taken place – is, of course, a Capitoline one, dedicated to the central trinity of Jupiter, Juno and Minerva. But any member of the Roman pantheon could be represented there, and Mars was once a member of the Triad anyway. (Of course, most deities have other temples of their own – some of them based on earlier places sacred to the Celts, like the spring belonging to this ancient river god – but at public festivals all of them are ritually invoked and can be worshipped at the Capitoline shrine, or even – like Janus! – offered special sacri-fice.)

'Images of Mars are always welcome, I sup-pose,' I said.

Cantalarius made a doubtful little face. 'Though this one's hardly handsome. Take a look – see what you think yourself.'

I lifted a corner of the cloth a little gingerly, revealing quite the ugliest statue I have ever seen. The face was crudely carved, as if a child had drawn a figure on a slate, and the eyes and teeth were inlaid afterwards. The result was to give it lopsided staring eyes and distort the mouth into an evil twisted leer – more like a demon than a deity. It was so horrid it was almost comical.

I grinned and behind me I heard Maximus give a stifled gasp. My neighbour laughed.

'You see? Would you not want to be rid of such a thing? It's my belief that might be what's bringing down the curse. I told my wife so. Truth to tell, I think she hated it herself. At all events I swayed her in the end.'

'If it goes to the temple there's no disrespect,' I ventured, doubtfully. 'And if you two had nothing else to sell...?'

He shook his head. 'Nothing else of value. A few bronze bowls, that's all. More of her great-uncle's handiwork. At first she was reluctant to let me take them, too – because if this fails, and she does divorce me and go back home again...' He trailed off unhappily.

'She would need a bit of dowry to make another match?' I finished. 'But she did agree that you could have them, finally?'

A sigh. 'Events persuaded her. This morning our last land slave caught the fever – we've already lost our other slaves to it. If he dies we shall have no help at all and I cannot work the farm myself. That finally convinced her that things were desperate. She let me have it all.' He spat on his hand and rubbed his ear with it in the ancient gesture to ward off a curse. 'If it's not enough to bribe the wretched priest to come, the gods knows what I'll do. She will divorce me, certainly. In that case, I might just as well be dead – as no doubt I will be, if I really am accursed.'

There did not seem to be an answer I could make to this, so I said simply, 'Well, I wish you fortune. Perhaps your luck will change. I'll bring you what I owe you – that would be a start, at least.'

This time he did manage a wry smile. 'Citizen, what I need is a miracle – not a few sesterces – but thank you all the same. Now, if I'm to find this priest and get back home tonight I had better hurry, or it will freeze again. Even a mule will stumble if there is ice enough – and I can't afford to lose these animals as well. They are pretty well the only healthy things we have.' So saying he pulled his hood up round his ears again and, jerking his laden mule behind him, he started down the track.

I glanced at Maximus, who had been standing back but obviously listening to this whole exchange. 'Unhappy fellow!'

My young servant nodded and watched him move out of sight. 'Sometimes, Master, there are worse things than to be a slave. We do not have his troubles.'

A piping voice surprised me. 'Well, I'm a

slave and I'll have troubles of my own, if we don't hurry to the villa very soon.' I'd forgotten the existence of Marcus's young page, who had been behind me all this time. 'My master will be waiting, and he does not care for that.'

He was right of course. I nodded. 'Then we'll hurry.' And we did.

NINE

Marcus may have been expecting me, and impatiently at that, but when I got there he did what rich men often do to emphasize their rank – he kept me idling in the atrium for quite a time before he was announced. (It might have been a quarter of an hour, though it seemed much longer because I was alone – Maximus had been led off to the servants' waiting room as soon as we arrived.) My patron often used enforced delay as a form of reprimand, so when he did come I was relieved to find that he seemed quite affable.

'Ah, Libertus, my old friend,' he murmured, extending his ringed hand for me to kiss and motioning his attendants to bring in seats for us.

I made the obligatory obeisance, going down on one knee, but he signalled me to rise and sat down on the gilded folding chair which had been set for him. He motioned me to the smaller wooden stool – where my head would be appropriately lower than his own – then he sent the household servants off to bring a table in, together with a tray of honeyed figs and wine.

Then, to my surprise, he shooed away the slaves to wait outside the door. I must have looked astonished – Marcus is rarely without attendants at his side – but he put one finger to his lips and gave me a knowing look. 'One cannot be too careful. Isn't that what you are always telling me?'

It almost made me smile. It was true. I had repeatedly warned him that slaves had ears and eyes and tongues – and were not merely 'living tools', as he tended to suppose – but I had never before known him to pay the slightest attention to my words. However, today he was obviously taking special care. I managed to compose my features into a duly serious look.

'This is to be a private conference!' He looked around theatrically, as if to make quite sure we were alone, then carefully selected the plumpest of the fruit and leant back to gaze thoughtfully at me. 'Libertus, I think you know why I have called for you?'

It was hard to know quite how to answer that. 'You wished to speak to me about the sale of Silvia's portion of her late husband's business?' I said, as gravely as I could. 'If Lucius's other backer will not provide the loan, you are minded to invest in the enterprise yourself?' I had chosen the expression with some diffidence. Marcus is famously cautious with his cash.

But he nodded almost blithely. 'I might even offer to do so anyway. I was talking to the lady Silvia last night and the more she told me of Ulpius's affairs, the more attracted to the prospect I became. It seems a pity that Genialis should be allowed to close it down.'

So that was why he'd wanted to stay in town last night to dine with his new ward! Not merely for the pleasure of her company, but to ask her a few questions about her late husband's trade. However, I knew better than to say such things aloud. 'The lady is observant and intelligent,' I observed. 'If she was acquainted with Ulpius's associates, no doubt she was able to tell you a great deal.'

'Indeed she did.' He took a bite of fig and waved it in the air. Marcus had a way of looking smug when he felt that he had been particularly shrewd and he was wearing that expression now. 'Not that I made it obvious, of course, but I managed to turn the conversation to the life she used to lead, and she furnished me with the names of several men with whom Ulpius used to trade. It seems he entertained them at his home sometimes and she'd met most of them. Afterwards I had my page prepare a list for you.' He reached into his inner toga folds and produced a rolled-up piece of bark-paper.

I took it from him and was about to look at it, but he waved a lofty hand. 'Read it at your leisure. You will want to study it in detail, no doubt. I've given you the names of his chief associates – that should save you quite a lot of work. But there's no need to thank me.' (I hadn't thought of it!) 'It will give you extra time for a more searching enquiry into their affairs.'

After that I did not dare to open up the scroll. I muttered a conventional, 'A thousand thanks, patron, you are most gracious,' but secretly I gave an inward sigh. Even at a glance it was quite obvious that the scroll contained at least a dozen names. This 'searching enquiry into their affairs' would clearly take a great deal of my time (for which I was unlikely to be paid) and involve my presence on a good few trading boats – which were certain to be swaying in a most unpleasant way, even if they were tied up against the quay. However, Marcus was my patron and no hint of reluctance could be allowed to show.

'You still wish me to investigate these men?' I hazarded, as meekly as I could, securing the rolled-up paper behind the purse-pouch on my belt. 'Hasn't Silvia told you most of what you want to know?'

He smiled. 'She told me a good deal about their various characters – and very entertaining some of that was too – and what commodities they trade in as a rule. You'll find that information on your list. But she is just a woman and there are things she could not know. Genialis is threatening to close the business down by selling Silvia's share of it – I suspect that's merely to increase the price he wants from Lucius, but it may be that there is some other reason that I don't know about. I look to you to find out if there is. Discover what these men are worth, whether they are honest and – naturally – what their status and their backgrounds are. In short, whether the warehouse is likely to continue to be prosperous. If your report is favourable, I will offer to put up the loan to Lucius. But I need to find out soon. As you know I expect to be setting off to Rome, and if I am to invest in this at all I shall need to settle it before I go.'

He said it lightly, but my heart had sunk. I had forgotten of his plans to offer Pertinax advice. 'How long – exactly – does that give me, Excellence?' I enquired.

He gave a small dismissive wave. 'Oh, several days at least. Even if written confirmation came today, we shan't be setting off now until the Ides are past. I had hoped to leave sooner and simply rest that day, since the fifteenth is always an ill-omened time, but I find that Julia – my wife – is rather indisposed. Nothing serious – too much rich food at the New Year feasts, I think. Entirely her own doing, that's the worst of it. She suddenly developed a taste for pickled eels. I warned her that they'd disagree with her – but you know what women are.' He made a deprecating gesture with his hands, as to a fellow-husband who would sympathize. 'I'm postponing our departure until she's strong again. That should give you time enough to find out what you need.' He spoke airily, as though it were an easy matter to win people's confidence and learn all their secrets within four days or so.

I made a little bow. 'I'll do my best, of course.'

He smiled indulgently. 'Oh, and another thing: discover whether any of these people is prone to gambling. This fellow Lucius in particular. I gather from Silvia that Genialis likes to have a flutter now and then – and it may be that his half-brother did the same. That sort of weakness often runs in families and gamblers attract gamblers, everyone knows that.'

I was surprised, and said so. 'I knew Genialis was a gambler, but Ulpius never seemed to me the sort of man to stake his fortune at a game of dice. The two were only half-brothers after all. And what makes you think that Lucius is involved at all?'

'He may not be. That is what I want you to find out. But Silvia changed the subject when I mentioned it to her, and I would like to know. One does not entrust good money to a man who takes unnecessary risks.' He took another thoughtful bite of fig and – in the absence of a servant – poured himself some wine and made a gesture that I should follow suit.

I did so, though in my case I didn't fill my cup. I'm not a lover of bitter Roman wine, but it would have been improper to refuse. 'But surely you're relying on his taking chances – to a point? Deciding to attempt to borrow capital in order to buy Genialis out is itself a risky business, don't you think? Especially when he hopes to manage everything himself? Without an active partner, such as Ulpius was, Lucius would have to make all the decisions on his own,' I went on, feeling I'd earned approval with a sound judicious point. 'What to trade and when, how much to pay for each commodity,

128

how long to store it and what to charge for it.'

My patron gave me a searching sideways look. 'But for Silvia's sake, surely, it is better to have Lucius in charge? Genialis only wants to sell the business, anyway.'

He was right, of course, but still I pressed the point. 'But, Patron, there are always factors even the best manager can't possibly control – poor harvests or bad weather out at sea. Trading ships are often lost in sudden storms and even if they make it into port their cargoes are sometimes broken, wet or spoiled. Remember all that, when you are tempted to invest. One incident at sea and Lucius could easily be ruined.'

Marcus gave me a triumphant smile. 'That's why the contract with his lender – whoever that might be – will make him personally liable for any loss. With his property as surety, of course.'

Suddenly I understood why he was so interested in this. 'So anyone who backed this venture really could not lose? If Lucius makes a profit, you would share in it – but if he loses, it is his affair?' I shook my head. 'Though he might take out insurance, I suppose? Don't the money-lenders offer some sort of policy?'

'Only at considerable expense – which would be his, of course. And if he did not do so – as I say – in the last resort his house and warehouse would be forfeit to the lender anyway.'

'All without the backer doing anything?' The scheme was breathtaking in its simplicity.

Marcus took a cup of wine and beamed at me across the rim of it. 'I see you understand the matter perfectly.'

It was so elegantly simple that there had to be a flaw. I sipped at a very little of my wine before I dared to venture, doubtfully, 'But, Excellence, no doubt Genialis understands all this as well. In that case he is likely to keep Silvia's share – or effectively sell it to himself – on exactly those same terms.'

Marcus shook his head. 'I don't think that's the case. Silvia tells me that his gambling debts are very high – he needs this money to be clear of them. That's why he offered himself as guardian and proposed to marry her. Genialis has even publicly declared that he wants to realize the assets straight away and close the business down, but Silvia believes that he really intends to let Lucius buy him out, and all this talk of closure is a ruse to raise the price. Which Lucius, she thinks, will probably agree, because he's desperate to protect his livelihood.'

'But suppose that Genialis has perished in the snow?' I said. Marcus says he values the way I see all aspects of a thing. 'You would then be her legal guardian, wouldn't you? In that case there would be no need to offer loans. You could simply keep the business and let Lucius run it as he's doing now.'

Marcus favoured me with his most knowing smile. 'But even more important, if that proves to be the case, to discover how things stand. Besides that way one has no guarantee if things go wrong, and one naturally wishes to make the greatest profit possible – if only for Silvia's own sake. After all she may wish to wed again some day. And it does seem probable that all this will arise. I forgot to tell you – they have found the horse.'

It took me a moment to work out what he meant. 'The one that Genialis borrowed from Bernadus to come back to Glevum on?'

'Exactly so. We had news this morning before we left the town. A message was delivered to my flat. That Syrian slave of Genialis's...'

'Adonisius?' I put in helpfully.

'That's right.' Marcus nodded. 'Apparently he rode off to find Bernadus yesterday, as we had told him to, having failed to find him in the town, but he had hardly got halfway to the country house before he found this animal roaming in the snow. The reins were broken but the saddle was still there. No sign of a rider, though he stopped and searched. The creature could have been wandering for miles. With the recent snow-melt there were not even decent tracks: too many people had been riding through that way.'

'And we are quite certain that it was Genialis's mount?'

'Adonisius is. Said that he'd helped to saddle it and would have known it anywhere, even without the distinctive white blaze on the nose. Besides, he took it to the villa afterwards and Bernadus has confirmed that it was his.' Marcus drained his wine cup. 'Since it was found wandering quite close to the estate, it appears that it was trying to find its own way home, but there's no sign or clue as to where it might have been. Though we can be quite certain that Genialis never got to Dorn – the household there sent a messenger to Bernadus to seek him yesterday.'

'But how did they know that Genialis had been staying at the house? Doesn't that suggest he's been in touch with them?'

Marcus shook his head. 'He sent word with the official post, it seems, on New Year's Day itself, when he first decided not to travel all the way. Silvia confirms it, so there can be no doubt. It seems the earlier messenger came from Dorn as well.'

'How do you learn all this?'

'Bernadus sent the Syrian back this morning at first light with the news – together with Lucius's servant who had stayed there overnight, after he had been asking at the inns with no result. The two slaves rode straight to Lucius of course – they could not know where Silvia was lodged – and Lucius came to me. Managed to just catch us before we left.'

'We? So the lady Silvia accompanied you here?' Like an idiot I looked around as if I expected to find her in the room.

Marcus looked disdainful. 'She could not travel in my gig, of course – that would not be proper for a lady of her class. Anyway, Bernadus had kindly sent back word that I could use his horse – until such time as he's back in town himself – so I rode it home and left the gig to follow later on.'

I nodded. Exactly as I'd thought.

'I had intended to obtain a hiring cart for her since a gig is not suitable for a lady of her rank, but Lucius suggested an alternative,' my patron went on with a smile. 'He has a proper carriage which he'll make available and later in the day she will come here in that. But first she is waiting for her luggage to arrive. Bernadus realized she would now be wanting it – since of course she was taking everything to Dorn – and offered, in his message, to send it back to her. Lucius sent the Syrian off again post-haste to accept the arrangement and escort the cart. As soon as it arrives it will accompany her here.' He popped another fig into his mouth. 'The main roads are clearer now; they should arrive tonight.'

'You intend to lodge her in the villa here?' I exclaimed, wondering again what Julia was going to make of that. 'But surely you are shortly setting off for Rome?'

He waited till he'd swallowed before he answered, stickily, 'When the slave market is open in a day or so I will take her back to town and find some staff for her and she can continue to live in her old home, though officially under my protection legally. I suppose I'll have to find some guards for her while I'm away. I have provided her a maidservant already, as you know.'

'That will be costly!' I took another sip of wine. I meant it too. A full complement of slaves, and replacements for whatever household items Genialis sold – from what I saw he'd nearly stripped the place.

He arched a brow at me. 'There should be no

problem. With Genialis dead – as I think that now we must assume he is – Ulpius's estate will come direct to her. As guardian I can use that to pay for she what needs – though I would like to leave enough to earn some income too. She will need a personal *stipendium* as well – some sort of small allowance for herself – though I would continue to have oversight, of course.'

'Unless she gets remarried,' I reminded him.

He grinned cheerfully and took another fig. 'Which I rather think she might. Lucius will make an offer for her, I suspect.'

'And surely as her guardian you would not object to that?'

He made a magisterial face. 'I would have to think about it very hard. I have my duties as a guardian and there are grounds for refusing permission for the match. For instance, if she marries him she'll lose her status as a citizen.'

'Of course!' I spoke as if I'd thought of it myself, though in fact this aspect of affairs had not occurred to me. Any married woman takes her husband's rank. 'In that case she may not welcome such a match herself.'

Marcus shot a sideways look at me. 'Oh, I suspect she would. She's clearly fond of him and I'm not sure that rank means very much to her. Her father was merely a freeborn man, like Lucius, himself and – from what she says – not even an especially wealthy one. Everything she has she owes to Ulpius, including her status as a citizen. I'm not sure that she values it as you and I would do.'

'So she would be content to marry Lucius and become a simple freewoman again?'

My patron put his goblet down, and cracked his finger joints – a sign that he was in the happiest of moods. 'It needn't come to that. If I became his partner...?'

'You would still sell her portion of the business to him?'

'I'll make him a loan so he can purchase it.'

'Though the money would come from Silvia's estate?' The circular nature of the intended deal began to dawn on me.

That smug smile again. 'I would use an intermediary, of course. He need not know who lent it until afterwards. Don't look so horrified. If I simply give permission for the match, her inheritance will come direct to him and she stands to lose her status and her wealth as well, if there's the kind of storm at sea that you were warning of. This way he gets what he is asking for, I get a chance to make some money out of it and he and Silvia can be citizens as well.'

I sipped at the last remnants of my wine. 'You think you can arrange it?'

'I imagine so.' He gave me an arch look. 'If it could be argued that – with all his trade – he'd contributed enough to the welfare of the state, then I could put in a word with our new Emperor, recommending Lucius for a grant of citizenship.'

'For a small consideration?' I felt I was beginning to get the hang of this. 'A continued portion of the trading profits, perhaps.'

He frowned at me reproachfully. 'Don't look so disapproving, my old friend. It would be a good solution, don't you think? That way everyone would gain. I can't see a single flaw in it.'

'Provided Genialis is genuinely dead,' I pointed out. 'Falling from his horse does not necessarily mean that he was killed. Even Gwellia pointed out that he may be simply hurt, and sheltering till he's well enough to move.'

Marcus selected the last few sugared fruits and looked sourly at me. 'Libertus, must you always take a contrary view? Yesterday, as I recall, you were urging Silvia to accept that if her husband was missing – in this weather – he was likely to be dead. And that was before Adonisius found the horse.'

'Excellence,' I murmured, feeling slightly piqued. 'You ask me for advice. The best that I can give you is to wait a day or two and make no assumptions till we learn the truth. If you behave as though the man is dead – by spending Silvia's portion or selling parts of it – you trespass on his legal potestas. So if he happens to turn up again, he would have a legal case to claim *injuria*, for loss of status, theft and the denial of his rights.'

Marcus scowled. 'I cannot leave the woman without a guardian. It is likely that he's perished in the snow.'

'But you can't be sure until they find a corpse. Surely the prudent thing is to instigate a search? Then it's clear that you've done everything you can, and any judge would recognize that fact,' I said, deliberately hinting that this might come to court. From what I'd seen of Genialis, there'd be no gratitude for Marcus's attempts to 'rescue' Silvia.

'A search?' Marcus held up the final fig and popped it in his mouth. 'Fortunately, Lucius had the same idea. The matter is in hand. He and Bernadus have already sent a party of their slaves to scour the woods and I have despatched several of my own from the town apartment – they should be there by now, searching the whole area between the villa and the town.'

'Nobody looking on the road to Dorn at all?' I saw his expression and added hastily, 'I ask because we can't be certain, even now, that Genialis came this way at all. As the lady Silvia pointed out – if that was the case, why didn't the messenger from Glevum pass him on the road?'

'And if he went the other way – to Dorn – why ever should the horse, when riderless, pass the villa where it lived and walk on down the road?' Marcus countered, with acerbity.

He had a point, of course, and I meekly bowed my head. 'As you say, Excellence.' Marcus by now was rising to his feet and I realized that the interview was at an end. I scrambled upright too and sketched a hasty bow. 'I will read this list of names, and make enquiries. And into this man Alfredus Allius as well – since he is your potential rival in this deal. Where should I report if I discover anything?'

'Oh, come to my villa. I should be here, I think, making arrangements for our travel overseas. If I find myself in town I shall send a message to let you know I'm there.' He held a hand out in dismissal but I did not go.

'There is one question, Excellence, with which I need your help. I had a contract with Genialis for a pavement, as you know, which I completed – almost certainly before he died, from what we hear of when he set off on the horse. If I can prove that, can I claim from his estate? And if so, to whom do I apply, if you yourself aren't here to plead for me?'

Marcus looked flattered, then gave a little laugh. 'Ah, the pavement. Have no fear for that. The lady Silvia was most concerned that you'd fulfilled your contract and would not be paid – the work was completed in her house, after all. So, as I hold temporary potestas she has asked me to make sure that you receive the promised fee. How much did he owe you?'

I told him and he whistled. 'As much as that?'

'I have witnesses to the exact amount,' I said.

'I'm sure you do,' he muttered tetchily. He clapped his hands and two young slaves arrived, so quickly that I was convinced they had been listening to all this at the door. 'Bring my wooden coffer from my desk!' Then, as they scampered off he turned to me again. 'I doubt that I have that much money in the house, but I'll give you what I can.'

'As you say, Excellence,' I murmured sweetly. 'And I trust you won't be out of pocket very long. The lady Silvia's inheritance will reimburse you the expense – unless Genialis can be found, of course, in which case he will be responsible himself and you might even claim a little interest on the sum – since you will have made him an informal loan.'

Marcus brightened perceptibly at this and when the slaves returned he paid me the full fee – as I'd hoped he would. That would solve my nagging problems with the money-lenders: the debt was due for payment at noon in two days' time, and after that the interest rose with every day's delay. I hadn't mentioned it to Gwellia, of course, though I'd been worrying how I'd repay it without Genialis's fee, but this would cover it four times over – which was a huge relief. I thanked my patron, bowed and was about to take my leave when to my surprise he called me back again.

'Perhaps in the circumstances, my old friend, on second thoughts you'd better join the search for Genialis yourself. If anyone can find him – dead or alive – it's you.'

'But these enquiries? This list of names...?' I gestured to my purse.

'You can look into all that after he is found. I'm quite certain that, with your assistance, the search will not take long. You'll work out what has happened – as you always do!' And with that he swept off, followed by his slaves, leaving me to pick up Maximus from the slaves' waiting room and make my own way back towards the gate.

TEN

When I got home and told Gwellia, she was not best pleased. 'Husband, your patron has no thought for you at all. You have not had a day at home for almost half a moon, because of the weather being as bitter as it is, and now no sooner are you safely at your hearth than he wants you to return to town. While it's still freezing nightly and the roads are treacherous!'

She was speaking forcefully, busying herself noisily with preparing food and from the way she banged the lids against the cooking pots I could see that she was genuinely upset. So I thought it wiser not to remind her that my search for Genialis might even take me out along the northern road to Dorn – a long way from Glevum on the farther side. Neither did it seem tactful to confess (as I'd intended, now that I had the wherewithal to clear the debt) that I'd borrowed from the money-lenders in the town and needed to go back urgently to pay them what I owed.

I just said gently, 'Marcus is my patron; I really have no choice. Anyway, I would have to go to town again quite soon. I have a trade to attend to.'

'And what chance have you of that? He wants you about his business rather than your own. Not that he'll pay you anything of course!' She started chopping turnips with such violence that you would think my patron's neck was underneath the knife. 'No one would believe you had a household with a wife and slaves to keep!'

There was little I could say to counter this, since what she said was generally true, but I pulled out my purse. 'At least he paid me for that pavement!' I murmured peaceably. I was about to tip the contents out for her to see, hoping that the sight of two gold aureii would lift her mood, when I remembered my appointment with the money lenders and decided to keep the one coin hidden in the bag.

I put down the other on the table top, like a street magician producing coloured balls. 'Enough to pay off Cantalarius twenty times – and even to hire a mule from him for a day or two, if you're concerned about the weather and think that would be wise!' I said, expecting first surprise and then her gruff agreement to this compromise.

She put down the bowl of turnips she had been adding to the stew, wiped her hands carefully on her apron skirt and picked up the coin with a sort of awed respect. 'Marcus gave you this?' She sounded so incredulous that I thought for a moment she was going to test it in her teeth. But she just weighed it in her palm and laid it down again. 'Perhaps I spoke too harshly. This is to reward you for helping with the search?'

'It's the money that Genialis owed me,' I explained. 'I'd contracted for that pavement and I did the work on time. Marcus himself was witness to the fact.'

'Julia must have told him we were in want of cash, and convinced him that you should be paid. Well, it is kind of her. She has always been particularly generous to us – like the other day, when I went there for oil.'

I shook my head. 'It wasn't Julia's doing this time, it was Silvia herself,' I said. 'She apparently insisted that – since I had fulfilled the contract in her house – Marcus, as her guardian, should ensure that I was paid.'

'So this came from her estate?' My wife made a little disapproving face. 'I might have known he wouldn't pay you so handsomely himself. But I like the sound of Silvia. An honest woman, by the sound of it?'

'A lively one, as Marcus may find out to his cost,' I told her. 'I would almost say "self-willed". But she's rich and pretty too – which is no doubt why he offered to step in as guardian. She is coming to the villa later on today, so perhaps you'll meet her there.'

Gwellia had gone back to adding turnips to the stew. 'Rich, pretty and self-willed? That sounds dangerous.' She raised an eyebrow with a wicked grin. 'I wonder what Julia thinks about her guest?'

It was exactly the thought that had occurred to me, but for some reason I felt moved to say,

'Oh, Silvia won't be there very long. Marcus proposes to acquire new furniture and slaves on her account, so she can move back to her town-house again before he and Julia go away to Rome. Assuming that Genialis is not found alive, by then.'

But Gwellia wasn't listening. She picked up a spoon and stood looking quizzical. 'Rome? Why ever does he want to go to Rome again? Surely he arranged all his affairs when he and Julia went there just a year or two ago? What makes him think of travelling all that way a second time? And at just the worst time of the year to make the journey, too!'

I stared at her. I had forgotten that – since Marcus had not after all returned from Glevum yesterday – he could not have sent the promised message to the house; and when I got home myself I had not thought to tell Gwellia any news except my own. And Cantalarius had last called here days and days before, so it was quite possible that – though the news had travelled quickly all the way from Rome – out here in the country, in the house alone, she had not learned about the happenings which had shocked the world.

'I forgot that you were unlikely to have heard! Momentous news. The Emperor is dead.'

She gasped and sat down on the bench, her face an actor's mask of disbelief. 'Commodus? Dead? Great Minerva! When?' Her shocked expression slowly softened to a wicked grin. 'Some brave man plucked up courage and murdered him at last? Well, if that's the case, I hope the man who did it wins a laurel wreath – though I suppose it's more likely that he's been marched off and executed horribly by the imperial guard. Either that, or been elected Emperor himself! What exactly happened?'

'There are conflicting stories. I don't know which is true.' I outlined the various rumours which had reached me in the town. 'But one thing seems quite certain. Guess who is nominated to the purple now? No other than our own ex-governor, Pertinax!'

'The one you met once in Londinium? Did you not dine with him?' Gwellia shook her head. 'Think of that! My husband – dining with a future Emperor!'

I interrupted her rapture with the commonplace. 'My patron's patron,' I reminded her. 'That's why Marcus wants to go to Rome.'

'I suppose it is his duty,' she agreed. 'To congratulate his friend and witness his formal installation, I expect. Hoping for some preferment too, do you suppose?'

'Marcus wants to go and give him some advice,' I told her, with a grin. 'Says Pertinax is far too honest to be an Emperor. He's anxious to set off as soon as possible – though he's afraid that Julia won't want to go so soon.'

Gwellia gave me a most peculiar look. 'You're sure that Julia intends to go at all?'

'Well, I assume so, if her husband wishes it!' I was startled into this abrupt reply. 'Though of course I haven't seen her since I heard the news. She wasn't at my meeting with Marcus, naturally, and in any case I hear she isn't feeling well.'

My wife got up slowly and went back to the stew. 'Not feeling well? You might say that, I suppose.'

She had such a strange expression on her face that I was quite alarmed. 'You don't think it is something serious?' I urged – and when she did not answer, I took it for assent. I shook my head. 'I'm sure that Marcus would have told me if it were.'

'It's possible that Marcus does not know the cause himself.' Gwellia sprinkled a few herbs into the cooking pot, sniffed and – seeming satisfied – put the lid back on it as she said, 'Especially since he's been away these last few days – no doubt busy with his duties in the town.'

I stared at her. 'You think she's kept her sickness from him? It's possible, I suppose – Marcus seemed to think she'd simply feasted far too well, or eaten things which disagreed with her. But there is a dreadful fever in the area which can strike you down quite suddenly, it seems. Cantalarius lost almost all his slaves to it. Let's hope it isn't that. When I last saw her she seemed in blooming health, but of course you've seen her since. Did you think then that something was amiss?'

Gwellia gave me a most peculiar smile. 'I do not think "amiss" is quite the word I'd choose. Some people would think it merited a thankful sacrifice.'

For a moment I could not work out what she meant. Then, belatedly, I realized. 'You don't mean...?' But of course she did. Once you had thought of it, it was self-evident. That glow of health, the liking for strange foods, and then the sickness following. 'You think she is with child?'

'I'm sure she thinks she is. Of course she did not say so, in so many words, but she apologized for being late – said that she was suffering from sickness every day – and gave me a smile that told me everything. No doubt she wants to wait until she's absolutely sure before she raises Marcus's hopes.' She grinned at me. 'Husband, you are noted for your deductive cleverness! Surely the idea had occurred to you?'

'I am no expert in such things,' I muttered sulkily – and then wished I had not. Gwellia had been snatched with me and sold to slavery, so we'd spent twenty years in servitude, apart. What had happened to her in those years I never asked, except to know they scarred her terribly. But it was not hard to speculate. Any slave girl is her master's toy, though any children that she bears are sold or killed at birth – and Gwellia in her youth was very beautiful.

She was still lovely now, though rather pained at my remark. I said quickly, 'But you are a woman. I've no doubt you are right. So you think that she may not accompany him to Rome? Not even to pay homage to his friend the Emperor?'

146

Gwellia was sprinkling more fresh herbs into the pot. 'I think she would be foolish to even think of it. Travelling such distances is hard and dangerous enough, what with the chance of meeting bears and brigands on the way, and any passenger is always shaken half to bits. For her to attempt it when she is with child, unless it is a real necessity, is simple foolishness. I only hope that Marcus will permit her to remain.'

'I'm sure he will,' I murmured. 'Marcus is unfashionably devoted to his wife.'

She put the lid back on the stew again, stemming the fragrant steam that floated out of it. 'He claims to be affectionate to you, as well – but he still demands that you come and go on these frozen roads to town. I shall be worried until you're safely back, even if you do arrange to hire a mule. I suppose you're sure our neighbour will agree to that?'

'I think he'll be delighted,' I replied, grateful to have something positive to offer her. 'I met him on the way to Marcus's. He was on his way to try to bribe a priest to come out in the morning and make a sacrifice.'

'To raise the curse he's certain has been laid upon his land? He told me about that. He and his wife have had a dreadful year, it seems.'

I nodded. 'And you won't have heard what happened at the Janus feast.' I outlined what had happened. 'So now they're desperate – ready to give everything they have to bribe the priest. So the chance to earn some honest money by hiring out a mule will seem like an answer from the Fates, I rather think.'

'Don't forget you owe him something, too, for bringing me the news.'

'One aureus should more than cover everything,' I said. I opened up the drawstring of my purse, and – feeling treacherous – added the gold coin from the table to the one already there. The small change I'd been carrying, left over from what I'd borrowed in the town, I pushed towards my wife. 'And this is for you – so next time you want to buy necessities you will have plenty in your purse.'

She smiled. 'It will replace the money in the sandal fund. I used the last of it for Cantalarius. Which reminds me, do you want to go and call on him tonight? You have another hour before it's really dark, and the fresh bedding is already cut and set to dry. The slaves are only gathering more reeds to make a new basket so I can store the eggs. One of the boys can easily be spared to walk with you.'

I shook my head. 'There is no point in my calling over there today – Cantalarius did not leave for Glevum until it was past noon. If I go now, I should be lucky to find that he'd returned from town – and besides it will no doubt start to freeze again quite soon. I'll call on him tomorrow.'

Gwellia looked doubtful. 'But if this priest is coming, then you can't well interrupt. You don't want to spoil the ritual again.'

'That will happen in the morning, if Cantalarius has his way. I'll go and call there tomorrow afternoon. I should still have time to ride the mule to town – and get there soon enough to make a start on things.' In time to reach the money-lenders before the close of trade, I meant.

'So I suppose you'll be away again a day or two at least?' Gwellia gave a deep, exasperated sigh. 'Well, at least this stew will make a warming lunch, and I'd better wrap up some bread and cheese for you to eat tomorrow night – you can buy things the next day from the street vendors.'

'You're good to me,' I murmured, reaching out to her. 'You know I won't stay longer than I need.'

She wriggled from my grasp and gave a knowing smile. 'And in the meantime, if you have a little time to spare...'

I could see that she was planning some household task for me, repairing the enclosure with fresh pointed stakes or helping the slave boys with the egg-baskets. I said quickly, 'Not for a moment. I have work to do tonight. Marcus has given me a document to read.'

Gwellia lit a taper and set it at my side. 'You'll need this light then; it's too dark in here. What is it, anyway?' She peered across my shoulder. 'Looks like a sort of list.'

'The names of Ulpius's associates,' I said importantly. 'I am to investigate their probity and wealth.'

'Well, why don't you ask Lucius?' she said. 'He was a partner, wasn't he? Surely he could tell you what you want to know.'

It was a good suggestion but there was a flaw. 'The trouble is, I am to be discreet. Marcus does not want Lucius to know that he has any interest in these individuals.'

She shook her head. 'But surely the search for Genialis gives you an excuse? If Silvia's guardian wants to close the business down – and you say he made a public declaration of the fact – then that might concern these people very much. Perhaps it was one of them who sent that messenger to him. They might have a motive for luring him away, or even for seeing that he perished in the snow.'

I nodded thoughtfully. 'That message never reached him, but in principle you're right. So I could question Lucius about them on that excuse alone – he need have no idea that Marcus is involved. Thank you, wife. An excellent idea. That could save me hours of fruitless questioning elsewhere.'

I meant it and I showed my gratitude by calling in the boys and weaving egg baskets with them till it grew too dark to work.

ELEVEN

I lay awake a long time, all the same.

I decided that I would tackle Lucius alone by calling on him at his warehouse in the town. I reasoned that – even if he'd been offered hospitality at Marcus's overnight after delivering Silvia and her luggage to the house – he should be back in his Glevum warehouse by late afternoon. Of course I would have to pay the money-lenders before I went to him, but the docks are famous for working after dark – ships need to load and unload to catch tides and winds – so I calculated that, with luck, I could still arrive in time to find him at his desk. My excuse would be to volunteer to join the search: I could find out what progress had been made so far, and perhaps I could slip in some questions about his trading partners too.

However, it was important that those questions seemed as casual as possible, and only to be related to the search – as though these were people I'd heard of for myself. I must give no hint that I had seen a list: so in the morning, as soon as I awoke, I turned my attention to my reading task. I spent several hours memorizing names and all the other information on the scroll.

Gwellia, gods bless her, did her best to help. Reading is quite difficult for her, but she asked me questions till I had the facts by heart, served me a lunch of quite delicious stew, then gave me a packet of the promised bread and cheese and packed me off to see about the mule.

'And take a servant with you! Minimus for choice – since you promised yesterday you'd take him the next time you went out. I don't want you roaming those icy roads on foot. Remember what happened to that poor old herb woman.' Her voice was gruff, which meant she was disguising tears. 'Of course it will be different once you have a mule. Those creatures are more sure-footed than a man and they travel faster too. Now, I know I can't expect you to come home again tonight.' She brushed aside the servants to tie my cloak herself. 'But given that you hire the animal, you should be home again quite shortly, shouldn't you?'

'Not if I'm to join the search for Genialis,' I replied, reluctant to see the disappointment on her face. 'And then there's Minimus. He isn't very big, but I doubt that Cantalarius's skinny animal would carry both of us. So I could only travel as fast as he can walk. Though I suppose that I can drop him back here, on my way past to town.'

The boy's face fell. I could see that he was fearing that I'd take Maximus again – who was a good deal smaller, despite the name his previous owner had bestowed on him. 'I could stay in Glevum, Master!' he proffered, eagerly. 'That way you would only have to get me there today – and I would be waiting for you every other evening when you came. I could keep the fires burning so the workshop will be warm when you arrive, and make it much easier for you to live in town.'

I made a doubtful face. If I took him with me, the trip to Glevum would take twice as long and if I was to search for Genialis on the road to Dorn, I was not likely to spend much time in the workshop anyway. I looked at Minimus, wondering how to tell him so without upsetting him – and displeasing Gwellia as well – but he gave me such a pleading look that I could not find the words.

He must have sensed that I was wavering. 'Let me come with you, Master. I promise you'll be glad. In any case, it wouldn't be for very long. In a few days' time the weather will improve, and then you and I and Maximus and Master Junio can all walk together each way every day, just as we always have. In the meantime, I'll bed down in the shop and attend you when you're there – and I could deal with any customers who call. You never know who might and you could lose valuable business otherwise. I'll just take my heavy cloak to be a blanket overnight, then all I'd need is a little bit of food, or a few sesterces to buy a pie or two.'

But Gwellia was already putting extra oatcakes, cheese and hard-cooked eggs into the supper bag and thrusting it into my servant's hand. 'A very good suggestion, Minimus. You go with your master. And mind you take good care of him – and of yourself, as well. Now, be off, the pair of you, or it will be too late to bargain for the mule and still get to Glevum before dark. And make sure you check whether it could carry both of you – even if it's only for a mile or two – that would help you get there before Lucius leaves the docks.'

There was even more urgency than she supposed, of course, since I had other things to do when I arrived, so I nodded and promised that I would. 'We'll be home as soon as possible,' I added in farewell, taking her briefly in my arms. 'Come, Minimus!'

But the boy already had his cloak around his neck, his sandals buckled and the food bag in his hand. 'At your service, Master!' He flung wide the roundhouse door, scuttled before me to open up the gate, and a moment later he was walking proudly at my side along the lane.

It did not take us long to reach my neighbour's farm – only a mile or two past my patron's villa – and when we got there could see the mules, in a small woven pen just inside the palisade. They looked extremely skinny, but still clearly useable, and they were chomping at something in a stone trough by the hedge.

There was no servant at the enclosure gate and we walked in unchallenged past the mules, and into the area where the farm buildings were: mostly store houses, circular, decaying and roughly thatched with reeds. A group of

154

charred remains showed where the barns had been – I remembered that my neighbour had spoken of a fire.

A mangy dog, tied up against a post, gave a half-hearted growl as we approached and strained against his rope, but we were in no danger of it reaching us and that was the only animal in sight. No pigs or piglets wallowing in the sty, no geese or chickens clucking in the mud. A thin trail of bedraggled rain-soaked wisps of hay and a pitiful lowing from a half-ruined shed nearby suggested the presence of a few sheep perhaps – but the sound was so weak that it was heartrending and a glance into the granary pit showed little sign of feed. It was clear at once that the whole farm was in decline – there was not even smoke ascending from the roundhouse roof, whose thatch was in any case in great need of repair. I could see why Cantalarius believed that he was cursed.

'Not even a fire,' I said to Minimus. 'And I don't believe that there is anybody in.'

My servant shook his head at me and gestured to the barn. I glanced around and realized that we were not, in fact, alone. A skinny child in ragged slave's attire – who looked no older than five or six, but was so undernourished he might have been far more – had sidled from the doorway of the shed and was watching us suspiciously with bright mistrustful eyes.

'I am a neighbour from the roundhouse down the lane,' I told him, hoping that this explanation would allay his obvious fears. 'You belong to Cantalarius, I suppose?'

A sullen nod was all the answer I received.

'I'm looking for your master,' I prompted, hopefully.

The boy made no response to this at all, so after a moment I added, 'Is he not at home? Can you tell me where I could look for him?' I took a step towards him.

The effect was startling and immediate. The boy began to gibber something, though to me – at least – it made no sense at all. It was not another language, either, as far as I could judge – just a rush of guttural noises while he waved his arms about and backed away as far as he could go, against the wall.

'Don't be frightened,' I implored him. 'I intend no harm. I have come about...' But I got no further. The boy had slithered past me, made a sudden dart for it and was running as fast as his skinny legs would carry him away from the farmyard to the hill beyond.

I stared at Junio. 'If that's the only servant Cantalarius has left, no wonder his wife believes that the household has been cursed. Let's hope this morning's ritual went off well and has helped to change their luck.'

Minimus, behind me, had hastened to the house. 'Well, the priest has clearly been here. The offering has been made.' He gestured to a little garden shrine beside the door – built in the Roman fashion and looking out of place inside this sorry Celtic farm. There was a plinth behind it – no doubt intended for that hideous statue that I'd seen – but now containing only a small bronze figurine, a portable image of the household Lars. However, the altar had clearly been in use: a pile of half-burnt feathers on the top and a pool of fast-congealing blood around the base, suggested a very recent sacrifice.

'Probably that ram that he was promising,' I said.

Minimus nodded. 'And not very long ago. I can still smell the smoke. Of course the celebrants can eat it afterwards. Do you suppose the priest may still be here?'

I shook my head. 'That isn't burning pigeon or sheep that you can smell. That is something else.' I glanced around, trying to locate the direction of the faint but pungent odour in the air. It was strangely familiar, though I couldn't for a moment work out what it was.

Minimus was wandering here and there around the court, but suddenly he stopped and beckoned me. 'You're quite right, Master! There is a fire on the hill. Look, you can see from over here.' He gestured past the shed towards the slope behind the house. 'Up there, where that peculiar slave boy went – that must have been what he was running to.'

I walked across and saw what he was pointing at. From somewhere just behind the summit of the hill, a dense black smoke was curling slowly up and – though the winter air was very crisp and still – the distinctive aroma was getting stronger all the time. Now there was no mistaking that remembered smell.

'A funeral pyre!' I said. 'Oh, dear gods! Poor old Cantalarius, the curse has struck again. He told me that his last remaining land slave had been taken ill with that fever that killed the other slaves. It doesn't seem as if the sacrifice has helped. Poor souls. I suppose now that poor gibbering slave boy is all that they've got left – and what use will he be, if it comes to working fields?' I turned towards my own slave with a rueful smile.

Minimus, however, looked ashen-faced. 'So perhaps it's not the moment to ask to hire the mule? Don't you think we ought to leave our errand for today?' He was already backing up the path.

I'd forgotten that my little red-haired slave (who had been raised in Roman households till he came to me) was likely to have this superstitious attitude. It was not the proximity of the corpse which worried him, of course – one often comes across dead bodies on the road and public cremations take place every day – I knew it was the mention of a curse, and the possibility of our offending the angry underworld.

I gave him my best reassuring smile. 'On the contrary,' I told him cheerfully. 'There could not be a better moment to propose this deal. The blood of sacrifice is hardly dry and someone has come to offer a good price to hire a mule! Cantalarius will be sure the gods are giving him a sign. In his position, would you not feel the same?'

Minimus nodded rather doubtfully. 'I suppose

you're right, Master. Do you want me to go up there and let them know we're here?'

I shook my head. 'I think the slave has managed to convey the fact, somehow. That looks like Cantalarius climbing back across the hill – wearing his toga too. Obviously he's been officiating at the rites.' I said this in some surprise. He didn't have to do that for a simple slave, or indeed provide a proper funeral at all – he must have taken the death of this one very hard indeed.

'And there's a woman with him,' Minimus agreed. 'That must be his wife. It seems they've finished the important rites and left that peculiar servant behind to tend the pyre.'

I watched the pair with interest as they walked back down the hill. I hadn't met the lady – only heard of her – but even from this distance I could see that she was young. She wore a long belted tunic, in the Celtic style, with a plaid cloak over it, a dark veil draped across her upper face and hair, and she walked soberly enough – but the ankles were shapely and the waist was trim. She was strikingly tall and athletic as she moved – in contrast to her husband's squat, misshapen form – all of which was rather a surprise.

I knew from Cantalarius that he'd married recently but I'd not expected his wife to look like this: men of his appearance were lucky to find a bride at all. No wonder he was so much in her thrall. Of course, it was possible she had an ugly face, or had survived some youthful scandal, or possessed a biting tongue. The latter, probably, I decided with a grin: remembering that the ill-fated Janus sacrifice had been at her demand.

Yet one had to have a certain sympathy for her, I thought, surveying the decaying remnants of the farm and the crooked ugly husband by her side. Who could blame her for believing in a curse? What a marriage she must feel that she had made! I was glad that I was bringing happier news. 'Cantalarius!' I raised my voice and waved.

He peered towards me, shading his eyes against the winter sun. 'Citizen Libertus? Is that really you?' He began to hurry down towards me, slithering from time to time on the uneven slope. 'What brings you to my farmstead?'

I smiled and patted my purse to indicate the reason for my call.

He reached me, breathing rather heavily – probably from the exertion of his abrupt descent – and stood staring disbelievingly at me. 'Surely you haven't come all this way, simply to pay me what you owe?'

I nodded. 'I knew that you would be in want of it. But I confess that there is another reason, too. Something has arisen and I have to go to town with some despatch.' I had adopted my best official tone. I was not about to tell him about Genialis and the search – the more he knew about my needs, the more he was like to charge me for the mule – when it occurred to me that he might already know. In fact it was more than probable. Cantalarius had been to town the day before and had presumably received a visit from the priest today – and news of the disappearance would be common knowledge now.

So I said to my neighbour with a smile, 'You were expecting a visitor from Glevum this morning, I believe? So I suppose you've heard the news?'

Cantalarius gave a sharp intake of breath, and a look of horror spread across his face. 'What news would that be, citizen?'

TWELVE

So, apparently he hadn't heard at all. Perhaps the rumour-mongers were not interested in an incomer from Dorn. 'An important Roman has gone missing in the snow,' I told him.

He gulped. 'Somebody of consequence, I suppose?'

'Considerable consequence, in his own mind at least.' I grinned. 'I think you've heard of him. The man who wanted to offer the Janus sacrifice this year, and was so discomfited when you produced the ram. Perhaps it would have been luckier – for everyone – if he had contrived to make the offering.'

I half expected that my neighbour would have been amused, but he simply muttered, 'Of course it would have been. As things were, it could hardly have been worse.' He met my eyes briefly, then turned his glance away. 'You say that he's still missing? You mean, he's not been found?'

I shook my head. 'It seems he set out in the snow, some little time ago, and no one's seen him since. There are people searching for him even as we speak. And that's where you come in. Is it possible you have a mule – one which

162

could carry a second person, perhaps, if he was small and didn't weigh too much?' I realized that Cantalarius was looking more and more appalled, so I added hastily, 'I don't mean all the way to town, of course, only a mile or two in an emergency? I'm sorry to ask that, but I promised that I would.' By this time he was looking so dismayed that I heartily wished that I'd ignored my wife's request and hadn't promised her to ask anything of the sort.

My neighbour didn't answer: he simply stared at me, as though Jove had struck him with a thunderbolt – until his young wife, having completed her scramble down the hill, came hurrying across to join us in the court, snatching off her mourning veil to get a better view.

One look at his expression was enough to make her say, 'What is it, husband? Not more trouble, by the gods? Tell me it isn't a message from the temple?' Her voice was shrill and anxious and she sounded close to angry tears. She must have been attractive at one time, I suppose, but her face was getting lined with too much care and hunger, and her eyes were wild and tear-filled as she looked at him. 'I told you it would happen. I knew you shouldn't have tried to offer that abomination to the gods!' She glanced towards the altar plinth, now empty apart from the statue of the Lars.

Her husband simply shook his ugly head. 'This is no messenger from the temple, wife. This is our neighbour, from the roundhouse down the track. He's come here asking me about a mule.' He turned to me and added doubtfully, 'Though I am still not sure I understand exactly what he wants.'

I gave them what I hoped was an encouraging smile. 'I know you keep a mule – or two of them in fact – and I know that money has been very short. I thought you might be grateful if I came to you. I am prepared to pay, of course, provided that we can agree a reasonable sum, and if I am successful in my enquiries, I'll mention your cooperation to Marcus Septimus.' I smiled at the woman. 'That may do more to change your evil luck, even than offering the gods your ancient friend.' I gestured to the plinth.

I rather expected to be rewarded with at least a smile. The promise of a personal commendation of that kind – especially when Marcus lived so close nearby – was usually more effective than a bribe, but to my surprise the woman gave an anguished cry and clutched her husband's arm. 'Didn't I tell you, husband? Now look what you've done!'

Cantalarius ignored her and went on looking grim. 'You spoke of enquiries, citizen? What enquiries are these?'

'I thought I'd made it plain,' I answered patiently. 'In this cold weather it's almost certain that the missing man is dead and since there are questions concerning his estate, my patron has asked me to investigate. I am sorry to disturb you at your funeral – and of your last remaining land slave too – but if I'm to join the search, I shall need an animal. Without one I can hardly walk the roads to Glevum in this chill, let alone go searching for a corpse.'

The woman was no longer listening. She was still tugging at her husband's toga folds. 'You shouldn't have done it – this is all because of you.'

I looked at her in some perplexity, but Cantalarius seemed suddenly to have recalled himself.

'You want the mule to join the search for him?' He raised his brows at me, then disengaged his garment from the clutching hands. 'Woman, you are overwrought,' he said, with a firmness that I'd never heard in him before. 'This is not what you suppose. Go away into the house and let me handle this.' He spoke with such authority that, to my surprise, she let go meekly and did as she was told. Her husband watched her out of sight and then turned back to me.

'You must forgive my Gitta,' he said, in something like his normal tone of voice. 'You can see she's not herself. It has been a dreadful day...' He motioned to the smoke which was still rising on the hill.

I nodded. 'The death of that last land slave must have been a bitter blow,' I said, then added in an attempt at sympathy, 'But perhaps this morning's sacrifice will serve to change your luck.' I gestured to the altar. 'You used your original ram, I suppose? And I see you offered a bird or two as well. Well, perhaps it's done the trick. You must agree the auguries look good. After all, the blood is hardly dry and here I am offering to hire your mule from you.'

He looked at me intently. A cloud seemed to have lifted from his brow. 'You think that little sacrifice alone might pacify the gods? Even without the involvement of a priest?'

I was about to offer more assurances but suddenly I realized what he'd said. 'Without the priest?' I echoed. 'You mean that after all he would not agree to come?'

Cantalarius turned away and kicked a pebble with his toe. When he spoke his voice was curiously calm. 'Oh, he agreed to come all right – I even went out with my mule to meet him on the way – but he did not arrive at the appointed place. I thought at first that he'd simply changed his mind, though I'd paid him everything we had.'

'Including that ancestral god of yours?' I said.

He nodded. 'Including that, although he jeered at it. But evidently even that was not enough.'

I stared at the altar. 'But what about the sacrifice?' I murmured stupidly. 'It's obviously been made.'

'I was so desperate and furious that I made the offerings myself – though my wife insists that I should not have done it on my own. She is convinced that I have only made things worse.' He made a wry face. 'She is beside herself with worry, as you may observe. So when young Sordinus came hurrying to the pyre–' he

166

gestured to the hill, where fitful smoke still curled into the air – 'and made signs to us that there was someone here...'

'Your wife thought I'd brought a message from the temple?' I supplied.

He nodded. 'Sordinus cannot talk, of course, so he could not explain. Perhaps Gitta was expecting an apology – or at the least for the goods to be returned...'

'Or even that the priest had come at last,' I finished. 'But by that time, of course, it would have been too late. You had already made the sacrifice. And your poor land slave was already dead.' I gestured to the pyre.

'Gitta is inclined to blame me for that too,' he muttered bitterly. 'Thinks it is a judgement from the gods.'

'Because you were making the sacrifice yourself? But surely you've performed such rituals before?'

'Many times, citizen. And at this very altar. As paterfamilias I've made a lot of offerings at the household shrine. But I'd moved the statue, and what's more I'd vowed upon that altar that there would be a priest today – promised the gods a proper sacrifice this time, and once again I failed. So the death of the land slave was the final straw. It happened just as I was lifting the sacrificial knife. That's what upset my wife. She is sure that I have angered the ancestral deities and increased the curse instead of lifting it.'

I nodded. Suddenly her agitation did not seem so strange. 'But you went ahead and finished the acts of sacrifice?'

He shrugged. 'I had to do something, citizen. I couldn't interrupt the rituals again, or Gitta would have left me there and then. I'm not sure that she won't do so, even now. It's all the fault of that confounded sacerdos. If he hadn't ruined my attempt at sacrifice in town, all this would never have occurred.' He spoke with such feeling that I was surprised.

'You are not convinced that you have raised the curse yourself?' I said. 'Of course, he promised he would come and I can see that you are angry, but consider this – if he had turned up and made a mess of it again, wouldn't that have been still more unfortunate?'

He looked thoughtfully at me. 'You are right, of course. And I confess that I was furious with his failure to appear. Though now that I realize it was not his fault at all...'

I interrupted him, surprised. 'Why not, if he had agreed a fee? You had a legal contract, didn't you?'

It was his turn to look astonished. 'Did you not just tell me he was missing in the snow, and although they'd searched for him it was feared that he was dead?' He saw me staring in surprise, and added mournfully, 'The man who was to make the Janus sacrifice, you said.'

And then – at last – I understood his shock. 'You thought I meant the priest! What did you suppose? That your curse had struck again and all this had happened on his way to you?' I shook my head. 'Well, don't worry. This is not

168

about the priest. I was talking about the man who wanted to provide the ram. Genialis, the would-be councillor.' Cantalarius still looked puzzled so I added helpfully, 'The man that I was making that hurried pavement for.'

An expression of bemusement crossed my neighbour's face. 'So the priest...?'

I put my arm around his crooked back. 'I'm very much afraid that he has simply let you down.' I realized he was shaking with relief, and I said, to comfort him, 'I'll mention that to Marcus when I see him, too – if you had a spoken contract, you have a case in law. It's not much consolation, I'm aware – especially where a member of the priesthood is concerned. He'll only claim you simply made a donation to the shrine, but all the same, the intervention of our most senior magistrate might persuade him to attempt some compromise. And in the meantime, I'd still like to hire your mule.' I tried a sympathetic smile. 'Perhaps the fifth part of an aureus will help persuade your wife that the sacrifice you offered was not a bad thing after all?'

He managed to summon a rueful smile at this and summoned Gitta from inside the house. She still seemed ready to hector and complain, but once her husband had explained affairs to her, she brightened up remarkably, and when she heard about my offer for the mule, she was positively anxious for him to seal the contract, there and then.

'It is surer profit than attempting to sell leeks

and cabbages,' she said, suddenly business-like and adopting a judicious air. 'Let him hire both of them, husband, if he likes, and look for this unlucky councillor.'

I was about to protest – I didn't want to do anything of the sort – but Cantalarius was already waving this aside.

'I shall require one animal to go to town myself – with the money that Libertus has agreed to pay, we shall have enough to buy some more feed for the stock. With luck we may keep the rest of them alive until the weather breaks.'

I beamed at her. 'You see? That sacrifice your husband made has obviously worked – the gods are seeing fit to change your luck at last.'

She seemed about to speak but he prevented her, raising a hand and looking indulgently at her. 'Perhaps the citizen is right. Things are looking hopeful, for a change. Nonetheless, wife, one of us should go back and attend the funeral pyre – otherwise we shall offend the netherworld again. We are already in danger of not showing the dead enough respect. You go back and take over the lament. Sordinus cannot do it, and it must be done. I will take the citizen to select his mule then I'll come to you and conclude the rituals.'

Gitta nodded. 'Perhaps I was wrong about that offering after all,' she said.

Then she turned and went hurrying off, while her husband led me and Minimus back to where the mules were kept.

THIRTEEN

When we reached the wickerwork stockade pen, Cantalarius raised the rope loop which secured the woven gate and escorted myself and Minimus inside. The field was small and muddy and the two animals were at the other end, snuffling at the wisp or two of hay still lying in the trough.

'You have contrived to keep these fed throughout, I see?' I said.

'I had to, neighbour,' he said glumly, 'or we would have starved, ourselves. I needed them to take my wares to town to sell. Or to offer to the temple, come to that. Though it has not been easy, once or twice. Between these mules and trying to keep that unblemished ram alive we've had empty bellies more than once this moon – animals that starve to death have little meat on them. Though Gitta did manage to make some soup from two poor scraggy ewes, with some of the blighted cabbage which was not fit to sell.' He gave a mirthless laugh. 'At least with all the servants dead there are fewer mouths to feed.'

I nodded. 'There must have been some hard decisions, I can see.'

A strange expression spread across the ugly face. 'The truth is, neighbour, I've done a stupid thing – though I did not wish to tell you when my wife could hear. But things were desperate. I had to feed the mules...' He trailed off, uncomfortably.

'Go on!' I prompted. 'If you have been begging, I shan't inform on you.' Beggars are officially forbidden in the town but people who are driven to it have my sympathy.

'I wish it were that simple,' he said soberly, making me wonder for a moment if he'd been stealing feed – for which of course the penalty was severe.

'Fortunately, since you are a Roman citizen, even theft is not a capital offence,' I hazarded, though the alternative – four-fold reparation and a swinging fine – was not much comfort, I could see. They'd seize the farm to pay it, and he'd lose everything.

But that was not the trouble either, it appeared.

He shook his head. 'It's like this, citizen Libertus. When I went into Glevum to the temple yesterday, I had to cross the market-place, of course. I found there was a little hay and oats for sale – someone had succeeded in bringing in a cartful from their store, though naturally they wanted an enormous price for it and by that time I had given everything I had to bribe the priest. But I was desperate. I was right beside the forum and ... I don't know how it happened, but temptation was too great...' He stopped and looked at me.

'You borrowed from the money-lenders!' I exclaimed. I saw his expression of surprised relief and gave him a wry smile. 'Don't worry, friend – you're not the only one.'

He was silent for a moment, as if he couldn't quite work out the force of that. Then he said, slowly, 'You went to them, yourself?'

I nodded. 'I think that half the town has been reduced to it.' In a burst of fellow-feeling I reached out and patted him on his crooked arm. 'And don't fear I'll tell your wife. I haven't told mine, either. Your secret's safe with me. Besides, when I have paid you for the mule you will have the wherewithal to clear the debt. Or some of it, at least.'

After that it did not take us long to shake upon the contract for the hire. I was to have the stronger of the mules for as long as I required, with permission to use it in any way I wished, on condition that I provided food and stabling for it and returned it 'before the Ides in as good condition as I found it' – a proviso I agreed to easily enough, as it was hard to see how the poor beast's condition could well be worse.

Then it came to payment. I'd agreed a fifth of an aureus, of course, and there was also the two sesterces that I already owed – but I had no coin smaller than an aureus itself, and I had fully expected to have to leave one here as a kind of surety for the animal. However Cantalarius reached down his tunic-neck and produced a leather purse that dangled on string, and to my amazement he unloosed the cord and solemnly counted out my change: a gold quinarius-aureus (or 'half-aureus' as he called it) and seven silver denarii, saying as he did so, 'Seventy-eight sesterces, I believe that's right?'

'You borrowed all that from the money-lenders?' I exclaimed. Suddenly my humble debt seemed insignificant.

He sighed. 'An aureus – they would not lend me less, though I only needed a fraction of that sum.'

I nodded. 'And it must be due by now.' There'd been a rush, of course, and – unlike me – Cantalarius had no powerful patron to protect him, so the money-lenders could dictate their terms. 'But if you get back today,' I told him earnestly, 'you can repay it all before the interest starts to mount too much. And maybe even have enough to buy a bit more feed – supposing that it's still available. Though I suppose you'll have to finish at the pyre before you go.'

'Exactly what I hope that I'll have time to do!' He was already hurrying over to a stone store hut near the gate, and producing a pannier saddle which he and Minimus threw across the mule. 'So you understand that I need to hurry back?'

I understood him better than he thought. I was in haste to reach the town myself, so I was glad to give a hand to tie the saddle on, and a few moments later I was on the creature's back. 'Do you think that she could take my slave as well?' I murmured, as Minimus took the rope and prepared to lead us out on to the road.

'I'd give her a minute to get used to you – but she's the stronger one and she is used to taking loads.' Cantalarius held the gate open to let us through.

'Till the Ides, then – or sooner if the weather breaks!' I called out cheerfully, as Minimus tugged the tether and we bounced out on to the road. The poor mule was so bony that I feared to break its back but it was walking willingly enough.

'She's called Arlina!' Cantalarius shouted back. He closed the gate of the enclosure after us then turned and hurried off towards his pyre.

'What makes you smile, Master?' Minimus enquired, turning his head to look at me. Up to then he had been staring at the path, picking his way with care among the icy stones.

I grinned at him. 'I was laughing at the name he gives the mule. The word means "oath" in Celtic, so it doesn't promise well! Though she seems tractable enough while you are leading her. I wonder if she'd walk without the rope? Let it go a moment.' I pressed my knees into the mule to urge it on.

In fact, I need not have been concerned. Arlina proved amenable enough in either mode – indeed she even seemed to know the way and, when we reached the junction where my round-house was, turned without the slightest prompting on our part towards the ancient track to-wards the town. It felt quite strange to ride straight past my home like that, but Gwellia

175

glimpsed me and came running to the gate.

'I'm glad to see you've got the mule!' she called. 'But don't go taking any risks with it.' She saw that Minimus had slowed the animal, and she shook her head at him. 'Don't stop now – you'll only have to hurry later if you do, and it's such a skinny creature it might not have the strength!' She stood at the gatepost and waved us out of sight.

I was starting to have confidence in the animal by now and a little further on, where the road got steep and difficult and Minimus was beginning to slide and stumble on the ice, I paused and pulled him up to sit in front of me. To my delight the mule seemed wholly unconcerned, so we rode in this fashion until the town wall came into sight.

Of course I had nowhere to accommodate an animal at my shop (as I had said to Gwellia earlier) but one of the hiring stable owners just outside the southern gates was a man with whom I'd had dealings once or twice before. In this dreadful weather he was short of trade and he took Arlina willingly enough – though at a fee of course. So we left the creature, hungrily munching silage in a stall, while Minimus and I went hurrying into town.

It was well into the afternoon by now, and very cold indeed, and many of the forum stalls were starting to close down, including some of the money-lenders ranged around the wall. I sent Minimus away to light the workshop fire while I sought out the man I had borrowed from. I managed to catch him, but only just in time, just as he was gathering up his goods and preparing to depart.

He was a swarthy fellow, with small greedy eyes and a suspicious frown, and it was clear he was not altogether pleased to find me there. 'Back to pay your loan off before it's even due?' he grumbled. 'Trying to deprive me of my proper interest, I suppose.'

Nonetheless he sat down again, took my proffered aureus and (after I'd called upon a passing citizen to witness that I'd paid) tried it in his teeth, put it in his coffers and counted out the change. After the deductions it did not seem very much, and I was very glad that I had not been forced, like Cantalarius, to borrow more that I could possibly afford.

The thought persuaded me to say – in some vague hope of preventing the man from packing up and thus costing my neighbour interest for another day – 'I may not be your last customer, even now. The citizen Cantalarius is hoping to arrive tonight and pay back what he owes.'

As soon as I had spoken, it occurred to me that my words were more likely to have the opposite effect and make the money-lender leave at once, but in fact he made no move at all – just looked up at me with a suspicious air. 'Cantalarius? What has that to do with me?'

'Perhaps you weren't the one who lent to him?' I murmured, foolishly.

The fellow shook his head. 'Not me, citizen. I would not have lent him anything at all. And after that business in the temple, I don't know who would! That man is obviously cursed.' He spat on his finger and rubbed it on his ear, as if he needed to ward away ill-luck for simply having mentioned Cantalarius by name. 'I wouldn't even let his shadow fall upon my feet, for fear of his ill-fortune rubbing off on me.'

'Because of what happened at the Agonalia sacrifice?' I said, privately thinking that this attitude explained my neighbour's troubles in obtaining loans. 'But surely the offering to Janus has been safely made by now – and I happen to know that Cantalarius has made a cleansing ritual of his own.'

The money-lender stared. 'But the trouble at the festival is only half of it.' He saw that I was puzzled. 'Don't tell me that you don't know what has happened now!'

'I'm aware his last remaining land slave died today,' I answered. 'It's most unfortunate. But there's been a propitiation to the gods – even a donation to the temple here – and things should be better now.'

'Who cares about a land slave?' The fellow clambered to his feet and pulled his coloured head-dress closer round his face. He was shorter than I am, and he smelled of spice, but he leaned close to me and murmured in the direction of my ear, 'It's those missing Romans that have started all the talk. First that Genialis fellow—'

I interrupted him. 'You heard that he was missing?'

He looked at me as though I were an idiot. 'Well, hasn't everyone? It's no secret, citizen. Alfredus Allius was in the forum earlier, making a formal announcement to his creditors.'

'Alfredus Allius!' I exclaimed. There was another man I'd have to interview.

'That's right, citizen. He was a close associate of Genialis, it seems. In fact he lent him money, but the fellow disappeared – and no one else gets paid till he turns up again, alive or otherwise.' His pig-like eyes were watery with mirth. 'Most likely otherwise. Allius claims he has been missing for a day or two at least and now there is a search for him. Though I'll wager that if they find him, they'll find him dead.'

'What makes you sure of that?'

'I told you, citizen, it is all around the town – he was connected with that Janus sacrifice and there's a curse on everyone who was concerned with that. Mind you, there is another rumour that he laid that curse himself, because he wanted to donate the offering.' He stopped and looked at me. 'Why are you so interested in all this in any case? You mentioned that accursed Cantalarius, – you are not a friend of his, I hope, or you'll be bringing ill-fortune on everyone, yourself!'

'I've had business dealings with him, that is all,' I said, feeling like a traitor as I spoke. 'I've hired a mule from him.'

The money-lender wafted spice at me again. 'Then I should get it back to him as soon as possible, if you don't want to be the next to feel the anger of the Fates. They say it's touching everyone that has to do with him. Even the temple priests are not exempt, it seems. And now they've found that body in the ice...'

'Body!' The word was startled out of me.

But I had shown too much interest. 'You want more information, citizen? You can attract ill-luck, you know, by too much talk of it. I'm not sure I should take the risk of saying any more. Unless, of course, you wanted to make it worth my while...' He rubbed two fingers up against his thumb in the universal sign that money was required.

I found a sestertius and held it out of reach. 'This if you earn it. Now tell me what you know. They have found a body – but it wasn't Genialis, is that right?'

'I haven't seen it, citizen, so I couldn't swear to it!' He eyed the money greedily. 'All know is that they say it was the priest.'

'The priest?' I was turning into Echo, in the legend of the Greeks.

'The one who let the ram go at the Janus festival,' he said. 'Or half of him, at least. First they were looking for him shortly after dawn – he hadn't gone to the morning sacrifice – and then some peasant came rushing into the forum with the news. He and his brother were looking for firewood on the forest path and they saw this pair of feet and legs sticking from a pile of snow out on a pond. Though Jove only knows what the old man was doing in the woods in this inclement weather anyway.'

On his way to visit Cantalarius, I thought, when some unpleasant accident had befallen him. So that is why he hadn't turned up at the farm! I wondered how Cantalarius would feel when he found out. Perhaps there really was a curse!

My informant was still telling me his tale. 'Anyway, when this peasant went to take a closer look, he found that legs and feet was almost all there was left of him – there wasn't any head, or any chest and shoulders come to that.'

That caught my interest, of course. 'If there's no head, then how can they be sure it is the priest?' I said, wondering if it might be Genialis after all.

'There are lots of theories about that, but I believe it was the sandals that they recognized. A very fancy pair. That's what brought the peasant rushing into town. He thought he'd seen the old priest wearing them – and the temple sent slaves out to verify the fact. They must have done so, because they brought the body back this very afternoon. There won't be a big state funeral, I understand – that would take some time to organize and they want to cleanse the temple as fast as possible. It's an evil augury to have only half a corpse. Looks as if he found his way into a frozen ditch and drowned: he was lying head downwards in the ice. Everyone is saying it is the curse, of course.'

'So what happened to the rest of him?' I said, half to myself.

The money-lender shrugged. 'The gods alone know, citizen. Looked as it if had been hacked away or gnawed – though his clothes were still there with him, mostly floating underneath the ice. Apparently they've brought those back as well. Perhaps a wolf or something got the rest of him. And that is all I know.' He made a lunge towards the coin.

I pulled it back and held it high above his reach. 'An underwater wolf?' I shook my head. 'I don't believe that, townsman, any more than you! Though I suppose it might be Druids. Have they thought of that?' The old religion had been banned of course, but there had been Druid rebels active hereabouts – often targeting the Roman soldiery and hewing off their heads to hang in sacred groves, as an offering to the woodland gods. 'A priest might be a target for them, I suppose.'

The money-lender stared at me as though I were insane. 'When did Druids ever hack off more than just the head? Or leave a body where it would not instantly be found? I told you, citizen, it is the curse at work. Mind you, it's my belief he brought it on himself. The man was old and sick, by all accounts, and should have been retired from the priesthood long ago. Couldn't be relied upon to perform the rituals. I wasn't at the sacrifice, of course – I'm not a citizen – but I've heard it was his fault that it had to be postponed.'

I nodded. 'He let the ram get free and spoil the sacrifice.'

He spat on his finger and rubbed his ear with it then fingered a good-luck amulet that he wore round his wrist. 'Well, if he did offend the gods, he's paid the price for it. And so will we, if we keep on like this. I said before, one can attract a curse by dwelling on its power.'

I was no longer listening. I was trying to make sense of all that I'd just heard. 'It can't have been the same body that Cantalarius saw,' I said, scarcely aware that I had said the words aloud. 'That was days ago, before the feast. So there must have been two separate corpses at the pond. I wonder if that earlier one was Gen...?' I shook my head. 'That can't be so; the body was being rescued then by passers-by, so if it had been a wealthy Roman in a toga we would have heard of it. Someone would have wanted a reward – just like that peasant who came running in today.'

But I had dropped my guard. The money-lender made a lunge and seized the coin, and – even before I could protest – he had bent down and snatched up his cushion and his box and was scuttling away across the forum, his coloured head-scarf bobbing as he ran.

FOURTEEN

For a moment I stood there, staring after him.

Of it course it was possible that his shocking information was only partly true: some half-heard story that had spread around the town, getting more and more distorted as it went. Or it might be a confusion of different incidents – after all there had been a body at the pond some day before. Everybody knows how rumours alter as they spread.

And then it struck me. Why was I supposing the same pool was involved? The money-lender hadn't mentioned where the corpse was found. I was beginning to conflate the two events myself. This was probably not even on the southern side of the town. Though, come to think of it, if the body was the priest's, I thought I knew a reason why he might have gone that way.

I shook my head. I could not really credit that the corpse was his. A priest does not go missing from the temple unobserved – he would always have an acolyte or slave attending him. Besides, he'd been alive and active only yesterday, talking to Cantalarius in the afternoon – no doubt there would be witnesses to that – so even if he had died overnight, how he could be half-eaten in so short a time? Unless there really was a curse, of course.

But I didn't honestly believe there was a curse at all. Call me cynical, but when there's a violent death that's unexplained, I usually suspect a human cause. This began to look like murder, and a nasty one at that. But who would want to murder a harmless, rather doddering, ancient priest – let alone divide his corpse up afterwards? And – more important – who would ever dare? The earthly penalties for such an act were terrible enough, but nothing compared to the almost certain retribution by the gods. Even rebel Druids would baulk at such a thought.

In fact if half a body had been found today, I thought, perhaps it was really Genialis after all. I could invent a plausible story to account for that. Suppose, for instance, that he'd fallen off his horse, been found by the wayside by a pack of starving wolves, dragged into a snow-drift while they were eating him and then abandoned when they were frightened off? That would make more sense of the timetable at least. And it was just possible. A pair of fancy sandals were no proof of anything, whatever the members of the temple said. Genialis, I remembered, had fancy sandals too.

There was one obvious flaw in this convenient theory, though. If this was Genialis, what had happened to the priest? Presumably he wasn't at the temple now, or no one would ever have supposed that the legs and feet were his. But how could he have got out unobserved?

Surely he would never have set off alone for Cantalarius's farm, and in the dark – since he was missed before the morning sacrifice at dawn? Or had he, for some reason, done exactly that? In which case, was it possible the rumours were all true and was this really the corpse of the old sacerdos, foiling my poor neighbour's hoped-for sacrifice again?

My mind was going in circles. I was back where I began. It was obvious I must discover more.

My first thought was to call into the temple and enquire. For one thing, I could ask about the movements of the priest and find out, for instance, who had seen him last; and for another I might even get a look at the remains – if they really had been brought there as the money-lender thought. That would settle the question of whose legs they were – Genialis was much stouter than the skinny priest. But wouldn't the temple have noticed such a thing themselves, if the wrong body had been brought to them? Well, there was only one way to find out.

I hurried to the temple, but as I climbed the steps I found my way was courteously barred. An apologetic but determined temple slave had stepped out from between the pillars and was standing in my path – quite deliberately to stop me getting in. It was not difficult for him to do. He was a man of vast proportions: not quite the tallest person I had ever seen, nor quite the widest either, but approximating both. He was olive-skinned and looked as if he'd once been beautiful – though now his neck and arms were wreathed in folds of fat – and he was resplendent in his dark-red temple slave tunic.

So it was rather like encountering a hill in uniform, as he appeared in front of me, blocking my view and saying in a strangely high and piping voice, 'I'm sorry, citizen. The shrine is closed today.'

I tried to see round him, but he moved to block my view. 'But I have business...' I protested.

He shook his head, jangling the golden hoops that dangled from his ears, and folded his huge arms across his chest. 'No entrance is permitted this evening, I'm afraid. There's been a tragic incident and the necessary rituals of cleansing are taking place. I don't know when the temple will be functioning again. There'll be a formal announcement on these steps tomorrow at midday. Other shrines are open if you wish to purchase votive offerings. If you have a prayer or curse tablet that you particularly want to present to one of our three Capitoline gods, and you are in a hurry, I can attend to that for you – or deal with any donation that you hope to make.'

'I'm only here to make enquiries,' I said, still trying to peer around his massive bulk, though without success. Whatever was going on in the shrine, one couldn't see from here. 'The old priest of Diana – I hear his body was discovered in a pond?'

'I can't confirm that nor deny it. My orders are quite clear. I must not encourage rumours!'

This was clearly intended as serious rebuke, but in that childish treble voice it was rather laughable. 'A full public statement will be issued in due course.'

'I ask because a neighbour of mine was expecting the priest to call on him today,' I said, adopting a duly apologetic tone. 'To officiate at a different cleansing ritual. I understand that some donation to the temple had been made, on the understanding that the priest would come. But, of course, if something dreadful befell him on the way...' I let the words trail off.

The mountain inclined a little towards me at the waist. 'I think there's some mistake. He did have a visit from a supplicant yesterday, I know, offering donations to the shrine and hoping he would undertake some private offerings – he was boasting about it in the courtyard afterwards. But he had no duties outside the shrine today – none, at least, of which we servants were informed. He was expected, as usual, at the morning rituals...'

'Expected?' I echoed. 'So he did not appear? So he is missing! I imagine the alarm was raised at once? You say he did not attend the morning rituals? So people have been searching ever since first light?'

A faint pink tone suffused the olive face. 'Not entirely, citizen.' He looked furtively to either side then leaned a little closer and said, confidentially, 'He was elderly, you see, and did sometimes miss the early sacrifice. But then it was time to break our fast and eat the offerings

– you know that when the gods have had their share, the rest often is taken to the kitchens to be cooked and then distributed among the priests and temple staff – and that was something that he did like to attend. But when they sent to fetch him, he could not be found. His cell was empty and his bed appeared unused – though he was there long after vespers, I can vouch for that myself. I saw him standing at the window of his cell.'

'What was he doing at that time of night?' I matched his tone. 'Watching for someone? Did he seem in distress? Or didn't he tell you?'

The mountain shook his massive head reproachfully, making the earrings jangle even more. 'Of course not, citizen. There was no distress at all. I could see what he was doing. He was praying to the moon. Perfectly normal – he was a priest of Luna, after all.'

I nodded. 'And of Diana and Fortuna, I believe. Of course Diana has always been connected with the moon.'

'Exactly!' the slave replied. 'So I was not surprised. The night was bright and cloudless and he'd thrown back the shutters – though it was very cold – and was doing his nightly devotions in the dark. He was old, of course, and not as scrupulous at rituals as perhaps he used to be, but he was still a servant of his deities. So of course I did not speak to him – I would not have dared disturb him at his prayers.'

'But you're quite certain that you saw him then?'

'There is no doubt of that. I've seen him lots of times, before. Last night I was crossing to the shrine of Jupiter to set the altar fire for the morning ritual and I could see him clearly, in the window space, worshipping the goddess with his arms outspread – just as he always did. It has occurred to me before that it might be dangerous – standing for a long time in the cold like that, at his age, in this weather, without a cloak and hood – but it's not my place to say anything, of course, and obviously I couldn't interrupt him at such moments anyway. But then, when they found him later, dead and frozen in the ice – you can see that it seemed like a kind of irony.'

'So they did find his body head-down in a pool? And was he half-missing, as the rumours say?'

He straightened up abruptly and reverted to his former tone, brisk and official. 'You may deduce that if you care to, citizen. You did not hear it from me.' His high voice was even squeakier than before. 'I know my duty. I am saying nothing more. The temple will make a formal announcement on the steps, when there is agreement on exactly what occurred and what is the best way in which we might proceed. They have called in the augurers to consult the birds. Now, citizen, I think this conversation has lasted long enough.' He took a single step towards me as he spoke.

I don't know what I thought that he might do – pick me up and carry me bodily down the steps, perhaps, or call for reinforcements to summon the town watch and have me dragged off to the city jail – but I judged that it was prudent to retreat.

'I am sorry to have troubled you at an unfortunate time,' I said, with a pretence at due humility. 'I'll try to come tomorrow and hear this statement read.' With that I backed respectfully away, till I had reached the steps, then turned and hurried down them into the street again.

The huge slave watched me for a moment. Then, seeming satisfied, he disappeared among the temple pillars – where no doubt there was a stool and he could sit, on guard in case some other would-be temple-goer arrived.

I was not altogether disappointed with my visit though. I had gleaned more information than he'd meant to give. For one thing, I could have faith in Cantalarius's account of his visit yesterday – it had occurred to me to question it. But the temple slave had borne him out in all respects: he had been to see the ancient sacerdos, who'd been alive and well and (more im-portantly) in good health afterwards – since he was not only talking with others in the courtyard later on but involved in normal rituals till the middle of the night.

Yet by this morning he had disappeared – and not officially going out to the farm, as might have been supposed or (as my slave friend had pointed out) someone in the temple would have heard of it. Besides, if he'd set off to perform a sacrifice, ritual cleansing would be called for before he left the shrine and an attendant, with equipment, would have been arranged for him. So what had happened to the old man in those intervening hours?

I was now certain that the story about the pond was true – my conversation with the slave had convinced me of that – and the priest was missing, so the body might be his. But how had he left the temple unobserved? That seemed impossible. There were slaves on watch all night, guarding the sacred fires, and he could not have reached the entrance without their seeing him. And there was no other way into the site, which – apart from the main entrance which I had just approached – was surrounded on all sides by a high stone wall, deliberately tall to hide the mysteries within. Perhaps a younger man might just be strong enough to scale it and escape, or scuttle up a sacred tree and wriggle out along a branch, but for an aged priest it was inconceivable – especially in the dark when it was freezing hard and everything was slippery with ice. (In fact, the feat was known to be extremely difficult, even for an athlete in the light of day: the last man to try it, for a dare, had broken both his legs, and been thrown into the city prison for his pains!)

So, given that no supernatural power had been at work, how had the priest got out of there at all? Had he, for some reason, adopted a disguise? Or had he been smuggled out against his will? I shook my head. Neither explanation seemed remotely probable, given that the temple was a busy place, with slaves and attendants in every corridor.

I don't know how much longer I'd have gone on standing there, chasing the same thoughts without effect, but I was interrupted by a hearty voice and a hand upon my shoulder.

'Libertus, my good fellow! I am glad to find you here. It appears that we are looking for each other! We have just this instant come here from your shop. Your slave informed me you were on your way to me – but he also mentioned that you had business to attend to in the forum first, so I came back this way in the hope of seeing you! And here, indeed, you are.'

I turned to find a beaming Lucius, looking especially tawny in a russet cloak and accompanied by the same slave that I'd seen before. I greeted them with pleasure – it was getting late by now, and I had been worried that I would not find the trader at his desk. I told him so.

'You would not have found me, I'm afraid. I have not been back in Glevum very long, and I merely called into the warehouse then, to check on everything and see if there was any news. I spent the night with Marcus at his country house,' he went on, with a hint of pride at the implied distinction this bestowed.

I gave the bow that he expected. 'I heard that you were taking Silvia out there?'

He nodded. 'We set off late yesterday when her effects arrived, but the main road was so difficult that it took simply hours, and Marcus

insisted that I should dine with them and offered me a bed – and somehow that lengthened
into my remaining half today.' He stroked his
beard in a thoughtful way. 'His Excellence was
kind enough to ask me about this loan I hoped
to get – I suppose he is concerned on Silvia's
behalf – and no doubt I talked too much about
the business and the hopes I have for it. He is a
courteous listener – though it seemed to interest
him.'

'Perhaps it genuinely did,' I muttered bitterly.
How like Marcus to set a task for me and then
– without warning – embark on it himself! 'So
you didn't leave his villa until this afternoon.'

'Exactly. And even then the military road was
difficult – there are carts and wagons queuing
up for miles. I suppose they haven't been able
to get here recently – and it has taken me till
almost now to reach the town. I merely called
into the warehouse, as I said, and then went
straight to you.'

I made that bow again. 'I am honoured, naturally – but, forgive me, Lucius – what made you
do that?'

'Your patron mentioned that you wanted to
have a word with me when I got back,' he said,
as though this were self-evident.

I was so thunderstruck that for a moment I
could not answer him. Surely even Marcus
would not be so thoughtless as to require me to
ask questions without seeming to, and then tell
my subject that I want to talk to him! However,
Lucius was looking at me, visibly nonplussed,

and I managed to say, through gritted teeth, 'Did he mention what I hoped to talk to you about?'

Lucius brightened. 'Well, of course he did. He told me that he's enlisted you to help us in the hunt for Genialis – since it is important to Silvia to know if he is dead. Some of my servants have been in the search party today, so as soon as I had news, I came straight to find you at the shop.'

I had misjudged my patron. I breathed slowly out. 'News? So have they found him?'

'Not so far, citizen,' Lucius replied. 'They have scoured the area near the main road all day with no success, and eventually Bernadus called off the hunt tonight, so people could get home before it froze again. But they mean to search tomorrow, a little further off. If you really mean to join them I will send my cart and take you to the area if you like.'

'So that was why you came to find me? That was kind of you.'

He smiled. 'It suited me to come, in any case. Silvia thinks that I should ask for your advice.' He placed a companionable hand on my arm. 'Besides, I hear you were proposing to eat bread and cheese tonight, so I wondered, citizen, if you would care to dine with me? I believe there is roast Gallic fowl and pork to offer you – it came from a consignment which was shipped in just today. And spiced mead, which I understand that you are partial to. Come, citizen, what do you say to that?'

FIFTEEN

It was very tempting – especially the mead – and the occasion would obviously give me an opportunity to learn more about the people on that list of Marcus's, but I shook my head.

'My slave,' I muttered apologetically. 'He'll be expecting me. He'll be anxious, in this weather, if I do not appear.'

'You are very solicitous of your servants, citizen!' Lucius gave a wry glance at his own, the stolid, sullen-looking boy with pimpled skin. 'But have no fear of that. I have already warned him that I was going to ask. I think he was only sorry that you were not there, so he could come with you and share in whatever is left over with my slaves. And there should be ample – even with an extra guest.'

'Extra?'

He smiled. 'My kitchen is preparing additional food tonight, in any case. Alfredus Allius is due to dine with me. The man that I am hoping will lend me capital. Your slave said that you know him?'

Alfredus Allius! There was that name again. There was no declining the invitation now! 'I have met him once,' I answered, carefully. 'He was a witness to that contract that I had with Genialis. Though, from what I heard in the forum earlier, there may be a small problem with that loan. Genialis owed him money, it appears – and he cannot even meet his debts until it's paid.'

I had expected Lucius to be cast down by this, but in fact he seemed relieved by the intelligence. 'That's excellent!' he cried. 'I was going to have to ask him to delay, until we know what is happening to Silvia's estate, though I knew he was in a hurry to invest somewhere. But now, it seems, he'll say the same to me. And since you two are acquainted there can be no awkwardness!' He stroked his auburn beard. 'And there'll still be time for you and I to talk, or rather for me to ask for your advice. Before he comes, perhaps. Allius does not generally arrive till after dark.'

'Then I should be delighted,' I replied. 'Though I'm hardly dressed to dine in such exalted company.' I was wearing only a warm tunic and a cloak – one doesn't choose to wear an awkward toga on a mule. 'And I have no attendant with me, as you see. Perhaps you could spare a slave to light me home?'

'Of course.' Lucius gave that bluff laugh of his again. 'And as to what you're wearing, give no thought to that. I don't have a toga to boast of anyway. Mine is a humble household, my friend. I'm a simple man – and the presence of two citizens at my table is an uncommon privilege, whatever they are wearing at the time.' It

197

was an exaggeration – he clearly had dealings with the rich and great – but it was courteous. He gestured round the forum. 'So, if you have finished here, we can escort you to my quarters straightaway. Or do you still have business to attend to at the temple, perhaps?'

I shook my head and he signalled to his pimply slave to lead the way. 'I hoped to call in at the temple,' I explained, as we began to follow. 'But they have closed the shrine today for cleansing rituals.'

'Not because of the problems at the Agonalia, surely?' Lucius said, taking my arm to aid me across a pile of frozen snow and making me feel like a great-grandfather. 'I thought that had been dealt with days ago.'

'This is more recent. There's been an accident to one of the old priests, and they are anxious to purify the shrine. You haven't heard the rumours?'

He shook his head. 'I haven't been back in Glevum long enough to talk to anyone. Except yourself, of course. What are you waiting for?' This last was to his servant, who was hovering at the entrance to a narrow alleyway.

'It's quicker this way, masters, if you can manage it.'

I nodded, and we turned that way, though the ground was still treacherous with patches of black ice and the occasional heap of frozen piled-up snow.

We picked and slithered our way in silence for a little while, then Lucius said, 'Is this what happened to this aged priest? You mentioned an accident? What did he do? Slip on the courtyard ice and kill himself?'

'Rather worse than that. They discovered half the body in an icy pond, miles outside the temple, earlier today,' I told him, as we paused at a corner to let a hand-cart pass.

'Half?' He whirled around to face me. 'But...?'

'You are wondering if it might be Genialis?' I suggested.

He looked nonplussed a moment, then nodded ruefully. 'I see you read my mind.'

'The same thought had occurred to me, at first,' I told him with a smile, 'but I've been thinking since. The two men were of such different builds, there could hardly be confusion anyway. And the temple is obviously sure it is their missing priest, because they sent a party out to bring back the remains – and they would not have done that if there were any doubt. The mere presence of any corpse within the shrine would call for hours of purifying rituals – let alone a priest, and a half of one at that.'

He made a face. 'A corpse would call for cleansing rites, wherever it was brought. But I suppose in a temple it requires much more.'

I grinned. 'Fire and smoke and water and the gods know what besides, and no doubt special ceremonies and sacrifices to propitiate the various goddesses he served. I think that they were beginning all that when I was there. Not that I could see what they were doing at the shrine – they've posted a giant servant at the gate, who wouldn't even let me talk to anyone.'

Lucius brayed with laughter. 'I see. I wondered what your interest in the temple was. I had not taken you for a religious man – at least not where the Roman deities are concerned. Though you went to the Janus festival, I think? The first time I met you, you and your patron had just come from that abortive sacrifice.'

'Only the first one, when it had to be postponed,' I said. 'In the afternoon I took advantage of the thaw and went back to my roundhouse, before the pathways froze. The Agonalia is not one of the obligatory rituals – not like the Imperial birthday sacrifice – and my home is quite a long way out of town. Quite near to Marcus's in fact – the land was originally part of his estate. You would have passed it, when you were out there earlier.'

'If I go there again, I will look out for it,' Lucius said graciously, as we turned the corner to the docks. 'And, speaking of your dwelling, here is mine.' He indicated a building in the quayside area. 'Not a fancy residence, but it suits me well enough. Office and warehouse this end and living space behind – and I'm lucky enough to share a proper kitchen in the court.'

'You are well-provided for,' I said and meant it too.

Many people had no formal cooking-space, and unless – like Marcus – they were very rich indeed, most apartment dwellers had no fire at all and depended on the vendors in the street, or the hot-soup kitchens, if they wanted a warm meal. No wonder Lucius was proud of his abode. And since he boasted a shared kitchen and was inviting citizens to dine, then more likely his home had several rooms – at least a dining area and a separate sleeping room – which was better provision than I had myself.

On the other hand this was clearly a poor place compared to Ulpius's house. It was close beside the river wharves and the associated smells were already reaching us – which was perhaps the reason that his living space was situated at the back, and did not have a separate front entrance directly to the docks. If the owner hoped to marry Silvia – as my patron seemed to think – he must be relying on the house which came with her estate. Surely he could not expect to bring her here?

Yet he was quietly boastful as he said, 'Come!' and ushered me inside the heavy warehouse door, which the spotty servant was holding wide for us. Lucius threw his cloak back and waved a proud, expansive hand. 'There you are, citizen. What do you think of that?'

I have been in such warehouses before, so I was prepared for the general size and layout of the place, but it was still impressive: a huge stone building sectioned into parts by waist-high wood partitions – with a different commodity stored in each area. Despite the recent weather, the warehouse seemed jam-full: there were few window spaces and it was dim inside, but the flickering light of torches on the wall revealed sacks and wooden crates of every shape and size, stone jars and amphorae, piles of sheepskins and heaps of metal bowls, to say nothing of a stack of rough-hewn timber near the door. How could Genialis think of forcing it to close?

Lucius was clearly expecting some response. I said what I was thinking: 'You have a lot of wares.'

He gave me a delighted smile. 'A varied range, it's true, although we tend to specialize. We concentrate mainly on little household luxuries. "Sell to the moderately rich – things for their wives and daughters," Ulpius used to say. That's where the profit is: glass beads, horn combs and perfumes and all that sort of thing. Or fancy dining ware.' He had seized a torch that was burning in a sconce and was enthusiastically illuminating the various products as he spoke, bouncing down the central aisle like an excited pup. 'Of course we import the usual oils and food and wine, and I brought in that silver fir-wood over there for a carpenter who wants it for making pails and bowls. Easier to work with and it doesn't grow round here.' He paused and looked at me expectantly again.

'I had supposed that with the cold snap you might be short of stock,' I said inanely.

He shook his head and gave a little sigh. 'Unfortunately, it is quite the opposite. Most of this stuff is orders – already spoken for – and simply waiting to be sent on to purchasers: but of course there hasn't been the transport, with the snow. The potted snails and dormice and the wine and oil will be all right, of course, but some of the other things are suffering a bit.'

'Like these?' I gestured to an area where a deep pile of heaped-up snow – obviously brought in from out-of-doors – had been compacted to a solid mass, which was now melting slightly, revealing sacks beneath, while the water formed a little puddle on the floor.

He gave a ghastly grin. 'A trick I learned from traders from the north. In winter they store their roe-deer venison that way, so I was hopeful that it might have worked for me. But now I'm not so sure. I don't often deal with perishable goods – and this, I fear, is going to start to rot and I shall have to throw it in the river at a total loss. But for other things, the cold has had the opposite effect. There's a consignment of pigments over there which has frozen in its sacks and I don't know if it will still be usable.' He led me to the place. 'Fortunately, I never deal in slaves or animals, or anything that needs attention while you're storing it, but as I was saying to Marcus earlier today, if I can't get some things delivered in a day or two, I stand to lose my profit, if not my customers.'

'But you do handle perishables now and then?' I said, a little doubtfully. 'You mentioned that we were dining on Gallic fowl, I think?' I hoped our meal had not come from the sacks that we'd just passed. There was a faint unpleasant odour there, despite the ice, and I was glad to have moved onwards down the aisle, where the air was heady with cinnamon and other Eastern spice.

Lucius must have seen my dubious look and laughed aloud. 'Quite fresh, I assure you, citizen. One of the first consignments to get here for some time – bigger ships can't get this far up the river when there's ice. The trade-captain had attempted to bring them here alive, three dozen crates of birds and several pigs, though most of the creatures had perished in the cold. Normally we would have taken all of those – exotic fowl-meat has a value anywhere – but as you see, at present...' He used the torch to gesture round the room.

'You have no room to store the birds?' I supplied.

'Exactly, citizen. My stewards took some living ones for me to use myself, but the trader had to sell the others in the town for whatever he could get – which won't be much, I think. The pork will do all right, but there is not much sustenance in a Gallic fowl and when food is scarce and dear, people will buy other things for preference.'

'But you agreed to have them anyway?'

He did that laugh again. 'Ah, but now he'll take my sheepskins and some wood when he sails for Gaul – I've been waiting half a moon to find a boat to carry them – so we both stand to profit from the deal. Trade is a funny business.' He gestured to his spotty servant, who was sulking close nearby. 'The office door

please, Pistus, and then you can let the household know that we are here.'

We had walked the whole length of the storage space by now and had reached a large
partition wall which had two doors in it. One of
these the servant Pistus was now folding back,
revealing what was clearly the office area,
containing a desk-table and a pair of stools, and
book shelves full of scrolls and parchment-
leaves. An ancient slave was seated at the desk,
binding a new iron nib on to a writing stick. An
oil lamp stood by him, but it was not lit and he
was working by the fading daylight through the
open window space high up on the wall.

He looked up and saw us, and made as if to
rise, but Lucius waved him to continue with his
work. 'When you've finished that pen, Vesperion, you can shut up for the night. Put up the
shutters and I'll send in your meal.' He turned
to me. 'That is my steward. Been with me for
years – I'll let him have his freedom, if this deal
comes off, though I expect he'll want to stay
and work here as a freeman if he can. I'd be
glad to have him for a year or two. I give him a
sleeping mat down there beside the door and he
acts as a sort of watchman for the goods – can't
be too careful, though my neighbours and I
share the cost to keep a burly guard outside at
night.' He smiled. 'Now, if you would like to
come this way?'

He led the way in through the other, smaller
door, through which the spotty slave had
already disappeared, and which opened on to a

little corridor and so into the house. I was pleasantly surprised by what awaited us.

I found myself in a spacious inner area. It had only one high window space, like the office next to it, but was lit by a dozen tapers in stanchions on the wall, and agreeably heated by a brazier at each end. It was not a fancy room. The floor was paved in simple kiln-fired brick, the plaster on the walls was painted plain ochre with a border of black lines, and there was not an ornament in sight, only a little niche with a statue of the Lars. The only furniture was a rustic table bench and a pair of rather crudely crafted wooden stools – yet the effect, though basic, was warm and welcoming.

Lucius placed his torch carefully into an empty sconce, took my cloak, then indicated the nearer of the stools and sat down on the other one himself. He clapped his hands and the pimply slave appeared through an inner doorway opposite. 'Take these cloaks away and put them somewhere dry. Have warm spiced mead and sugared figs brought in, and then leave us to talk.'

The servant bowed and went away, but left the door ajar. Through the aperture I could see another passageway, obviously leading to further doors beyond. It was clear now that my guess about the house had been correct. There were several rooms on this floor and there was evidence of at least one more above. I could hear something – or someone – hurrying around up there, then the rattle of quick footsteps down what sounded like a stair. A moment later Adonisius came into the room.

He seemed about to speak to Lucius, but when he saw me he stopped in some surprise. 'Excuse me, masters, I had not intended to intrude. I did not know that you had company.'

Lucius smiled. 'Libertus has consented to come and dine with me. But I am glad to see you anyway. You can give him the latest news direct – though I've already told him that no trace has been found. I presume that nothing's happened since I last spoke to you?' He turned to me. 'Adonisius has been assisting with the search. Indeed, we have placed him virtually in charge – no one knows Genialis more thoroughly than he does – and Silvia has kindly made him available as long as he's required.'

'Of course, he is formally at her disposal now,' I said, remembering.

Lucius nodded. 'At least until his master's body's found.' He smiled. 'And he has already proved his worth. After all he was the one who found the horse!'

I looked at the Syrian, who was wearing a proud smile – which in a man less attractive, might have been a smirk, but on Adonisius simply added to his charm. 'You heard about that, citizen?' His tone to me was soft and courteous. If Silvia decided to sell him later on, I thought, he would command a price as handsome as himself. 'I searched for the body for a long time, then, but could not find the slightest trace of that,' he said. 'Though Bernadus was extremely pleased to have the horse.'

Lucius barked with laughter. 'Pleased enough to let you keep the one he'd lent to you – until this search is over, anyway.' He jerked his head at Adonisius and said, addressing me, 'Of course, there is no risk. This slave is a considerable horseman, citizen. Genialis used him as a mounted page.' He raised a brow at me. 'Among other things, I understand.'

I ignored the innuendo. 'And yet Genialis set off riding on his own, when he left the villa? That was a little strange?'

Adonisius gave a courtly little bow. 'I was surprised myself. I was making ready to accompany him, in fact, but he said that he had private matters to attend to and he wished to go alone.'

'As others in the household could no doubt testify?' I softened the implied insult with a smile.

He did not take offence. 'I am sure they would. It was remarkable. Generally he liked me to accompany him.'

'And you have no inkling where he went and why? Clearly it was not what he'd originally planned.'

'Unfortunately, citizen, I cannot help you there. He was not a man to confide in anyone. One did not ask questions; one was simply expected to obey. He was getting restless, I was aware of that. Increasingly restless as the days went by. And irritable too. To be honest, citizen, we were glad to see him leave.'

'But you have no idea why he decided to?

There was no messenger or anything like that?'

He shook his handsome head. 'Not until after he had left the house. It may have been something that he thought of suddenly. My mistress thought he might have gone to make a scene about the Janus sacrifice – he was offended because he could not donate the ram. But he did not say as much. Simply that there was a pressing matter he must deal with straight away. So important that he must leave at once but he hoped to see my mistress in Glevum on Agonalia day.'

I frowned. 'Which was a change of plan, of course? Up to then he had been intending to take his bride to Dorn.'

Adonisius and Lucius exchanged a glance at this, but again it was the Syrian who spoke. 'Exactly so. I think that everybody was surprised. However, I did wonder at the time...' He tailed off and glanced at Lucius again, as if requesting permission to say more.

Lucius nodded. 'His master was a gambler, citizen, as perhaps you knew – though Adonisius is too loyal to say so openly. The thing is, citizen, when I heard of this, I assumed that he was worried about some creditor who was threatening and the day was due for repayment of a debt – which, of course, Genialis could not pay. He had expected to have married Silvia by that time, I expect, which would have given him control of all she owned – but the weather had prevented him from getting back to Dorn. Perhaps he wanted to see the man and sue for a delay. He would not want Adonisius to witness such an interview.'

'Though he owned him?' I was incredulous.

'Perhaps because he meant to offer me as payment,' the slave said, ruefully. 'Or, more likely, he would simply ask for time, promising to pay as soon as he was wed. But the lady would contest the marriage if that promise could be proved. Frittering away her dowry in advance – without her formal assent in front of witnesses – would give her legal grounds to challenge in the courts and I'm sure my master was aware of that. Perhaps that's why he didn't want me there.'

'Because he thought that you would tell her? But a slave cannot inform against his owner!' I exclaimed.

He coloured a little. 'That's quite true, citizen, in a general way. Of course I can't speak out against my master lawfully, but I could have reported events to someone else – Lucius for instance – who would have the status to investigate and take it to the courts. I doubt I would have, when it came to it – though I was very sorry for the lady Silvia – but my master may have feared to take me with him, all the same.'

'I don't believe that for a moment,' Lucius said. 'Your reputation for discretion was what he valued most.'

The slave boy looked flattered. 'I expect you're right. All this is speculation anyway, but I'm still inclined to guess that he went out to some secret meeting of that kind and died as a result. Perhaps the messenger who missed him could have averted this – if, for instance he was bringing gold from Dorn?'

I pursed my lips at him. 'You think that your master was murdered by this supposed creditor?'

Adonisius shook his head. 'I did not say that, citizen,' he said, reproachfully. 'I suppose it's possible. Abducted him perhaps – why would a creditor want to kill a man who is likely soon to have the means to pay his debts? But in that case we would certainly have had demands by now.' He shook his head. 'It's far more likely that in the snow my master missed the path and a branch or something pulled him from his horse. He was too good a horseman to have fallen otherwise...' He paused and wrinkled that perfect olive brow. 'Unless perhaps he was overtaken by the cold. Either way, I'm sure he's lying in a pile of snow somewhere. But we have searched a half a mile on each side of the road, and we have not found him yet. If there's still no sign tomorrow we shall move out nearer Dorn. No doubt he had enemies in that direction too.'

'And have you told the other searchers what you think?'

He shook his head. 'Of course not, citizen. It's not my place to voice opinions of that kind – but I think that Lucius agrees with me. He'd come to much the same conclusion for himself.'

I glanced at Lucius, who gave his braying

211

laugh. 'There is some truth in that – though I had not thought the matter out so lucidly. You see, citizen, why I value this Syrian so much that I have put the search into his hands...' He broke off as the door behind us opened quietly and the aged steward from the warehouse shuffled in.

'Your pardon, master, but I think that Alfredus Allius is here. I was about to shut the warehouse when I saw a litter come.'

'Earlier than I expected him!' Lucius shot an anguished look at me. 'Very well, Vesperion, go back to your place. And Adonisius, go and greet our guest and escort him in to me. But take your time about it – show him round the warehouse on the way: point out the samian plates or something as you pass and try to impress him with the copper goods in store. I want a private word with this good citizen.'

SIXTEEN

When the servants had departed, Lucius turned to me.

'This hardly leaves time,' I said, 'for much discussion now. But what was it that you wanted to talk to me about?'

'It's your advice I'm after. It won't take very long. The thing is, citizen–' Lucius tossed back his mane of tawny hair and for a moment I almost imagined that he blushed – 'I wish to be a suitor for the lady Silvia. I suspect that Bernadus would secretly like to offer for her, too, but that would mean divorcing his present wife, who brought a substantial dowry with her, which he can ill-afford to let her take away again. So do you think your patron would countenance my suit? Or perhaps you would even put in a word for me?' He caught my eye and added sheepishly, 'If Genialis is not found alive, I mean, of course.'

'I think that Marcus might be persuaded to consider it,' I said, attempting to put on a doubtful face. Then, fearing that this sounded a bit too confident, I added, 'I mean, if no better offer can be found. He will be anxious to ensure that she's well provided for, but since she's not a virgin to be bargained for, he may consult her wishes in any marriage arrangement he makes. Which would favour you, I think. Though you realize what that would mean for Silvia?'

'You mean because I'm not a citizen?' He sounded anxious now. 'If I'd been born inside the walls of Glevum, instead of half a mile outside, I would have qualified! As it is I don't know what to do. I don't suppose there's any chance that His Excellence would sponsor me for my citizenship diploma, while he is in Rome? I know that he intends to see the Emperor, who is a friend of his.'

I nodded, trying to judge how much I should disclose. At last I hazarded, 'It might be that Marcus would condescend to put in a word for you, if you could find some way to make it worth his while.' I glimpsed an opportunity and grasped it with both hands. 'Meanwhile you must convince him that you can keep a wife – that your business enterprise is sound, and your contacts, for instance, are honourable men. Or that you and your associates are not prone to gambling...' I broke off, realizing I hadn't put this very tactfully. I'd managed to raise all Marcus's questions, but listed in that way they sounded arrogant – almost as if I were a praetor questioning in court. I glanced up nervously to see if I'd given Lucius offence.

But not at all, it seemed. He had risen to his feet and was smiling eagerly. 'Of course. That would be easy, citizen. I can show the record scrolls. That would tell him everything he wants to know. Apart from the usual records – of profits, cost and loss – Ulpius used to keep a note of all the suppliers and importers that we used: where they traded from and what they traded in and how reliable they'd proved to be. He used to put a little mark beside the ones he did not trust, whether because of gambling or otherwise, and a cross to indicate the ones that we should never do business with again. And the same with customers.' He shot a glance at me. 'If I gave you that information, could you contrive to pass it on?'

'Give me the records and I'll see what I can do,' I promised silkily, though inwardly I heaved a happy sigh. I stood up too, as courtesy demands.

I thought he was about to go and get the records then and there, but we were interrupted by the spotty slave, bringing – at last – the promised tray of fruit and mead for me and a handsome-looking jug of wine for Lucius. However, Lucius waved him impatiently away.

'Not now! At the moment it is inconvenient. Take it away and wait until I call for you. And when you do come bring another goblet and some different wine – I'd forgotten that we still had this in the house. It's the rubbish that Genilias gave to Ulpius once. It isn't fit to drink. Go and get rid of it at once – and throw the jug away. Bring us something else. There is some of the best Rhenish in that amphora still, I think. And don't be so long about producing it, next time. Our other dinner guest is an important man.'

The servant sighed. 'I'm sorry, Master, for the long delay, but we had to wait to use the fire so we could heat the mead.' He padded off again.

Lucius turned to me. 'The disadvantage of shared kitchens, I'm afraid. Fortunately our meal is in the clay-oven, and has been for hours, so there will be no problem over that. However – to conclude the matter we were talking of just now, you will speak to your patron in support of me?'

I nodded and he came across to slap me on the back.

'I thank you, citizen. Silvia thought you would. And you believe that there is hope?'

It was time to backtrack slightly. I pursed my lips and said judiciously, 'I think there is a chance. Not immediately, of course, but in a year or so.'

Lucius looked startled. 'Why not sooner if Marcus will consent? She is Ulpius's widow, not Genialis's – and there is no need to wait the customary full ten moons from now. I'm aware that it is usual, in case the lady is with child, but Genialis was prepared to marry her at once, and I would be more than glad to do the same. If there is to be a child, then Ulpius fathered it, and I am happy to acknowledge that and rear it as my own. In any case it's most unlikely – there would be signs by now.'

I shook my head. 'All the same, there would have to be a decent interval – especially if Genialis's body is not found. In the absence of a corpse, there is no proof that her former guardian is dead and it may take some time for Marcus to make a formal application to the court – especially since he plans to go to Rome within the moon. But he will need the legal sanction, if he's to take charge of her affairs and have the right to find another husband for his ward. And, incidentally, to deal with Genialis's estate. I know the man had debts, but there was the house in Dorn. Presumably, since he was a councillor out there, his residence is of a certain size. Who will that go to?'

Lucius shrugged. 'I've no idea at all. I hadn't thought about it. No doubt – being in public life – he's made a proper will, with seven witnesses and all that sort of thing. If not, I suppose the state will benefit.'

I raised a brow at him. 'Or Silvia, as his nearest relative? Would she not have a claim? He was her guardian and she was married to his brother, after all.'

He nodded doubtfully. 'Though Silvia says that he was heavily in debt – what with his gambling and his financing of public works in Dorn, to secure his election – so I doubt there'll be a lot left over, anyway.' He ran his fingers through his tawny hair. 'Would that make a difference to your patron's attitude...?' He broke off as there was a tapping on the door that led out to the warehouse. 'Enter!' he called and Adonisius came into the room on silent feet.

'Alfredus Allius, masters!' he announced, standing back to let the visitor come through.

Of course I'd seen Alfredus several times before: not only in the snow when he was witnessing my contract for the pavement and at the ill-fated Janus sacrifice, but also at a distance at the basilica in his capacity as a minor councillor. However, he was not a man who stood out in a crowd. I had always found him instantly forgettable, and even here, in a humble freeman's house – where he was clearly the most distinguished guest, wearing a toga and a curial one at that – he somehow contrived to lack presence and prestige.

Partly this was the product of his looks. There was nothing about him that distinguished him: he was of middle-age, of average height, and neither fat nor slim. His hair, which was of medium length, was nondescript and brown, and though he was not ugly he was hardly beautiful – his regular features were resolutely plain. Even his toga was only moderately white. All the same, it bore a very narrow purple stripe, an indication that he was a councillor-magistrate, though of the lowest rank.

I gave a little bow in salutation, very conscious of my own improper dress and preparing to frame an explanation and apology for it. Even a narrow-striper demands a certain deference.

However, having exchanged the proper greetings with his host, he was already blinking short-sightedly at me and saying, in his strangely flat and nasal voice, 'Ah, the pavement-maker! I remember you. I witnessed a contract

218

for you, I believe.'

'For Genialis,' I corrected as courteously as I could. 'Though you were never called upon to see it was fulfilled. However, the work was duly witnessed by a magistrate, and I have been paid.'

The grey eyes looked dispassionately at me. 'Then you're a lucky man! Not many of his creditors can say as much.'

There was an awkward moment, then Lucius clapped his hands, and at once the pimply servant sidled in, bearing the tray of refreshments as his master had required. He set it down and was about to serve the wine, but his owner shook his head.

'Adonisius will serve us. You go and find an extra seat for us – the folding stool from my bedroom will suffice. And when you have done that, you may tell the kitchen we will dine as soon as possible.'

The boy dashed off to do as he was told, and a moment later I was sipping mead while my companions drank the Rhenish, which was clearly excellent.

'Just as well the captain of the vessel had some sense,' Lucius was saying, holding his fine glass goblet to the light. 'He had to jettison some cargo in a storm, to save the ship – with of course a total loss to the owner of the goods – but he had the wit to save this wine at least.'

'And what happens if it goes overboard and is actually retrieved, but is damaged by salt water when it gets to shore? I suppose the shipper bears the losses in a case like that?' Alfredus was asking questions eagerly. Obviously his experience with Genialis had made him cautious about lending capital.

'That depends on what contract he has made. In any case, it's generally worth the risk. There is good money to be made from wine.' Lucius, in his enthusiastic way, began to discourse on the various types of wine, and where they could most profitably be traded to and from. 'There is a ship tomorrow loading up for Gaul, and I'm going to bargain with the captain to bring me back a few amphorae from the vineyards there. Would you care to come and watch, and see the arrangements that are made and how these things are done?'

I think they had forgotten that I was there at all – which wasn't very courteous to me, but in fact I did not mind. It was all information I could give to Marcus afterwards. So I was content to sit and listen and savour my warm mead, which was the best I'd ever tasted – delicately warmed and flavoured with sweet spice. I would have been ready to finish the whole jug.

However, it was not very long before the slave came back, saying that dinner was ready if we wished and Lucius led us through into another room. It was fairly Spartan, the floor and walls completely unadorned. The three small dining-couches around the table took almost all the space and the brazier in the corner gave off little heat – unless, like Alfredus, you were reclining next to it. However, we were provided with the usual courtesies – linen napkins, and the spotty slave to wash our hands and feet. He even offered us a spoon and dining knife, in case we were not carrying our own, and there was a small libation to the household Lars, brought in for the purpose in a little travelling box.

The meal was not by any means a feast, only two dishes other than the meat, and everything was very plainly served: though this, in fact, was rather to my taste. I was glad to see that garum – that fish sauce that Romans like to put on everything – was offered in a jug and not put on the serving-plate itself. Alfredus, I noticed, poured a lot on his.

As the senior guest, he was naturally on Lucius's right, while I was on the left, so I had little opportunity to join the talk – and in fact for a long time, nothing much was said. But when we had moved on to dried berries, fruits and nuts, and the slaves had retired to clean the dinner-ware, Alfredus cleared his throat. 'Lucius, there was something that I wanted to discuss, but perhaps...' He jerked his head at me. 'A little later, possibly, when your other guest has gone?'

I was about to offer to withdraw and give them privacy – after all I had that promise of the record scrolls, which answered what I'd come for – but Lucius straightened to a sitting pose (a signal that we two should do the same) and seized my arm again, saying heartily to his other guest, 'You may speak freely. There are no strangers here. Libertus already knows about the loan I hope to get from you and why.'

Alfredus looked embarrassed. He took another handful of the nuts and cleared his throat. 'Then I'll confess it straightaway. I'll have to disappoint you, I'm afraid – unless or until Genialis comes to light. You've heard that he owes me money, I expect? No doubt that's common knowledge in the town.'

Lucius nodded. 'Libertus heard it in the forum, I believe.'

Alfredus made a face. 'I was obliged to make a shaming public statement at the basilica, in front of everyone, that I can't pay my creditors. If Genialis were available I would simply delegate – pass the debts to him, as the law permits – there is no requirement that he should agree. But it seems he's disappeared, and one cannot declare *delegatio* without the knowledge of the man involved – so I've simply had to ask for the customary length of time to pay.'

'Thirty days? And that will be enough?' Lucius sounded genuinely interested now.

'By that time, I hope, I can sell my usual crops again – I've not been able to do so with the recent snow – and that should be sufficient to pay my creditors. But it doesn't solve the problem of what Genialis owes to me. At present it is legally "impossible to pay" and so there is no immediate redress. If he's dead I'll have to sue from his estate, though that clearly won't be possible within the thirty days.' He gave a bitter smile. 'Just as well they've done away with old-style punishments for defaulters, that's all I can say.'

I remembered what Marcus had once told me about that. The ancient law provided that a man could chain his debtor up for the whole period – without the necessity of offering him food – and if the money was not paid in time, the creditors had the right, not just to seize his goods (as happened nowadays) but to share up his body in equitable parts.

'When did you discover he was missing?' Lucius asked. 'We weren't aware of it ourselves until a day or two ago.'

'I expected to see him at the Agonalia feast – it was the day the debt was due and I thought he would have travelled back to keep the feast: he had intended to, he said, in fact he was furious when he could not provide the ram. I spoke to Bernadus – knowing that Genialis had been to stay with him.' Alfredus tossed another shelled walnut down his throat and took a sip of wine. 'He was surprised, himself. He said that Genialis ought to be in town: he had left the villa several days before, with instructions that his bride-to-be should follow him to town on the day of sacrifice, and she had done so – though she'd left a lot of her effects behind.'

'He wasn't here to meet her, though!' Lucius said. 'The doorkeeper hadn't seen his master since the day he left.'

Alfredus frowned. 'So I understand. I tried the house, myself. There was a special meeting of the curia – in relation to the proclamation of the new Emperor – so I couldn't go at once, but as soon as it was over, I called there straight away. But the doorkeeper told me that his master hadn't come and Silvia had been taken into temporary potestas by His Excellence. That was the moment I began to fear that I'd lost my money. And the gold is not among the things that were left behind at the villa. I went straight to Bernadus's villa, the first thing next day, and he helped me institute a search, but...' He trailed off helplessly. 'The coffer was there, but it was emptied of its gold. It seems he's simply vanished and the money too.'

'Then perhaps he had it with him?' I suggested, brightening. 'Intending to repay you when he got to town. That might explain his disappearance, mightn't it? If he were intercepted by some robber on the road and found to be carrying a lot of money it is more than possible that he was murdered for his purse.'

In fact this seemed an obvious theory, now I had thought of it, and the more I considered it, the likelier it seemed. Violence and robbery on the public road is a crucifying offence so victims of such crimes are more often killed than not – dead men cannot identify a thief. And it would fit with what Lucius and Adonisius thought as well – that he'd gone off in a hurry to meet a secret creditor. I only wondered that I had not thought of it before!

But Lucius was making a disbelieving face. 'But surely thieves would just have dumped the corpse beside the road? That's what they generally do. And I've never heard of any thief who didn't try to seize the horse – especially a valuable animal like that – or at least the trappings, which are easier to sell. Yet when that horse was found, it still had its saddle on, although the reins were broken. What robber would do that? That saddle would bring a good price at any market stall.'

Alfredus had finished all the walnuts by this time and was eating almonds now. 'And if Genialis were carrying a large amount of gold, wouldn't he have had the casket with him too? Bernadus said he was carrying a purse, but that would not hold the amount of gold I lent to him. Besides,' he added, 'I don't believe that he meant to pay me back. In that case, why did he want the loan at all? There was nothing what-ever to spend it on while he was at the villa, and no opportunity of gaining extra funds. He was relying on some deal that he hoped to make, he said.'

There was some sense in all of this, but I did not give up without a fight. 'Or perhaps Berna-dus stole it, after his guests had left,' I suggest-ed doubtfully. 'Such things have happened.'

Alfredus gave that mirthless smile again. 'I don't think so, pavement-maker. Bernadus had agreed to act as surety – so if that money's missing, he must make it up himself. Only, since he is a sort of friend, I swore in the *stipu-latio* that I would not sue until it was proved "impossible" for Genialis to repay – so there is no legal way that I can call on him for it just now.' He turned to Lucius. 'So you see why I cannot – at the moment – offer you the loan.'

Lucius laughed and clapped him on the arm. 'Oddly enough, it does not matter much, while Genialis is unaccounted for. And if he's dead, I may not need a loan at all.' He looked at me and grinned. 'Supposing that my hopes of matrimony come to pass.' Then he sobered suddenly. 'But I thought you had recently sold a piece of land. Surely you didn't lend Genialis all of th—?'

Alfredus brought his fists down on the table with such violence that the bronze dish which had held the nuts bounced off and hit the floor. 'That is the worst of it! I have been such a fool! He swore – upon the altar, in the presence of a priest – that he would return it to me by the Agonalia, and even add a little interest. There were urgent expenses which he had to meet in Dorn – largely for his intended marriage to his ward – but he'd arranged to sell some business interests within a day or two, and this loan was simply to see him through till then. But I'm not sure that's true. Bernadus tells me he was laughing afterwards, when they were dining at the villa the next day, saying that he'd duped me, and this merely a device to find out exactly how much he dared to ask for those business assets. Though I don't understand how that could be.'

Lucius's smile had faded and he was looking grim. 'I think perhaps I do,' he said through gritted teeth. 'He knew that I was anxious to try

226

to buy him out, and somehow learned that you were planning to make a loan to me – though I tried to keep it from him. He wanted as high a price as possible, of course, but didn't know exactly what I could afford to pay. So he duped you into this – he now knew the maximum that he could ask of me, no doubt adding a little extra on for luck, including the interest that he promised you. So when he paid you back, you'd lend the gold to me and I would give it back to him again – that was the strategy. And it was not the wedding that he needed all this money for, it was his gambling debts.'

But I was hardly listening to this tale of perfidy. I turned to the purple-striper urgently. 'You say you swore your stipulatio in the presence of a priest? Not by any chance the ancient one that tried to make the Janus sacrifice?'

Alfredus looked at me in some surprise. 'How did you know that citizen? Of course, he hadn't made – or failed to make – the sacrifice to them, otherwise I should never have consented to involve him in the act. I wasn't very keen in any case – I would have preferred a senior magistrate – but Bernadus was insistent that we should ask the priest. A vow was better than a simple pact, he said, and this priest was willing to do things for a fee. So I agreed to it. And so did Genialis. Well he broke his vow – and now they are looking for his corpse, and serve him right.'

He said it with such venom that I was slightly shocked. 'But I thought you were a friend?

Were you not supporting him to be an aedile?' I was only guessing that, but he did not demur.

'A friend?' For a moment the pale eyes sparked with unaccustomed fire. 'A man like Genialis does not have real friends. Only people who are useful and people who are used.' He gave that little mirthless laugh again. 'I was fool enough to think that I was in the former group – but tonight I have discovered otherwise. Well if he has perished, he brought it on himself. The gods have punished him.'

Lucius gave a barking laugh. 'And the old priest as well – though that was most likely because he spoiled the sacrifice. You have heard the story of the finding of his corpse?' He told it, much as I'd related it to him, though omitting the grisly details of the missing upper parts.

Alfredus, however, was looking worried now. 'So there is no longer a witness to our vow. I wonder how that will affect things in the court. You don't think Genialis had a hand in that? We don't know that he is actually dead.'

'That is why we're mounting this enormous search for him. Libertus here intends to join it, in the morning I believe, and you are welcome to send a slave to help.'

Alfredus was already rising to his feet. 'I think I'll do that. I hope the corpse turns up. If he's dead there'll be no problem in suing his estate – Bernadus will simply be relieved of acting surety and I'm sure he'll testify for me, if there's no penalty to pay.' He bowed in our direction. 'In the meantime, gentleman, I will go back home and find a servant I can spare to join the hunt.'

Lucius rapped the table with the jug to bring the servants back. Alfredus's attendant (who, unbeknown to me, was being entertained by Vesperion in his warehouse lair) was sent for, and despatched to find a litter to take his master home. Meanwhile Adonisius went off to find my cloak and came back wearing a warm cape of his own, and carrying a lighted pitch-torch in his hand.

'If you are ready, citizen? I will escort you to your shop.' And together we set off into the night.

SEVENTEEN

The walk back to my workshop took much longer than I thought it would. Away from the docks, where an inn was brightly lit, and the prostitutes were lurking under every arch, I had expected that the streets would be deserted by this time. Unless people were invited some- where else to dine, as I had been, or had a night- time funeral to attend, most respectable towns- folk are usually in bed an hour after sunset at any time of year, and certainly at home with all the shutters up – especially in winter when the nights are cold.

But tonight there was a different feel about the town – a background murmur like a thou- sand far-off bees – and as we picked our way along the snow-piled streets, I began to hear an individual shout or two. More alarmingly, a fiery glow was visible against the evening sky – and it came from the forum, by the look of it.

Of course, fire is not uncommon in a big town like this: some careless soul who overturns a lamp, or uses a taper to find something on the floor and accidentally sets the bed alight. (I had a fire in my own workshop once, which half- destroyed the roof and – despite the efforts of the fire watch to which I paid my dues, who brought buckets from the river and tried to put it out – I've never been able to live in the upstairs rooms again.)

A night fire is always a public spectacle, of course – people will always leave their homes to watch, if not to help – but this evening it seemed to be rather more than that. Every hot-soup stall or wine shop we came to had lighted links outside, and was clearly doing a brisk and noisy trade, and there were flickering torches visible down every street we passed, with cloaked figures hurrying towards the centre of the town – despite the fact that it was getting very cold and the pavements were already treacherous. It was obvious that something unusual was afoot.

Moreover, the red glow which was visible above the roofs was now beginning to flicker with leaping yellow flame. I began to wonder if a wagon had caught fire: such vehicles, which are not permitted in the day, come rumbling into Glevum for an hour at dusk to make deliveries, and the air is often loud with the rumbling of wheels and the curses of the drivers as their carts get stuck in ruts. A cartload of logs might create a blaze like that. But the recent snow and the condition of the roads had put a temporary stop to most wheeled trade into town and there was scarcely a vehicle to be seen tonight – only an old peasant with a donkey cart, at the corner of a narrow alleyway, shovelling up a frozen midden heap to take back and spread to fertilize whatever crops remained.

He looked up as I passed him, glancing with envy at the splendid slave, and then realized that his little vehicle – which he had positioned to hold the torch that he was working by – had blocked the pavement and was standing in our path.

He straightened up and sighed. 'Want to come down this way, do you? Let me move the cart.' He tugged at the reluctant animal. It moved a pace or two. 'There you are. I think there's room to pass. Going to join that rumpus in the town, I suppose? Well, if you think it's worth it, then good luck to you!' He stamped his hide-bound feet impatiently as if to keep them warm, obviously waiting to move the cart again.

'Some sort of fire? It seems a nasty one.' I paused in the act of edging through the space that he had cleared, a narrow strip of pavement flanked by dirty piles of snow. 'Looks as if it's coming from the forum square. Do you know what's alight? I suppose it isn't the basilica?'

He gave a dreadful smile that showed, even by torchlight, his yellow, jagged teeth. 'Not unless some idiot's set fire to that as well. Though it wouldn't be surprising, if this mob gets out of hand. That's a triumphal bonfire they've lit. There's been cavorting in the forum for an hour or more – ever since the military legate got here, shortly before dusk, to announce the news he'd just delivered to the garrison.'

'News?'

'If you can call it that. The latest bulletin from Rome, at any rate. All properly signed and sealed on an official scroll, this time.'

'What's happened? The Emperor Commodus isn't dead at all?' That would explain the people on the streets and the lighting of a celebratory fire: people would be very anxious to be seen demonstrating loyal joy, especially those who had most loudly cheered the news of his demise. Paid spies would be taking note of everything.

But my aged informant shook his grizzled head. He had a piece of ancient sack tied round it as a hood, but it seemed to offer no protection to his ears and allowed his straggling grey locks to show. 'Oh, he is dead all right – his body was dragged around the city on the hook – and this new man Pertinax was installed instead. That's what all the celebrations are about.'

'I see!' I said. 'I'm very pleased myself, but I'm surprised that the people have taken to the streets – especially at night when the weather is so bad – just because their former Governor has been appointed Emperor.'

He laughed. 'It isn't that so much. Of course they're calling him the Great and Merciful – he rescued the hook-torn body from the crowd, as soon as his own accession was agreed, and insisted it was given proper burial. Or so the legate says. And he's declared an extra holiday next moon. But most of all, he's rescinded all the stupid edicts people hate so much. He's formally declared that Rome is Rome again, and not Commodiana, as it was supposed to be: the months have all reverted to their proper names, and aren't called after the Emperor's honorifics any longer, so no one can be flogged for forgetting which is which. That's what caused the real excitement here – people came rushing out on to the street, the instant that they heard, cheering Pertinax and pulling down all the statues of Commodus they could find. And the town watch hasn't stopped them – the crowd has done the same in Rome, apparently, and no one has been condemned to punishment, by order of the Great and Merciful.'

I glanced toward the distant flames, which were leaping higher now. 'How do you know all this?'

He shrugged his bony shoulders under the shrouding sack. 'Oh, I was in the forum when the message came – I'd brought in a few turnips, and I was selling those before I came out here to take away the pile. But I've got a farm to see to and a wife to keep. I'm not risking prison by setting fire to things and causing a disturbance in the street. I don't see that it matters at this stage anyway, whether they dragged Commodus behind a hook or not – and the new fellow may be Great and Merciful, but I don't know what difference he's going to make to me. I'll still be doing this same stinking job until the day I drop. But Hail Caesar anyway – I'd better say that, I suppose, or with my luck you'll turn out to be a spy. And good luck with your bonfire – I hope the gods approve.'

He spat on his chapped fingers – which were all that protruded from the rags wrapped round his hands – urged the donkey back into its former place, and turned to his unlovely task again. At least with the snow, I thought, his makeshift fertilizer would not smell so much.

I said to Adonisius, who'd been listening to all this, 'We'll go through the forum, then, and see what's happening. It's as good a route as any to the other side of town. My workshop lies outside the northern walls, of course, and the gate is now doubtless shut again till dawn – we'll have to find a sentry to open up for us.'

He bowed and murmured, 'As you command, of course,' but I could see from the glitter of excitement in his eyes that he was as curious as I was to see the spectacle. Indeed, as we continued on towards the centre of the town, I noticed that he'd visibly increased his pace – which meant that I was obliged to quicken mine, since he was the one who held the torch which lit our way.

In fact, when we got there, the crush was such that we could not get into the forum square at all, but standing in one of the narrow entry roads it was possible to glimpse, over the heads of others, what was happening within. The fire we had seen far off across the roofs was raging fiercely in the centre of the square, and it was clear that no wagon had ever been involved. The crowd had made a huge impromptu bonfire of anything flammable that came to hand – dried reeds, old clothes and broken furniture –

and were throwing on to it anything connected with the previous Emperor: wooden statues, painted images, and even coins and marble busts, though obviously the latter were never going to burn.

Anything connected with Commodus was at risk. I saw the wooden sign-board for a wine shop, which had borne his name, passed from hand to hand across the heads of spectators towards the fire, and when at last it was pitched into the flames the crowd gave a communal whoop of victory.

Another roar from nearer the basilica drew my attention to an amazing scene. A group of people, several of them clearly quite respectable, were clustered round the huge bronze statue of the hated Emperor – dressed in his favourite garb as Hercules – which for years had overlooked the steps. They had succeeded in throwing thick ropes around its neck and knees and were now attempting to topple the whole image from its plinth. As soon as others realized what was happening, dozens more came rushing forward to join in, and soon there were half-a-hundred of them, hauling on the lines, to the accompaniment of a rhythmic chanting from the spectators: 'Down with him, down with him, may he eat the dust!'

As I watched the statue wobbled, swayed a long moment and began to tilt. This was greeted with loud cheers. Then all at once it came crashing to the ground with a deafening thud and a force that shattered it, making the very earth beneath us shudder with the shock. Several people were very nearly crushed, and I saw one limp and lifeless-looking body being dragged away, but any grief was drowned by joyful cheers and shouts. The crowd was jubilant, and when the head came off the statue and bounced into the fire, the triumph of the onlookers was almost deafening.

A dozen amphorae appeared from somewhere in a trice, and immediately broached; and brimming wine jugs passed exultantly from hand to hand. People started dancing and a ragged song broke out.

Men joined in as they rolled the broken statue to the fire – but behind them matters took a darkly different turn. Where some had tried to scatter as the statue fell, others had been pushed against the wall, and a lot of shouting and shoving was going on, even as the statue was thrown into the blaze and a cheer was rising from around the fire. That part of the forum seemed oblivious to what was happening elsewhere.

One spectator looked up and, realizing that folk were being hurt, tried to shout a warning, but far from his neighbours taking heed of this, he was immediately spat upon and pushed quite savagely. 'Those who aren't rejoicing with us are enemies of the Emperor!' someone cried.

The mood was becoming ugly and rather dangerous. I turned to speak to Adonisius, but he'd been pressed against a neighbouring archway by the crush. I tried to signal to him that perhaps we should depart, but there was no escape. People were still surging forward to get a better view and it simply wasn't possible to withstand the flow. Having left the shelter of the wall myself, to look around for him, I found myself shuffling forward without intending to, forced to move my feet to keep myself from falling down and being trampled on. And all the time I was being separated from my attendant slave.

I was out into the forum now, though there was less room than ever. Beside the bonfire a more general skirmish had begun, fuelled by the wine perhaps. A few people were still cheering as the statue glowed, but more and more were joining the melee – and I was being firmly propelled towards it from behind. I looked around for Adonisius but he was far behind, still pressed against the pillar with his torch aloft. He saw me and signalled, but there was nothing he could do.

I peered around for some way to escape the pressing throng, but there seemed to be nowhere safe to stand. The public buildings were all locked and barred – as one would expect at night – and the market area was one heaving, shouting, surging mass. Even the steps to the basilica were thronged with cheering men. There was only one place where the crowd had not encroached and that was the temple, slightly to my left – though even the lower steps of that were crammed with spectators. However, at the top the sacred flame could still be seen, flickering in tranquil darkness at the entrance to the shrine, and there was no evidence of disturbance there – obviously no one wanted to offend the gods.

I tried to work my way towards it, weaving and shuffling sideways when I could – though I received a bruising on my back and ribs as a result. But I persisted and after what seemed like half an hour (but was probably much less) I did succeed in reaching the bottom of the temple steps. Getting up them was another matter, as I soon found out. The mass above me – though they were not actually joining in the now-general brawl themselves (perhaps out of some sense of deference to the shrine) – were still intent on what was happening and not at all disposed to move and let me through. One man – in a tradesman's cloak and tunic – even hissed at me 'Commodus-lover!' when I tried to pass, and people turned and jeered.

Someone spat and I was roughly jostled from behind. 'Must be a sympathizer, probably a spy. Otherwise he wouldn't be trying to go the other way.' I began to wonder if I was going to be attacked.

'I have business at the temple!' I called out, as loudly as I could. I meant to sound masterful, but my voice came out as a squeak, and it was doubtful anyway that anyone would hear – there was so much uproar from the crowd that I could barely hear myself. And it made no difference – people around me were still clearly hostile and the same hissing tradesman, encouraged by the mood, began suggesting loudly what might be done with me – 'Put him with his favourite Emperor and let him roast awhile' – and the cry was taken up by several of the crowd, who blocked my way.

I braced myself for people laying violent hands on me – and sure enough a pair of strong arms came from somewhere at my back, pinioned my own arms and seized firm hold of me. I tried to wriggle round to see who my assailant was, wondering what an appeal to Marcus's name would do, but there was no chance of either of those things. The grasp that held me was stronger than a vice, and when it picked me up so that my feet were flailing air, I could offer no resistance; I just dangled like a doll.

I tried to speak – to reason or to beg – but there was so much pressure on my ribs that I found that it was all I could do to breathe. Indeed I was close to losing consciousness. I closed my eyes, as if to shut the terror out, and was only half aware of being dragged along – part-carried almost – my toes making occasional contact with the steps, and although I could hear and smell the crowd on either side, it was clear the mob was parting to allow us through, no doubt to allow me to be thrown on to the fire. I think I actually fainted in the end.

When I came to myself I was sitting on a step, propped up against a pillar in the semi-dark. There was a small lamp glimmering just above my head and a strong smell of incense and spices in the air. For a moment I wondered if I'd been killed and had made the journey to the other world, but once my brain had cleared and my eyes had adjusted to the light, I could see that I was in the temple porch and the giant slave was bending over me.

EIGHTEEN

'Ah, good!' he said. 'I see you are awake. I feared I might have squeezed the life from you. I do apologize. But I had to get you safe. They would have harmed you otherwise, I think.' He gestured down the steps towards the crowd, who were still roaring like a thousand gales.

'You were my saviour.' I ran a rueful hand around my ribs. 'I'm still in one piece, too, though I'll be black and blue tomorrow. But thank you, from my heart.' I looked into his face, which looked even darker in the half-light here. 'What made you rescue me? You might have risked your own life doing that.'

'It was no more than my duty. You have business with the temple, I believe you said?' The high pitch of his voice was oddly carrying. 'I was standing right behind you and – since you'd been here earlier – I reasoned it was true. What is it, citizen? Something you failed to do when you were here before? Some little offering to the shrine, perhaps?'

I cast around for something plausible. I did not want to be sent off to face the mob again. 'There is a would-be councillor from Dorn,' I said, raising my voice above the shouting and

242

jeering from below. 'He has been missing since before the Agonalia. A man called Genialis...'

He nodded so that his giant earrings rang. 'The one who hoped to offer the Janus sacrifice? I remember him. He was very angry with me when I had to tell him that a donor had already been agreed. Missing, is he? I noticed that he wasn't at either sacrifice that day – but I supposed that he'd gone home to Dorn and the snow had simply prevented him from coming back in time.'

I shook my head and tried to rise, but found that I could not, so I had to go on shouting. 'He never got to Dorn. He stopped at a friend's villa and set off from there, apparently to return to Glevum. But he did not arrive. There is a ward – a certain Silvia – whom he had planned to wed and whom my patron, Marcus Septimus, has taken in his care, at any rate until Genialis can be accounted for.'

The mention of my patron had the usual effect. The slave became more deferential instantly and squatted down beside me so I did not have to raise my voice so much. 'So you wished to sponsor an offering to the gods to entreat his safe return?'

I felt every inch the hypocrite that I was being over this. 'Or at least that his body should be quickly found so that the lady's future can be properly arranged,' I said. That was safe enough. Since I was obviously going to be required to offer a small sacrifice – a pair of pigeons at the very least – I was content that it should be for such a cause. 'But the shrine was closed today, and it is unlikely that tomorrow I shall be in town – I am due to join the search for him at dawn.'

He smiled. 'Ah! So you have a personal interest in the case. I presume a lead prayer-plaque would meet the case for you?'

I nodded, relieved that he'd suggested such a minimum expense.

'Then give me the money and I'll see that it is done. One of the stalls outside here has a range of them, and will scratch any message on them that you wish. They'll have a bumper day tomorrow with curse-tablets, I'm sure – all calling down vengeance on the soul of Commodus – so I'll buy yours early. I'll nail it on the lintel of a cella, if you like. Which god would you like to have it written to? Jove or Juno or Minerva – you can take your pick. Or all of them together if you would prefer.'

I'm not a follower of Roman deities, but I knew enough to say, 'Juno, perhaps, since she's the goddess of marriage.'

'Very well. Then that will cost you a denarius.'

It was still a largish sum, but not as expensive as a pair of sacrificial birds. Anyway, I would have paid a great deal more, simply for rescue from the crowd. I rolled on to my side so I could reach my purse, loosed the drawstring and handed him the coin, together with a couple of brass asses that I found. 'Here you are. And a little offering for yourself.'

He put the coins into a small slot in his tunic-hem, as though that was a hiding-place he often used. 'Thank you, citizen, I'm glad to be of use. It's only a pity that the old priest has died. He would have placed it on the actual altar for you, for a fee – though he was apt to ask the maximum he thought you could afford...' He broke off, obviously conscious – as I was – of a sudden lull below.

'What is it?' I said dimly, as he jumped up to look.

He bared white teeth in an enormous smile. 'It is amazing what a difference a few soldiers makes. If you can stand up, citizen, you can witness it yourself.' He reached out an enormous hand and pulled me to my feet. I found they would support me, if I held on to the wall, and I looked where he was pointing and saw what he had meant.

A group of Roman soldiers was marching into the forum, two by two, through the same lane entrance that I'd used myself. Their shields were linked to make a barrier, and their javelins held at 'ready', level with their ears. The crowd that had been rampaging so triumphantly had fallen silent now: all skirmishing had stopped, and where a moment earlier there'd not been standing room, there was suddenly a pathway opening to the fire. People were edging away backwards from the shields, climbing on pillars and one another's backs to escape the crush, but mostly surging towards us up the temple steps – the only place that there was left for anyone to go.

'Come!' my rescuer said, and seized me by the arm – a fact which it bore witness to for several days. 'I must get reinforcements. This crowd cannot come in here!' He tugged me in the direction of the temple court, but already there were other shapes approaching through the gloom. One was hooded, and might have been a priest, but the others looked like temple-slaves or acolytes, all carrying tapers, their faces ghostly in the flickering light.

Nothing was said. They simply formed up in a line, as if to shield the inner sanctum from the rising tide of one-time rioters. But, all at once, it seemed that tide had turned. As the troops advanced towards the fire, so the mob began to melt away behind their backs, and soon there were people pouring from the forum through every exit – though there was hardly a lit torch among the lot of them. One unfortunate was trampled in the rush; his moaning body was rolled into the square and it was at this point that the soldiers moved.

'Halt! Stand still! The next to move is dead.' The officer, an *ordinarius*, barked the order in a clarion voice. He was clearly used to issuing commands and expected to be instantly obeyed. He was. People froze as surely as if they'd turned to ice – with the exception of his troops, who swiftly formed into a circle round the fire, so that all parts of the forum were in range of javelins.

The gaggle, prompted by the officer's drawn

sword, were quickly formed into a set of straggling lines. Another order and several of his soliders came and walked along the files, picking out obvious non-citizens from the crowd and setting them aside. Then: 'The rest of you may go! Back to your homes at once. Anyone found out on the street tonight will find himself in jail.' He stood back and let the subdued spectators straggle out into the dark.

A sort of peace had fallen on the square: there were a few people lying lifeless or moaning on the flags, and others with more minor injuries sitting in doorways, rather like myself – but otherwise only the group of non-citizens was left. It soon became clear what they were wanted for. A pair of Roman soldiers with their sword-blades drawn swiftly organized a bucket-chain to put out the fire, using water from the great tank in the fish-market and using the leather buckets which had been full of eels. As the pails of water passed from hand to hand, I recognized the cloaked tradesman who had hissed at me, now perspiring as he worked, and – to my relief – I saw Adonisius too, refilling emptied buckets at the pool. Already the flames were hissing and starting to die down.

I turned towards the line of temple-guards, who were observing all this quite impassively. 'I think that it would be safe for me to leave,' I hazarded.

They turned and stared at me, as if they'd not noticed my presence up till now and were not best pleased to find me there at all.

My giant friend spoke up for me at once. 'This man is not a trespasser. I brought him here myself. I had already met him earlier today. He came to offer a petition plaque. I told him I would see to it on his behalf.'

The priestly figure half-inclined his head, then he and the rest filed silently back into the court again. It was quite uncanny – all this co-ordinated movement without a single sound – or it would have been if a skinny temple-slave of perhaps twelve years or so had not lingered a little as the others left.

'Tomorrow there are likely to be a lot of plaques. And no doubt a penitential offering or two, as well!' It was obvious that he was bursting with some kind of news. 'Commodus may be dead but he was still a deity, and tearing down his statue from the Imperial shrine is a matter which will have to be atoned before the gods.'

My rescuer stared at him. 'You can't mean that the crowd broke into the temple, Popillus?'

I was boggling too. I could hardly credit it. Even if some people had taken too much wine, you would not expect anyone to desecrate a shrine. Especially not a Capitoline one. They would be too afraid of bringing down the wrath of Jove.

The boy called Popillus shook his head. 'They didn't come into the temple proper, only into the sacred grove around the back.'

'The one that houses the Imperial shrine?' I was so surprised that I interrupted him. 'But there's a six-foot wall! How did they manage that?'

'Someone seems to have found a ladder from that site just down the road where they are rebuilding that cloth-shop that caught fire – and it looks as if a group climbed over and wrenched the statue of Commodus from its plinth. Fortunately it was too heavy for them to carry off, otherwise it would have been smashed to pieces too, I expect. We've just found the ladder that they left up against the wall.'

'And no one in the temple saw anything amiss?' My slave friend was as astonished as I was myself.

Popillus shrugged. 'It was not the hour for Imperial sacrifice and we have been too busy with cleansing rites for that – and some of you were elsewhere anyway – attending the cremation of that old priest's remains.'

The giant nodded. 'Indeed. And you may tell them that it is duly done.'

Popillus looked startled for a moment, then pulled his cloak around his ears and hurried back inside.

I turned to my companion. 'The funeral's been held already?' I was surprised again. Usually such a ritual does not take place for days.

He shrugged his massive shoulders. 'The augurers decreed it was the safest thing. We couldn't have a desecrated body on the site and it wasn't fitting to have it lie in state. Six of us slaves were given charge of it, to see that it was quickly cleansed with sacred herbs, and then it was taken to a funeral site just after dark and burned upon a pyre – just a priest and a few of us temple-slaves to offer a lament and see that everything was done according to the rites. I was sent back to say the corpse had been consumed.'

'So that's what you were doing in the forum!' I exclaimed. It should have occurred to me before that it was odd – temple-slaves don't generally wander round the town. 'The pyre must have burned down very fast indeed.'

He nodded. 'There was so little of the body that it did not take long – even the cremation-pyre wasn't very large: though when the ashes are gathered later on, it is not quite certain where we're going to put the urn. The high priest thought that it should be given a proper monument out by the northern road, but the ground's too hard to bury anything, so it's going into the public columbarium until there is a thaw. We'll think about it then. But at least the body's been disposed of decently, and any question of a curse will have been lifted by all the rituals.'

'Except for the desecration of the Imperial shrine?' I said. 'Surely that will have to be pursued? Commodus was, after all, officially a god. In fact unlike his predecessors in the post, he hadn't even waited to be dead: he'd declared himself a deity while he was still alive.'

Another massive shrug. 'The culprits will be sought and punished, I suppose.' He gave a sly, most un-temple-slave-like grin. 'Though if he's really an Immortal, he may avenge himself. In the meantime no doubt you're right. The priests will have to make oblations to purify that shrine – and almost certainly they will require me to help. So I will leave you now. I will see your plaque is made and offered to the goddess, as soon as the stalls are open after dawn. Will you be safe returning to your house?'

I nodded. 'I have an attendant down there in the square.' I gestured in the direction of the bucket-chain, who – urged to their best efforts by threats and baton-strokes – had more or less put out the blaze by now. There was a pile of embers still smouldering in the dark, while charred and broken furniture and bits of statuary could be made out here and there. The forum would require hours of clearing up but there was no longer any risk of the fire spreading elsewhere in the town. 'I think the fire fighters are about to be dismissed. Though I don't know what has happened to our torch.'

The giant nodded. 'Take this one with you! You can repay the temple for it next time that you come. I will look out for you!' He unhooked the pitch-torch from the stanchion in the portico, and handed it to me.

Holding the light aloft, I thanked him heartily and picked my way with care through the scattered debris on the steps and down towards my borrowed servant, now waiting in the square.

251

NINETEEN

By the time we reached my workshop it was very late indeed. It had taken us a little time to get past the sentry at the northern gate – there was a warning out to apprehend anyone suspected of being rioters – and I felt that we were lucky to escape without finding ourselves locked up in the prison overnight.

Minimus had evidently been sitting up on watch, waiting to hear me come, and almost before I had time to knock the door, he had come out to unlock it and was ushering us in. He was quite reproachful as he took my cloak, more so than his status would properly allow.

'Master!' he cried. 'I have been terribly alarmed. I went out to close the shutters and I saw the smoke, and then a pie-seller went by and told me that there was a fire and people had been injured in a riot. I dared not leave the shop to look for you, but I was getting anxious that you had not come. I feared you had been hurt.'

Adonisius was looking rather scandalized at this familiarity, so I said hastily, 'Thank you, Minimus, for your kind concern. The fire delayed us, but we are unscathed. However this poor slave, who was escorting me, was coerced into carrying buckets for an hour to quench the blaze. I'm sure we could find him something warm to drink before we send him home?'

Minimus looked flattered by the 'we'. 'I've got some hot mead, Master. It was awaiting your return.' He led the way into the inner shop, where a cheerful blaze was crackling in the hearth and the smoke of several candles hung thickly in the air. The smell of hot spiced mead was rising from a pot beside the fire and a sleeping blanket had been set out on the floor for me. Never had my workshop seemed more welcoming.

Adonisius seemed to think so, too. When Minimus had brought out an extra stool and drinking bowl for him, and he was sitting by the fire sipping the hot, sweet liquid gratefully, he cast an approving glance around the room.

'When I get my freedom, this is what I'd like. A little cosy place to call my own, where I could earn a living and sleep snug and warm at night. Perhaps, in time, I could even have a slave to wait on me.' He smiled to show that this was not said bitterly.

'You have a trade?' I asked him. Most freed slaves don't dream of being shopkeepers.

'I could be an amanuensis or a clerk, perhaps. I can read and write and use an abacus. It's one of the things that Genialis bought me for. Though in the end he rarely called on me for that. I have some skill with horses and he preferred to have me ride as escort everywhere.'

'I thought that chiefly you were his personal

slave,' I said.

He stared into his mead as if he did not wish to meet my eyes. 'After a fashion, citizen. Several of us used to help him wash and dress, but I had special extra duties, as I expect you've heard, since he made no secret of the fact. Duties which I hated – but of course I had no choice. I shouldn't expect to make a living out of that.'

Now it was my turn to stare into my cup, heartily wishing I'd never raised the subject of what his skills might be. I've never shared the Romans' casual attitude to having sexual pets. 'You expect to get your freedom very soon?' I said, anxious to turn the talk to something else.

A delighted smile lit the handsome face. 'At least I now believe that it is possible. Genialis used to promise all the time, but every time I saved my slave price he'd increase the sum – saying I'd grown in value and would cost more to replace. But now Silvia and Lucius have sworn that I'll be freed, as soon as his estate is sorted out. I was publicly assigned to Silvia while my master was alive, so I will pass to her – and she'll let me purchase freedom, at a price we have agreed.'

'Assuming Genialis turns out to be dead,' I pointed out.

He gave a rueful laugh. 'Of course – although at this stage that is probable, I think. It's been too long for him to have been sheltering anywhere, and a man can't live for long out in the open in the snow.' He drained the cup and put the vessel down. 'However, the search for him will be continuing at dawn and I believe I'm taking part. If I don't hurry home, I shall get no sleep at all. Thank you for your hospitality.' He nodded at Minimus. 'And I admire your slave – perhaps someday, when I acquire the means, we might discuss a price?'

I cocked an eye at him, raising my drinking vessel in salute. 'I hope you find a slave that pleases you, but I'm afraid that Minimus is not for sale. Not at any time.' I realized that I'd sounded rather sharp and softened my blank refusal with a grin. 'Where would I find another slave who knows my eccentricities so well?'

Minimus, of course, had been listening throughout and he was grinning like a toad as he took a taper from the bench and led the visitor outside. I heard him bolt the outer door, but by the time that he'd returned I had finished off my mead and was preparing to curl up on my blanket on the floor.

'Thank you, Master, for what you said just now! It's pleasing, of course, to think he wanted me, but I'd hate you to sell me to anybody else!' he murmured, setting the candle on the bench again and kneeling to remove the sandals from my feet.

'Well blow out the light, then, before I change my mind!' I said gruffly, and he did as he was told, leaving merely the warm glow of the fire as he settled down himself.

Whether it was the excitement of the day or simply the effects of too much mead, I cannot say, but despite the hardness of the floor I slipped at once into oblivion. In fact I slept so soundly that I knew nothing more until I raised my head and realized that there was a tapping at the door.

I half-raised myself to instruct Minimus to answer it, but found that he was no longer lying at my side. In fact, he must have risen quite a time ago. He had already poked the fire into life and taken down the shutters at the window space, which were letting in the cold grey light of dawn. I struggled to my feet and called his name aloud.

'I am here, Master, in the outer shop. There's someone at the door.' Even as he answered I heard him open it.

'Is your owner ready? I am sent to fetch him for the search.' I did not instantly recognize the voice. I was expecting Adonisius, but this clearly wasn't him, though it was a speaker I was sure I'd heard before.

I did not have long to puzzle over this, as a moment later the two of them came in and I recognized Pistis, the pimply, sulky slave I'd seen with Lucius – whom I had mentally nick-named Pustulus. He was swathed from head to foot in an outsize woollen cloak and his feet were wrapped against the cold with binding rags. In one hand he was carrying a sack and in the other a couple of long pointed poles.

'Are you ready to come with us, citizen?' He looked even more sullen than he'd done yester-day.

'I won't be a moment,' I said untruthfully, reaching for my own cape and sandals to put on. 'I was rather late last night. I think there is some bread and cheese I didn't eat?'

Minimus had already fetched it and was handing it to me. 'You ought to have a warm drink, Master, before you leave the house. I'll put some wine to warm. And you should do as he has done and bind rags around your feet. It will still be freezing underfoot, and if you're in the forest there will be standing snow.'

'There is no need for that,' the sulky one put in. 'My master sent you these.' He thrust his hand into the sack and drew out what looked like a pair of untreated leather bags. 'You put them on your feet and pull the drawstring tight. A trick he learned from his trading contacts from the north. And these–' he produced another, smaller pair – 'Are for your hands. They're made of rabbit skin and still have fur inside.'

I had heard of rabbits though I'd never tasted one – they were an expensive delicacy shipped direct from the Hispanic provinces for the benefit of wealthy legionaries who'd enjoyed them there, which no doubt explained where Lucius had acquired these skins. Although I had never seen the living animal, I had some notion that they resembled goats. However, when I slipped the garments on, I realized why the creatures fetched so high a price and why some people took such pains to try to breed them here. The skins alone would be a luxury; they were as soft as kid and wonderfully silky in their furriness.

I was reluctant to take the mittens off again, but I removed them to gulp the wine which Minimus had warmed and splash a little water on my face and beard. Then I quickly put them on again, and said to my new escort, 'You can lead the way.'

Pustulus nodded and led me to the street, but skinny little Minimus was too quick for him. He made a point slipping of past and opening the door. 'Don't worry, Master, I will mind the shop. And I'll see that there is more than bread and cheese for you tonight.'

I turned to smile at him. 'And I'll try not to be home so late!' I said.

Beside me, I distinctly heard a bitter sigh. 'Well, I won't keep you on the streets all night,' my companion muttered, as we made our way towards the northern gate. 'I don't know what that Adonisius was thinking of – going to the forum when he wasn't ordered to, and getting mixed up in a public riot. Keeping the master waiting for hours after dark – so much so that he gave up in the end and went to bed.' He gave a short, affronted sniff. 'If I had been so late, I'd have certainly been flogged – but not Adonisius. Oh, great Minerva, not a bit of it! He can do no wrong it seems.'

I glanced sideways at the sullen face. 'Lucius is only a freeman, after all,' I pointed out. 'He could hardly whip the servant of a wealthy citizen. Adonisius still officially belongs to

Genialis, doesn't he?'

'I suppose that's true,' he answered grudgingly. 'Or to Silvia at least. Though you'd never think so from the way my master talks to him – more like a trusted steward than a borrowed slave. Today, for instance, he's excused from coming out with us – at least at first; there's a guest expected and my master wants him at hand to serve. I tried to protest – after all I am the household slave – and do you know what Lucius said? That Adonisius hadn't managed to complete his chores last night, and this way he could see to them as well. I would have been expected to stay up and finish them, even if it meant I didn't get to bed.'

'You do not care for Adonisius?' I said, and saw him hesitate. 'I was a slave myself,' I went on carefully, 'and I know from experience how awkward it can be, when some temporary incomer becomes a favourite.'

He shrugged. 'It's not for me to speak against my master,' he replied. 'But it does seem maddening – promising to help him find his slave price instantly, when I have served the house for years, and no one ever mentioned doing that for me. I shall be like poor old Vesperion, I expect – kept on till I'm too old to be use to anyone, then forced to beg for the doubtful privilege of going on working to survive, for a pittance entirely at my master's charity.'

It was said with such resentment that I could think of no reply, and for a few moments we simply stomped along, my clumsy foot gloves

259

squelching in the mud and melting snow – though they certainly succeeded in keeping out the wet. I was about to ask a question regarding Silvia, and whether Pustulus had met her when she was Ulpius's wife, but by this time we'd reached the junction with the northern road, where the promised cart was waiting by the tombs.

Pustulus waved an airy hand at it. 'Here you are. My master's vehicle. He has put it and the driver at the service of the search. Would you prefer to sit in front beside the carter, or in the back with us? They'll make a space for you, though I'm afraid we're only slaves and it won't be very dignified for someone of your rank. Some of them belong to your patron I believe. Perhaps you already know them?'

I peered into the cart and found that there were several that I recognized from Marcus's apartment in the town. There was a lot of whispering and nudging when they saw that it was me – they had not forgotten the last time that we'd met, when I was virtually a prisoner in the flat and had made that undignified escape.

Perhaps it was embarrassment that prompted me to say, 'I need not trouble you to squash up in the cart. I have my own transport – I have hired a mule, though it's in the hiring stables on the southern side of town. I will go and get it, and ride out after you. I know which way you're going, and if you travel slowly, I should catch you up.'

The driver grunted, clearly displeased at this idea, and there was a stifled giggle from his passengers.

'The mule will give me freedom to go home straight away if anything is found.' I looked at the grinning faces in the cart, and added slyly, 'After all, I am a citizen-client of his Excellence and my patron will be awaiting my report.'

That sobered them. The grins had disappeared. The driver turned to me. 'As you suggest, citizen, of course. I'll drive on as slowly as I can, until we reach the area where we mean to search. If you haven't caught us up by then, I'll leave a slave to wait where we turn off, to show you exactly which way to go next. We're heading for the forest but once we've left the military road you should be able to follow the cart tracks in the snow.'

'Very well!' I told him, and watched them drive away.

TWENTY

It did not really take me very long to fetch the mule. Of course, it was by now half an hour past dawn, so the gates were open and the whole colonia was waking for the day. An enterprising tradesman had set up a booth inside the arch, selling leafy garlands and strips of cloth on which the legend 'Long Live the Emperor Pertinax' had been daubed, and was already doing a brisk trade with visitors. Otherwise the town appeared as usual. Shopkeepers were busy sweeping down their slushy frontages, taking shutters down or laying their goods out on the freshly cleared pavement in the hope of attracting passing customers. Two slaves were struggling to the fuller's with a brimming urine pot, and the first street vendors were hollering their wares: 'Fresh milk!' 'Hot pies. Finest horsemeat. Cheapest in the town!' But there were hardly any other pedestrians as yet, and it was possible to walk quickly through the streets – though I did encounter a little flock of geese, being driven towards the market to be killed and sold.

The gooseherd looked up at me as I tried to pass. 'In a hurry, mister? You wouldn't like a goose? Make a feast in honour of the new Emperor? I'm prepared to take an offer, though I won't be selling cheap. There haven't been fresh birds like this for sale since Janus feast.'

I shook my head and thanked him and attempted to walk on, though his flock came flapping after me, hissing and pecking at my ankles till he shooed them off. However that was the only enforced delay I encountered.

In the end, I made a little detour of my own. The quickest route lay close to the centre of the town and as I passed the forum I could not resist going there to have a look. But by now there was nothing much to see. A contingent of soldiers had been hard at work, piling last night's debris into a hand-cart, which was standing by, laden with pieces of half-burnt wood and broken drinking pots. Now they were busy sweeping up the ash, leaving only a burnt place on the paving stones and an empty column where the late Emperor's statue used to stand as evidence of what had happened here last night.

The market booths were already opening, and even the stalls on the temple steps were readying themselves for customers. One owner was hanging up the cages of small birds which he would later sell as offerings, while another hung a notice above his door, advertising the engraving of curse and prayer tablets. That must be the one the temple-slave had meant. Any moment now, I thought, the slave would come himself, and as I did not want him to find me standing here, I hastened off towards the southern gate.

My mule was at a manger stall when I arrived, looking contented and well fed, and after a little bartering, I secured agreement that I could bring her back tonight if I desired. A stable slave had meanwhile strapped the saddle on, and with the help of a handy mounting-stone I was hoisted up – though I had to take my rabbit mittens off to hold the reins.

For a moment I thought that Arlina was not going to move, since no amount of digging with my strangely booted feet had the least effect on her, but a well aimed stick across the rump (wielded by the stable owner) seemed to do the trick, and she ambled into motion willingly enough.

'I should take this with you!' The fellow tossed the stick to me, and thus equipped I managed well enough. There is no law, of course, against riding through the town by day – only horse-drawn vehicles are prohibited – and soon I was trotting through the streets again, urging Arlina forward every now and then. Then it was through the northern gate and out on to the road, following the way the cart had travelled earlier.

I had the impression I was moving fairly fast – certainly quicker than I could have walked the route – but after an hour or so I still had not caught the cart, and I began to wonder if I had missed my promised guide. However, just when I was beginning to despair, I turned a corner and caught sight of him.

He pushed his hood back and I saw that it was Pustulus! He was sitting on a wall beside the road, looking cold and even more unhappy than before. I ambled up and reined Arlina in.

'This is where the cart went?' It was a foolish thing to say. As the driver had predicted I could see the tracks, veering off the main road and down a narrow lane between a little cottage and a wood store opposite. In the distance I could see a tangle of high trees where the cleared land ended and the forest wilds began.

Pustulus said nothing, just gave a sullen nod. It was not mere discourtesy, I realized: his lips and hands were turning blue and he was genuinely chilled from waiting in the cold.

'Get on the mule,' I said. 'And you can ride from here.' The offer earned me a disbelieving look, but I shuffled backwards and showed him how he could sit in front of me, as Minimus had done the day before. Pustulus still seemed a little hesitant, but he'd been loaned to me and an order had to be obeyed.

He came and clambered on the wall, from where I could assist him up on to the animal, and as I took his hand I realized that his fingers were almost numb with cold. I pulled my rabbit mittens from inside my belt, where I had stowed them when I took the reins, and handed them to him. 'And put these on! If your hands are frozen you will be no help at all.'

He gave me another startled look but did as he was told. I put one arm around his waist to steady him, since he seemed incapable of holding on himself, then reached around and with my spare hand flicked Arlina with the stick until she lumbered into motion once again.

It was not hard to follow where the cart had gone. This far from town the snow was fairly deep and undisturbed, except for a few footprints and the tracks of animals. The wagon had effectively cleared a rutted path for us and Arlina walked along it with confidence and surprising daintiness, and very shortly we were in the shelter of the trees. After a few minutes we saw the cart ahead, pulled up on a patch of frozen bracken by the road.

The driver, who was still sitting in his seat, swung himself down to the ground as we approached. 'Ah, there you are, citizen! I see you found the slave. The search party has spread out on the forest paths around here, but I have left the nearest area for you.' He made an expansive gesture with his hands, indicating the merest suggestion of a track which wound away between the hazel and ash trees and the massive oaks in front of us. 'If you hear me whistle, come back here at once. It will be a signal either that something has been found or that it is time to break off for a rest. And you'll be needing these! I told the slave to leave them in the cart.'

He reached into the back and produced the pair of poles, which Pustulus had brought into my workshop earlier. In order to take them I got down from my mount, followed – in an undignified slither – by my companion, who had taken off my mitts and thrust them at me surreptitiously.

'Thank you, citizen!' He flashed me a warm smile – the first time that I'd ever seen his face without a sulk. 'Allow me to assist you, in my turn.' He seized the mule and tied it to a tree, then took the poles and demonstrated how to use them to test the piles of snowy leaves beside the path. It was obvious I'd earned myself a friend.

'If anything is in there, you will feel it with the rod,' he told me earnestly. 'We found a couple of dead dogs yesterday.'

I nodded. 'Then I will come and try it for myself.' I turned to the driver. 'Is is safe to leave the mule?'

'Certainly, citizen, I will not be far away – though I'm to search the borders of this lane myself, Bernadus and Alfredus Allius have contributed another wagon-load of slaves and they will work towards us from each side, and we'll work out to them. That way they know the whole area has been scoured.' And so saying he produced a pointed stick himself and began to prod amongst the frosted bracken by the road.

Pustulus was already making for the trees and I pottered after him, still making my peculiar boot tracks in the snow, and together we began the painstaking business of the search. It was bitterly cold and I sent up a mental thanks to Lucius for the protection on my hands and feet: his northern traders clearly knew a thing or two. But even my unconventional boots could not keep out all the chill and very soon my feet had turned to blocks of ice: so how the slaves were faring, with only rags around their legs, it was difficult to guess.

The snow was patchier underneath the trees, but it was still hard work and it seemed like hours before we took a break. The driver gave the whistle – an especially piercing one – and slaves appeared from different areas of the forest on either side. It was obviously too cold to sit down on the ground, so we climbed up on to the cart. He doled out two pieces of dry bread and a wizened apple each, after which there was a swig of watered wine from a communal jug and then it was time to get to work again.

I was thoughtful as I went back to wielding my probe – something else for which I owed Lucius my thanks! Obviously he'd provided enough sustenance for me. I wished I'd had the sense to bring some foodstuffs of my own, but I hadn't thought of it. Even a slave meal like that was welcome in this cold.

My thoughts were interrupted by a cry from Pustulus. 'There's something here!' he shouted and I turned to look. The driver must have heard as well, because he gave that whistling once again and the other slaves came crashing through the trees from every side.

Pustulus had moved aside the leaves and snow by now, revealing the sorry sight which lay below. It was a body, but it wasn't Genialis, that was clear at once – just an aged crone who'd obviously been overcome by cold, still clutching the firewood she'd been out to fetch.

'She must have been there quite a little time, to be so covered with the leaves,' I said. 'But she's quite well preserved. At least...'

I tailed off as Pustulus turned her on her back. Her short patched tunic had been half-torn away, and telltale toothmarks in her side and thighs showed that we were not the first to find the corpse.

'A wolf, by the look of it.' Even the driver had left the lane by now and was taking an interest in what Pustulus has found. 'Bring her to the cart and later I will drive her to the military road. We'll leave her on the side and tell the army when we get back into town. They'll come and pick her up.' The army sent a death cart out from time to time to collect the unclaimed corpses and put them into the communal pit, along with paupers and criminals from town.

'But she might have family!' somebody exclaimed.

'If so, they would have looked for her by now.' The driver was dismissive. 'And if she had younger relatives they would have fetched the wood for her – not sent her out to get it and let her freeze to death.'

There might be a sick old husband languishing at home, but I did not point that out. Without a fire it was probable by now that he'd be dead as well. So I simply watched as several of the slaves took up the body and bore it to the cart.

They were just in the act of slinging it up into the back, when the sight of a lone horseman coming down the forest track caused us all to stop and stare. Whoever it was, he was moving very fast and waving one hand agitatedly. As he drew closer, I realized who it was. It was Adonisius and he was out of breath.

He swung down from the saddle. 'They have found him!' he told us breathlessly. 'Alfredus Allius's men have found the body in a ditch. The search is over. You can bring in all the slaves.' He turned to me. 'Though it's most peculiar. When I got there they had just begun to dig him out ... and ... well, you're the expert at solving mysteries. Perhaps you'd better come and take a look yourself.'

But I was already heading for the mule.

TWENTY-ONE

We left the driver rounding up the slaves to get back in the cart and return to Glevum and their duties there, while Adonisius and I rode off in company. Or almost in company. It was not easy for him to travel at the same speed as the mule – his horse went so much faster that every few minutes he had to stop and wait – but we kept up a sporadic conversation when we could.

'Silvia has been sent for, I suppose?' I asked on one occasion as I caught him up again, where he'd been idling his horse near a slight curve in the road.

He nodded. 'There is a messenger on his way to her. The slaves who found the body called at the nearest farm, and arranged for someone to ride out and let her know. They had already done that before I got to them, so there should be time for her to get to Glevum well before it's dark.'

'And no doubt my patron will accompany her,' I said, privately thinking that this made things difficult. I would have to go and find him to tender my report.

'They will go to his apartment, I presume,' the Syrian agreed. 'I'll suggest to Lucius that he should call on them as soon as possible. There'll have to be decisions about a funeral. They'll put the body on the cart and take it to Bernadus, I suppose, since he volunteered to house it, if it was ever found. We've sent a rider from that nearby farm to let him know, as well.'

'But doesn't Genialis have a property in Glevum?' I enquired. 'The townhouse that his half-brother used to own? That would surely be the proper place to take him, since it is obviously too far to go to Dorn?'

Adonisius reined his horse in, so as not to draw ahead. 'Except that the Glevum house is empty and there is no bed there to lay him on, no steward to oversee the funeral and no slaves to give him a lament. Apart from me, of course!'

'And even you were given to Silvia, I hear.'

He gave a sideways grin. 'I had no cause to love him, but I'll gladly mourn his corpse. Ah, here is the turning – you can see the print of hooves. And there's the group of slaves who found the corpse.' He gestured down the lane. 'I'll see you down there.' And he cantered off.

The forest here was nearer to the road, and between the trees I could make out the successful search party – a huddle of cloaked and hooded forms in a little clearing not far off the track. As I drew nearer I could see that they were slaves, accompanied by what was obviously a steward, dressed in the colours of Alfredus Allius. The cart that they'd all come in was drawn up further on.

Adonisius had already reached them and slipped from the saddle with his usual grace. From his gestures he was telling them that I was following, and the group all turned and stared at me until Arlina ambled up. The steward barked an order, and they shuffled into ranks and stood back politely while he showed me what they'd found.

The dead man was Genialis; I could see that at once. He was propped up in the hole, the head was turned towards me and his face was visible. His arms appeared to be clamped across his chest and his body seemed at first sight to be grotesquely standing upright in a frozen ditch. However, even before I'd got down from my mount, I could see that this was quite impossible – the ditch was far too shallow to admit his legs and indeed, where the slaves had partly scraped away the loosened snow and leaves, it was clear that the torso ended just below the waist.

'It was almost buried when we found it, citizen,' the steward said proudly. 'We were lucky to spot it – it was half-submerged in leaves.'

'You did well.' I turned to Adonisius. 'Is there more of him elsewhere?'

The handsome face looked startled. 'Not that we have found. Finding half a body is peculiar, of course – but didn't the same thing happen to some ancient priest you knew? I hear that only half that body was discovered in the ice.'

There was a little buzz of shocked surprise

from the assembled slaves at this. 'That's true!' I said, surprised.

Adonisius shook a baffled head. 'So now it's happened twice. There must be some connection, don't you think? As Lucius says, it can't be merely a coincidence.'

I stared from Adonisius to the corpse. 'But with the priest it was the other way about. The head and chest were missing and only the lower part of him was found...' I trailed off. It had suddenly occurred to me that I could not be altogether sure if that was true. 'Or so I am informed – I did not actually see the corpse myself,' I finished awkwardly.

But the Syrian wasn't listening. 'No head, citizen?' He sounded mystified. 'Then how could anyone be sure that it was him?'

I laughed. 'That's the same question that I have asked myself. Someone suggested that it was the sandals that he wore – but I privately suspect there might be other signs. In any case the temple has accepted him – they gave the remains a hurried cremation yesterday.'

The steward had been listening to all this and he stepped forward, doubtfully. 'That couldn't have been the bottom half of this one, I suppose? Pardon if I am speaking out of turn.'

'I don't think so, steward. That corpse was very fresh. The priest was seen alive and well the night before, but I'm fairly sure that this one has been dead some time – the flesh has got a faintly greenish tinge – though probably it didn't happen here. I don't believe this body has been here very long.'

'What makes you say that, citizen?' The steward was surprised. 'We heard he had been missing for half a moon or so and that he'd probably fallen off his horse and killed himself. Surely no one would bother to move his corpse about.'

'It might not have occurred to me,' I said, 'if our party hadn't found the body of an ancient crone today, in the part of the forest we were searching in. Sad business – she'd obviously been dead some little time, though very well-preserved. But she was also several inches underneath the snow. Yet Genialis was only "almost buried" – by your own account – and "half-submerged in leaves". That's obviously true; I can see what you have moved from round the corpse.' I stooped and ran a little through my fingers. 'Loose leaves with softish snow mixed into it. Yet it has been snowing hard and freezing since the day he disappeared.'

'But not the last three days or so,' the steward pointed out. 'There's been quite a thaw – it might have melted round him, I suppose.'

'In that case, he would partially have thawed as well and there would be much more putre-faction than there is. Let me take a closer look.'

Adonisius stood beside me as I knelt beside the corpse, obviously electing himself my second in command. 'Then perhaps he hasn't been dead for very long?' he offered, thought-fully. 'I suppose it's possible that he was set upon. Dragged from his horse, perhaps, and

275

shut away somewhere. Maybe they were hoping for a ransom, but he died – leaving them with an inconvenient corpse, which they disposed of recently by bringing it out here?'

I shook my head. 'And drew attention to themselves by cutting it in half? That does not sound plausible to me. Besides, as I say, it's clear that he's been dead some little time.'

'So, do you think this is somehow connected to the priest?'

'I suppose it must be, though I can't see how. I suppose that also happened in unfrequented wood. And there's another thing. It is quite clear what the crone was doing, off the beaten track – she was collecting wood. But what would bring Genialis so far from the road?'

'Lost his direction in the snow, perhaps?' the steward said. 'Or perhaps he was dragged here by some animal – we know that there are hungry wolves about. We've heard them several times while we've been searching in the woods.'

I looked up at him. 'Those are not gnaw marks – that looks like an axe.' I brushed the few remaining leaves away and examined what remained of Genialis with more care.

It was not a pleasant task. He had been a well-fed and unlovely man in life; in death he was frankly horrible. The plump face was white and bloodless, though with that faint greenish suggestion of decay, and it was frozen in a look of agonized surprise. The eyes were closed but they were still disquieting, as if they might suddenly open in a terrible blank stare. His rigid arms were clamped across his chest as stiffly as two spears and his torso simply ended in a jagged cut as though a market butcher had been at work, although his toga, cloak and tunic appeared to be intact, and were drawn up in muddy, filthy folds around his waist. Strangely – apart from smudges on his clothes – there was not much blood on him.

But something appeared to be adhering to his hair, and to his cloak and shoulders when I examined them: tiny wisps of something coarse and brown. I reached out a doubtful hand and contrived to pick up a tiny piece. I rubbed it between my fingers then had a sniff at it. 'Hessian, by Juno!' I exclaimed aloud. 'I do believe his head's been in a sack.'

'Perhaps he was imprisoned by whoever stole his purse,' said Adonisius, now kneeling at my side. 'And look!' He was pointing to the empty loop that still dangled from the belt. 'Someone stole his purse. It's not unknown for bandits to tie their victims up and put a bag around their heads – so that they can't see their attackers and testify against the culprits afterwards.'

I nodded doubtfully. 'Perhaps it is the obvious answer after all. Maybe there really is a half-crazed thief abroad who chops up his victims when he's done with them and stuffs them in a ditch. If the heads were missing I would have thought of Druids – but this is something different and much more sinister.' I dusted down my hands and attempted to stand up.

Adonisius reached out a hand to assist me to my feet. 'Then we must warn the town watch and garrison. If this is some kind of madman, then it's imperative he's caught.'

'I suppose so,' I conceded. I turned to the steward. 'Have your men wrap up the body and put it on the cart. You could even begin to offer a lament.'

The slave looked flustered. 'Well, I just hope that we don't have to ride with him! Unless our master sends another wagon out for us, I'm going to walk to town – I don't want to share the journey with half a murdered man. It's bad enough disturbing his corpse like this at all – I hear he was a stickler for the proper dignities in life – but to put him in a slave cart is another thing again. His ghost is likely to be walking anyway, seeking revenge on whoever chopped him up. You never know what harm...'

Adonisius interrupted him. 'There is no need to worry. If I am not mistaken, here is Bernadus now.' He gestured down the lane where a cloaked horseman and a mounted page had just come into sight.

It was indeed Bernadus, on a splendid horse, even more splendidly attired in an impressive dark-blue hooded cloak and leather boots. He rode easily for a stoutish man, and drew up beside me with almost as much elegance as the mounted page who had accompanied him.

'Citizen Libertus! Hail Caesar Pertinax!' he murmured, holding out a hand in greeting, but not troubling to dismount. 'They told me you were here. Where is this body – I hear that it's been found?'

I stood aside to let him see the place and he trotted his horse closer to peer into the ditch. One glance, however, appeared to be enough. He turned away, his face the same green colour as the dead man's skin.

'Dear gods! Nobody told me that there was only half of it. What have I agreed to! Still, it's too late now. I sent to Silvia to say I'm taking it – and I suppose I'd better do as I arranged. I'll have to find some funeral herbs to dress it with.' He swallowed hard. 'Lucius might have some – he imports that sort of thing. In the meantime I suppose we'd better take the body on the cart.'

'You could send a funeral litter,' I told him earnestly. 'Make it the first thing that you do, when you return to town, and leave these slaves to keep a vigil here meanwhile. The funeral directors will carry him for you – they provide their own embalming herbs and women who'll lay out the corpse as well. They even have professional mourners who will keep up a lament and they'll arrange the pyre and everything. It would be expensive – especially sending them out here to get the corpse – but I imagine that's what Silvia would prefer. Though no doubt you'll want to check the final details with her, and discuss arrangements for the memorial feast?'

He turned towards me with a grateful smile. 'Thank you, citizen. I'm glad of your advice.

279

I've never had to plan a funeral myself – my elder brother always does that sort of thing. You are quite right. I'll go to town at once, and try to make contact with the lady Silvia. I imagine that she will be on her way back to town from Marcus's by now. And I ought to talk to Lucius, perhaps.'

'I'll call on Lucius for you, if you like. But then I must go and find my patron straightaway. He'll be on his way to Glevum as we speak, I'm sure, but if he has not got to his apartment by the time I call, I'll take my slave and try to intercept him on the road ... I'll let them know what you intend to do, and no doubt they will find you at your villa later on.'

'Not the villa,' he said quickly. 'My poor wife is out there now and she'll be distressed. I'll have them take the body to my Glevum residence. I have a townhouse just inside the walls, and that would be a great deal more convenient. Do you know where it is?'

I shook my head.

'Well, if you'd like to follow me, I'll take you there,' he said. 'I understand you have an animal?'

'I have a mule,' I told him, pointing down the lane, where Arlina was munching morosely at wet leaves.

Bernadus threw his head back and gave a nervous laugh. 'Well, I can't accompany you to town on that. Give it to my slave, and you can ride my horse. '

Adonisius had sidled up to us. 'I could take it,

masters. He could have my mount.'

Bernadus grinned. He was enjoying this. 'Better that you ride back home yourself as fast as possible and let your master know what has been found. Libertus will be calling on him later on.'

The Syrian nodded, though he was clearly not happy at being thus dismissed. He climbed on to his horse and urged it down the track, while Bernadus's escort clambered scowling to the ground, abandoning his lovely animal to me.

'Ride that thing to my townhouse!' his master called to him. 'The Citizen Libertus will collect it there! Come pavement-maker!' He wheeled his horse and led the way along the lane.

TWENTY-TWO

I thoroughly enjoyed the journey back to town. It is many years since I had ridden such a horse and the next few minutes were a pure delight. Bernadus seemed surprised that I could ride at all.

'It is good of you to take such trouble and to have joined the search,' he called, cantering up beside me as we rode the snowy lanes. 'You hardly knew the dead man, as I understand?'

'I had a contract with him, that is all,' I replied, reining in my horse to talk to him. 'But my patron is acting as Silvia's guardian and he asked me to come. You, on the other hand, must have been his closest friend. I know he called on you to witness what we had agreed and you were very generous with your hospitality.'

The stout face flushed a little. 'Hardly a friend, citizen, as one understands the word. I don't think Genialis ever had a friend.'

I stared at him. That was the second time that someone had said that to me. 'But you were good to him. You agreed to act as surety for him, with Alfredus Allius, I heard. And I heard you invite him to your country house – "treat my house as your own" you said to him. Which

282

it seems he did. No casual matter either – you entertained him from the Kalends till the day he disappeared. And his ward and slave as well, I understand. You even left Glevum and went out there yourself to host them properly.'

I said this in the hope of provoking some response. It had occurred to me that of all the people Genialis knew, Bernadus had the greatest opportunity for killing him, since the party bound for Dorn had been staying at his house. As for disposing of the body, there was chance of that as well, as he had certainly been travelling up and down that major road, several times after his guest had disappeared. I had seen him at the Janus festival myself.

Moreover, it was his horse that Genialis was riding the last time he was seen – it would be easy for the owner to have it tampered with. It was quite the best theory that I had managed up to now. But what would be the motive, if the men were friends?

As if he had been reading my mind, Bernadus answered that question for himself. 'Citizen, since it is quite safe to tell you now, as he will never hear of it, I will confess the truth. I could not stand the man. Of course I would have done a great deal for the lady Silvia – as would any man who ever met her, I suspect. If I did not have a wife I would sue for her myself, now that her guardian is safely dead.' He seemed to realize that this wasn't very wise and he went on, leaning over to caress his horse's neck. 'As to the services that you remind me of, I had no

283

choice but to oblige him in any way he chose. He knew something that could have cost me everything – even my life – and he'd threatened more than once that he would use it if I did not do exactly as he asked.' He glanced around as if his mounted escort might be overhearing this, but of course there was nobody in sight. Arlina could not move at such a pace.

'Blackmail?' I whispered.

'You could call it that. There was a letter – written on a wax-pad, that is all – one scrape with a warm strigil would have rubbed it out – but he got hold of it. It was very foolish to have written it – it was only intended for my brother's eyes – several stupid jokes about the Emperor.' He paused and looked at me. 'I don't mean Pertinax, may the gods increase his rule; I mean the last Imperial idiot. Mad as a burnt bear and thought he was a god. Well, everybody said so – I'm not the only one. The trouble was that Genialis found the jokes somehow. I think he intercepted my private messenger. In any case he threatened to betray me – and pass the tablet to the Imperial spies. He said that he knew several of them, and I expect that's true. He's the sort of man who would. And you know what would have happened to me then?'

I nodded, though in fact I didn't know at all. One of the famous things about the Emperor Commodus was that he found inventive methods of executing 'foes' – which meant anyone who dared to say a word against his so-called deity. But one thing was quite certain:

Bernadus certainly had cause to wish Genialis dead.

'Of course,' he went on innocently, 'it doesn't matter now. Commodus is dead. But I didn't know that when Genialis disappeared, and when he left us I had an awful fright – especially when he insisted on going out without a page. I thought he'd gone to have some secret meeting with an Imperial spy. I would have promised anything to have avoided that.'

'Or done anything?' I prompted. 'Such as killing him?'

Bernadus looked startled, then gave a little laugh. 'I suppose I might have done that – if it came to it. But it seems that someone else had equal cause. And in case you are thinking that I did it anyway, I'll just point out to you that it isn't possible. The day that Genialis left us, I was in the house with my wife, my staff and also Silvia and that Syrian slave. They can all vouch for that.'

'But you have travelled that way several times since then.' There was no point in not telling him my thoughts.

'I never leave the house without an escort,' he exclaimed, as though I were mad to have suggested it. 'Especially when the weather is so bad. Come to that, I don't know any citizen who would. Genialis was the one who acted in a peculiar way, insisting that he didn't want his servant to accompany him. But he did say that. I heard him, and so did half the house. There can be no doubt of it.' He grinned. 'Anyway,

285

I'm not the only one who's glad to see him dead. I imagine that Alfredus Allius will be pleased as well. I hear that Genialis made a fool of him – made him a debtor in the sight of all the town, which threatens his re-election as a councillor. But now, at least, that problem will be solved – he'll get the money out of the estate.'

I looked at him severely. 'But weren't you the surety?'

He looked a bit unhappy, but he simply shrugged. 'I'm not sure where the law is going to stand on that. If a man can't meet his debts on time for reasons out of his control – and I imagine being dead is going to qualify – then the contract hasn't failed, and the surety will not be called upon. There will simply be a claim against the legatees.' He urged his horse a little faster.

I kept up with him. 'But Genialis had the money with him, didn't he?' I remembered hearing the story of the gold.

Bernadus did that dismissive shrug again. 'We didn't find it, citizen, if he did. After Silvia sent and told us that her guardian had not arrived in town, Alfredus Allius came to me and together we searched all his possessions carefully. We found an empty casket and some silver coins. But there was nothing in the way of gold – I have a household full of witnesses to that.' He dug his knees into his horse and pulled ahead.

But I was no mean horseman in my youth. I

whispered to my mount and we caught up again. 'Why did you search his luggage, councillor? Surely you should simply have sent it back to town?'

'Because Alfredus Allius came and asked me to. I think that we had cause. We both have a lively interest in that gold.' He looked away but could not hide a flush. 'Besides, he brought a letter from the lady Silvia, requesting the same thing. I would do a great deal to oblige her, I have told you that. But enough of questioning. I did not kill her guardian – and there's an end to it. Look ahead. We're nearly at the town.'

Indeed I could already see the first memorials, and soon we were trotting past the humbler graves beside the road. I glanced towards the muddy suburb, just outside the gate, where I had my workshop and where Minimus no doubt awaited me. But for the moment, I had other things to do. I followed Bernadus through the city gate, and very shortly he led me down an alleyway and into the stable yard of his town residence.

It was not as grand as Marcus's apartment, but it was quite impressive all the same. It was crammed in with several other houses in the street, but it was a proper building, owned from cellar to the sky, with a stable for two horses, and even a tiny courtyard garden at the rear with a painted shrine in it, a kitchen to one side and a few struggling clumps of lovage and sweet herbs around the walls.

Bernadus led me through this with a proprietorial air. 'Not a very big place, but it qualifies,' he said – meaning that it met the property requirements for election to public office in the town. 'Come into the atrium – that's where we'll bring him to.'

He ushered me into the reception area. It wasn't very large, and fairly sparsely furnished, but the table and two carved benches were of splendid quality, the wall-friezes were lively, and the mosaic floor – three half-dressed naiads wrestling with a snake – was competently done (even I had to acknowledge that). Bernadus waved a hand towards a bench.

'Wait there for a moment, while I find a slave and you can direct him to the undertaker's shop. I'll have to go and find a servant, I'm afraid. There should have been someone on duty at the door, but they're not expecting me and obviously they didn't hear us come. I only keep a small staff here in any case, when we're living at the villa.' He marched through an inner door and disappeared from sight.

I looked at my surroundings but my thoughts were somewhere else. I was still mulling over that business in the woods. What kind of killer left half a corpse? What was the point of it? A dreadful warning to the rest of us? Surely the other bits could be no use to anyone? There must be a reason, if I could think of it. But try as I might, I could not fathom it.

And who could possibly have done it anyway? Not Lucius: he wasn't present when Bernadus invited the party to his house, and so

– without a messenger – he had no way of knowing where they were. Besides, ever since Genialis had failed to arrive in town, Lucius's whereabouts could be accounted for – and by the most reliable of witnesses: myself and Marcus Septimus. And, presumably, Alfredus Allius today.

The same thing went for Silvia, of course, I realized with delight. I was reluctant to regard her as a suspect, anyway, but of course she had the most pressing motive of them all – she didn't want to marry her unpleasant guardian. She had been at the villa, certainly – but if she was an alibi for Bernadus at that time, then he was equally an alibi for her. Besides, this did not seem to be a woman's crime. Would she have the strength to carve a corpse in half? And when would she have the opportunity? A lady never left the house without a slave.

Alfredus Allius, then? That was possible. I had no very clear idea of where he'd been that day – and certainly he knew where Genialis was. That was something I should investigate.

I went on staring at the naiads stupidly. A niggling conviction was growing in my brain that there was something important that I'd missed. Surely there was some point that Adonisius had made, some detail that I hadn't paid enough attention to? I shook my head. It was eluding me.

My thoughts were interrupted by the return of Bernadus, now in the company of an attractive maidservant. She dropped me a small curtsey.

'Master says you're going to show me where to go to fetch the people to arrange the funeral.' She flashed me a shy smile. 'And the kitchen's sending up some fruit and wine for you. In the meantime, would you care to have us wash your hands? And your feet as well perhaps? There is water warming and I know you've been out in the snow.'

I found that I was blushing with embarrassment. I had entirely forgotten my peculiar boots – though I still had my mittens tucked inside my belt. I was trying to decide on the courteous response when Bernadus solved the problem by saying heartily, 'He is very welcome to the wash of course, and no doubt he would be glad of some refreshment too, but he may prefer to keep his footwear on. His mule will be arriving very soon, and then he will be wanting to go out again.'

As he spoke a pair of pageboys came into the room, one bearing the promised water and a towel, the other carrying a little tray of treats. My hands were rinsed and patted gently dry (the pleasure of warmed water had never seemed so sweet) and the slave girl fussed around us, with dried plums and wine.

Bernadus waved her impatiently away. 'Fetch your cloak. The citizen has other things to do. You are content to show her where to go, and call on Lucius?'

I had almost forgotten that I'd undertaken that, but I nodded. 'I'll do so very soon – though first I have a little business of my own.'

I had decided that I'd go back to the shop and talk to Minimus. He would be wondering where I was again. Besides, I had an errand that I wanted him to run. I had promised to report our grisly find to the town authorities, and my slave would be the perfect courier. I myself would go to Lucius – and very gladly too. It occurred to me that, like an idiot, I'd forgotten to ask him for those record scrolls. This would give me the opportunity to request them now – and when I saw Marcus, I'd have something to report even if I hadn't solved the mystery.

So when the escort at last came lumbering along with a reluctant Arlina, I was glad enough to leave. I took the slave girl with me, pointed out the undertaker's premises and – urging my ungainly mount along the slushy streets – made my way back to Minimus and the shop.

TWENTY-THREE

Minimus was delighted and surprised to see me come, and extremely flattered to be used as a courier. He found me my old writing tablet from the shelf and I scratched a short account of what I'd seen out in the woods, pointing out that there had been another corpse found near here recently left in a similar truncated state, then tied the tablet shut and sealed the knot with my seal stick and a blob of molten wax. I wanted this to be a formal document.

Minimus had bustled around with still more food and drink for me – including the remainder of the mead – and I must confess that I was glad of this more homely fare, but before I'd finished he had seized the writing block and was already heading for the door.

'First to the garrison and then to the town watch. That's right, Master?'

I told him that it was and that I'd see him back here at the workshop afterwards. 'I'm going to return my boots and mittens to Lucius and ask him for some records to show Marcus later on. After that, I think I've accomplished what I can. We'll take Arlina back to Cantalarius and have a day at home.'

'So you know who was responsible for Genialis's death? You can tell me, Master – I promise I won't breathe a word to anybody else.'

I shook my head. 'I haven't solved the mystery – perhaps there isn't one. Adonisius believes there is a crazed bandit out there doing this, and I'm beginning to agree with him. But at least the body has been found and Genialis is now clearly dead, so Marcus can leave a proxy to deal with the estate and go to Rome. I imagine that now Pertinax has been confirmed as Emperor, he'll want to talk to him as soon as possible.'

Minimus nodded. 'Then I'll await you here. I should be back within the hour.'

'And I won't be much longer,' I replied, pouring out the last drops of the delicious warming mead as he gave a little bow and hurried on his way.

I did not especially hurry over my repast. I told myself there was no special rush and I took the opportunity to think about the day. I was still convinced that there was some detail I'd missed, which should have led me closer to the truth. Despite my cheerful words to Minimus, I did not like to leave a mystery unsolved.

And what had all this to do with the body of the priest? I shook my head. I was going around in circles and I was wasting time. My patron would be on his way to Glevum now, and if I wished to intercept him and give him my report, I had better go to Lucius and get what I required.

I debated whether I should ride Arlina over to the dock, but decided against it and left her where she was, tied up in the alleyway beside the shop, where she was contently munching at the tanner's rubbish heap. I put my cloak and sandals on, picked up the boots and mitts and set off as quickly as I could for Lucius's premises.

I called at the warehouse, but he was not there. The ancient steward gestured to the dock. 'He and Alfredus Allius are over there, overseeing the loading of that timber pile and some other goods that he is shipping off to Gaul. The captain's anxious to get out on the tide. There hasn't been much trade for days, with all the ice, so the first ship to get to Gaul will command the highest prices. There's a crew, of course, but my master always goes to see that his cargo is stacked in properly, and this time he's taken Allius with him. And now they've got that slave of Silvia's to help.'

I thanked the steward and went out on to the dock. There was still a little ice along the shore, but the slaves who had been employed to keep the quayside clear were no longer needed and the ship was now drawn up beside the quay. A little further down the river bank Lucius was standing with his back to me, talking to the captain and to Alfredus Allius. They were all watching Adonisius, who was struggling up the gangplank with a heavy sack.

The slave turned and saw me, dropped his

burden on the deck and called, 'Here is Libertus, Master!'

Lucius whirled around, for a moment seeming quite alarmed. Then – as if he'd realized who it was – he came towards me with his hands outstretched. His face was wreathed in smiles. 'Ah, citizen. I hear the news is good. The search is over and they've found the corpse at last.' He glanced at the boots and gloves that I was carrying. 'Though there was no need to make a special trip to bring these back.'

I handed back my borrowed luxuries and – deciding that there was no need for formal courtesies – said with a smile, 'I was very glad of them. Thank you for your kindness. But returning them was not the only thing that brought me here. Bernadus was hoping you might have some hyssop or other funeral herbs to cleanse the corpse.'

He stroked his handsome auburn beard and frowned. 'I'm not sure if we do. We do keep herbs sometimes – though generally only the more exotic ones. But Vesperion will know. If I do have anything I'll send him off with them.' He must have seen my anxious face, because he asked, 'And is there something else that I can help you with?'

'You promised me some records,' I murmured doubtfully.

He gave his hearty laugh. 'That should not be difficult. I have had them out already to show my visitor!' He nodded at Alfredus Allius, who was coming up to join us as he spoke. 'He has shown an impressive interest in the business.'

Alfredus greeted me with courtesy and then said, in that undistinguished voice of his, 'Well, I'm still hoping to become a part of it. Perhaps it will now be easier than we thought, since Genialis is not merely missing, but obviously dead. I regret to say it, but that is welcome news. It will make investment easier for me. Though at the moment I am not wholly certain where I stand.'

I nodded. 'Since it was legally impossible for Genialis to repay his debt on time?' I said, trying to sound as if this was the sort of fact I always had at my command. 'Though I believe that you may still have a claim on the estate.'

He gave a frosty smile. 'You are well-inform-ed, I see. The only trouble is that it may take a little time.'

'Though there is not now a necessity for speed,' Lucius put in. 'And I'm sure Silvia will agree to have you paid, in any case, even if the gold is never found. She would not wish you to sustain a loss because of Genialis and his gam-bling – and as Libertus pointed out to me, there is the house in Dorn to calculate as part of his estate.'

Alfredus nodded. 'I am afraid the man will not be greatly missed. Though we shall all be attending the funeral, I suppose – no one wants to offend the nether world. Though if somebody has really carved the corpse in half, no doubt the spirit will be vengeful anyway!' He turned to me. 'I suppose that story's true? It is what

Adonisius told us when he came back from the search, but it seems so unlikely I can hardly credit it. I know how rumours grow. I believe you saw the body. Can you verify his tale?'

I was about to answer, when I realized what had been niggling in my brain – the piece of the mosaic which had not seemed to fit. I heard myself saying, very carefully, 'Oh, I can confirm that Genialis had been cut in half. And he was not the only one. The same thing happened to an old priest yesterday – as Adonisius pointed out to me.'

'Great Jupiter!' Alfredus looked at Lucius in surprise. 'Did you know of that?'

Lucius nodded soberly. 'Libertus told me of the incident himself.' He turned to me. 'Do you think that is significant?'

'Very significant indeed,' I said. 'And I'm sure that Adonisius thinks so too. He said so earlier. His master thought the two deaths were no coincidence, he said – but obviously his legal owner's dead and Silvia is his mistress if she is anything. I'm sure he meant that it was you who offered the remark.'

Lucius blinked, surprised. 'Well, so I may have done. It would have occurred to anyone, I think.'

'But not to someone who had not seen the second corpse – and could not know what had been done to it. And when would you have had that opportunity? Alfredus Allius has been with you since dawn, but he's just told me that you didn't hear about the condition of Genialis's body until Adonisius got back from the search. Yet the Syrian mentioned your remark to me shortly after the body had been found. He'd not been back here by then. So when did he manage to have this conversation he reports?'

Lucius looked flustered but he said, dismissively, 'He must have simply meant that I would see the parallel – not that I had actually done so, I suppose. I'm sure there's nothing sinister in his account. I've never had the slightest cause to doubt his honesty.'

'But how did Adonisius know about the priest? He wasn't in the forum when I described events to you, and he was with me after that until very late last night – and your other slave–' I nearly called him 'Pustulus' aloud – 'informs me that you had gone to bed before the Syrian got home.'

'I told him first thing this morning, I suppose.' Lucius was beginning to get a little roused. 'I don't remember. Ask him yourself.' He raised his voice and called to Adonisius, who had picked up his load again and was walking slowly up the deck with it: 'Adonisius, do what you're doing with that sack and come back here at once – the citizen has questions he wants to ask of you.'

Adonisius looked wildly at me and, before anyone else could make a move, he had stepped nimbly over ropes and casks and oars until he'd reached the far side of the ship, where it was lying furthest from the shore.

I realized suddenly what he was going to do,

and shouted, 'Stop! I want to see what's in that sack!' but it was far too late. He had already hoisted it above his head and dropped it overboard. It sank at once, as though it were weighted down with stones – as I was beginning to believe it was.

Lucius made a despairing gesture with his hands. 'I'm sorry, citizen. It appears to be too late for you to look at that. But I do not understand. There can be no problem about disposing of that sack – it had begun to stink. I personally told him to get rid of it – I'd actually intended to do so earlier. Alfredus Allius can testify to that.'

Alfred Allius looked from Lucius to me and back again. 'Of course I can, and gladly. It was only venison. Lucius and I discussed it earlier. It entails a small loss of course, but the contents were no longer useable, even by the pie-makers and hot-soup stalls. He tells me he'd have thrown it in the river days ago, but up to now the water was still frozen by the banks and it could not be taken where it was deep enough.'

'Then what was the matter with the midden heap?' I said. 'Except that dogs might show an inconvenient interest in what the sack contains? Because I think you know as well as I do, Lucius, what we shall find in it.'

Alfredus Allius was looking mystified. 'Gentlemen, what is all this about? I wish that you would take me into your confidence. If there's some mystery about what's being traded here, I should be told of it. I am considering an investment in the business, as you know.'

I nodded gravely. 'I don't believe that this concerns the trade in goods, but if I discover otherwise, you'll be the first to know. In the meantime, I want to interview that slave. Can I leave you to ensure that he is held until I come? I wish to have a talk to Lucius first, and I fear that Adonisius might try to run away. However, I am sure you have enough authority to make sure he's detained.'

Alfredus beamed. 'Of course!' The appeal to his purple stripe had rather flattered him. 'I'll see what I can do.' He gave his little undistinguished smile and hurried off towards the captain of the boat.

I turned to Lucius. 'Do you think that we should have this conversation somewhere else? In the office area of your warehouse, perhaps? I should hate to make a public accusation which I afterwards regret.'

Lucius glared at me. 'If you insist. You have your patron's authority for requesting this, I suppose? I may not be a Roman citizen, but I do have certain rights! I've no idea what this is all about.' He led the way, still grumbling, towards his premises.

I paused a moment before I followed him. I could see Alfredus further down the dock, gesturing towards the Syrian slave, who was still aboard the ship staring at the water where the sack had gone. The captain must have given an order which I could not hear, because an instant later Adonisius was seized roughly from the rear. Two burly crew members forced his hands behind his back then dragged him bodily across and lashed him to the mast. I nodded, satisfied. He would be safe until I wanted him.

Then I went into the warehouse where Lucius and his aged steward were awaiting me.

TWENTY-FOUR

Inside it was already dim, of course, despite the candlelight, but the trader signalled to his slave that he should shut the door. He walked along the central aisle, and I thought that he was going to lead me to the house, when suddenly he turned round as if confronting me.

'Now!' he said acerbically. 'I am a busy man.' He gestured to the empty spaces where the now-loaded cargo had been stored. 'What is this all about? I thought you came here wanting hyssop, but it seems that I was wrong. First there is an inquisition about who said what and when – though I can't see that it matters very much. And then this sudden interest in rotting venison. What is the point of that? I could understand if Alfredus had wanted to inspect that sack – he has a possible financial interest in my affairs – but I can't see what on earth it has to do with you. I can assure you that the contents were quite inedible. Not that I can prove it, either way. It is all at the bottom of the river now.'

I looked him coolly in the eye, trying to sound confident of what I said. 'I'm sure a grappling hook could be employed to fetch it up again.

My patron has enough authority for that. And don't I remember there were two sacks anyway?' I gestured to the empty storage place where they had lain. 'Your steward will have a record of the number, I suppose?'

For the first time Lucius looked a little less than confident, but Vesperion took a chalk slate from a slot beside the wall and made a great business of consulting it. 'Two sacks of venison, that's quite right, citizen. The other must have been disposed of earlier today when I was busy somewhere else.' He rubbed out the item with his sleeve to show that it had gone. 'But that it is all in order; I know that it was planned. My master's right – they had begun to smell and were becoming an embarrassment.'

'I am quite sure they were. But then I don't believe that it was venison at all.' I turned back to his master. 'Perhaps you did learn how to preserve things packed in snow from the northern traders, as you claim, but no one keeps a valuable meat until it rots – especially at a time when food is very scarce and there would be a considerable profit to be made. I don't know why I didn't question it before.'

Lucius gave a would-be casual shrug. 'So what are you insinuating, citizen?'

I was about to answer, but he saw my face and all at once he seemed to change his mind. He motioned to the slave. 'Vesperion, you should not be listening to this talk. You can go and collect together all the record scrolls – the ones that I was showing to Alfredus Allius. I promised this citizen that he could borrow them. And check if there is any hyssop left in stock.' Then he added, as the slave looked hesitatingly at the slate, 'Take that with you – what are you waiting for? Close the folding door behind you and stay there until I call!'

Vesperion sighed and did as he was told.

When he was safely out of earshot Lucius turned to me. His tone was sombre now. 'Well, citizen, I gather that – for reasons of your own – you've come to have suspicions of Adonisius. What, exactly, do you suppose that he has done?'

I shook my head. 'It isn't Adonisius I'm suspicious of – it's you. And don't dissimulate. I'm serious when I talk of bringing up that sack – and you know as well as I do what we shall find in it. A decomposing body, isn't that the truth? Or half a body, anyway. The lower half of Genialis, if I am any judge. And by your face, I see that I am right.'

He was about to make some protest but I held up my hand. 'When we do retrieve it, and I'm proved to be correct, you will do yourself more favours if you've confessed the truth. You know what Marcus's inquisitors can do. So, why not save yourself the torment and just tell me everything? Including how you killed him, as I suppose you did – though I must admit that it surprises me. I had not seen you as a murderer.'

He sat down abruptly on a pile of crates. All his bluff bravado had deserted him. 'I didn't murder him – not in the way you understand the word. It would be more accurate to say I made him kill himself.' He looked up at me with strangely empty eyes. 'Citizen, I swear he brought it on himself. I was convinced he'd murdered Ulpius, and it's proved I was correct. If he had been innocent, he would not have died.'

A small piece of mosaic tumbled into place. 'The wine!' I said, remembering the events of yesterday. 'The jug your servant Pistis brought in yesterday. You declared that it was "rubbish" and made him throw it out. But it wasn't rubbish, was it? It was poisonous – and Genialis had given it to Ulpius, you said. You made him drink from it himself at some stage, I suppose?'

He nodded. 'It was laced with poppy juice as well, though there was obviously some kind of poison in it too. Something slow acting – so when poor Ulpius got aboard the ship that fateful night, he was half-drugged and already staggering. I was always convinced that there'd been something of the kind, and that's what made him tumble overboard – Ulpius was far too experienced to have done so otherwise.'

'It was said that he was drunk.'

'I always doubted that. I've never known him take more than a cup or two of wine, and it was always much-watered even then. Especially if he planned to travel, as he sometimes did, to bargain for a cargo further east. There was not even any storm that night. So when this amphora came into my hands, I decided to invite Genialis to drink a bit himself – to prove my theory, or disprove it once and for all.'

I sat down on a small dividing wall beside a pile of little casks which smelt of perfume spice. 'How did you come to have it, anyway? I should have thought that Genialis would have disposed at once of any incriminating evidence like that.'

He shook his head. 'He couldn't do so, at the time. He sent it as a present to Ulpius, at his house – he made sure it was a night when Silvia did not dine, and of course he was not there to share in it himself – and afterwards the servants simply put it all away and nobody suspected there was anything amiss. I understand he ask-ed about it once or twice, once Ulpius was dead – but he couldn't draw too much attention to it by insisting it was found. Though, since he had control of what was in the house by then, he could make sure it wasn't served to anyone by accident. One of the many reasons he took Silvia away. However...'

I saw where this was leading. 'When they were packing up the contents of the house, it came to light?' I said.

'You are percipient, citizen!' Lucius said. 'He made sure that he was watching when they loaded up the wine, and when that particular amphora was produced, he seized on it at once and ordered Adonisius to smuggle it outside. He gave instructions to pour away the remaind-er of the wine, then break up the amphora and leave it on the midden heap – even saying that he'd check there afterwards. He pretended this was simply to prevent the servants stealing wine and getting drunk, since he didn't want to carry an opened amphora all the way to Dorn. But Adonisius had suspicions that there was something more.' He paused and looked at me.

'Go on,' I told him.

'So the Syrian spoke to Silvia – of whom he had naturally grown fond – and she saw the implications instantly. She told him to break up the amphora and put it on the heap – so Genialis would find it when he checked – but first he was to put the wine into a different pot and find an opportunity to bring it here to me.'

'On the promise of freedom, when his master died?' I said, to show that I was following.

'Exactly. And we were extra lucky there. Genialis assigned Adonisius to her, in front of witnesses, before he left Bernadus's country house that day, so now she has a perfect right to free him if she likes, without the need to wait for any legal settlement. She would have tried to do so anyway, I think, even if her guardian had survived the wine – but of course, it was as lethal as we thought. He didn't want to drink it, but I'd tied his hands and I was holding a blade against his throat...' He shrugged. 'It only proved what I'd suspected all along. He killed his half-brother to seize his assets and his wife, so it was a kind of justice – I think you must agree.'

'Justified revenge?' I murmured, thoughtfully. 'That plea might be accepted as mitigation by the courts. But why not take the matter to them in any case? If a man kills his brother, it means exile at the least. That would have solved your problem, without any risk to you.'

He gave me a wry grin. 'You forget that – unlike you – I am not a citizen. Genialis was a wealthy and influential man. You can imagine what chance I would have had. Besides, until I'd made him swallow what was in the flask I had no proof of anything at all.' He gave that rueful smile again. 'Though as soon as I told Genialis what it was, I knew from his face that my suspicions were confirmed. Not that there were any other witnesses to that.'

'So you lured Genialis out to meet you – where? And when? How did you contrive that you should be alone?'

'I sent a message back with Adonisius when he brought the jug. That was in the morning of New Year's Day, while his master was busy with a Kalends visitor and the last of the packing was being loaded on to the cart.'

'A verbal message?'

'That would not have worked. I wrote it on a little scrap of bark paper. Adonisius was not to give it to his master then, but to conceal it for a day or two and then produce it as if it had just arrived. I did not sign or seal the note of course – I affected to be one of his gambling creditors. I said that I had information which could ruin Lucius and if he brought ten golden pieces I'd tell him what it was. I knew he'd fall for that. He was not to bring a slave with him – if there was a witness there would be no deal – and he was to burn the message, which he didn't do of course. I found it on him when I took the purse. I've destroyed it now or I could show you what it said. He was to meet me, on the third day before the Agonalia – there is a little wood yard on a corner along the northern road...'

I nodded. 'I think I know the place. Go on.'

'About midday, I told him. That was the tricky part. There was a risk that there would be other people on the road at noon. Of course, I thought he would be riding back from Dorn, but as it happened they didn't get that far. However, with the snow there was no one much about, and that was not a problem when it came to it. The cold was quite a help in fact – it meant I wore a hood and it was not till we'd both dismounted that he realized it was me.'

'And you attacked him out there on the public road?'

'Hardly an attack!' He gave a rueful grin. 'I'm younger than he is and much fitter too. I simply twisted his arms behind his back, tied him behind his horse, and compelled him down the lane to where the forest starts. There I drew a blade, produced the phial of wine, and the rest I think you know.' He got up with sudden passion. 'The man was gambler, a murderer and a cheat, about to force poor Silvia into a loveless match – and incidentally he was going to ruin me. In my place, citizen, what would you have done?'

I stood up too and murmured thoughtfully, 'I don't think I'd have cut his corpse in two. Far less take half of it and hide it in the snow, and then pretend that it had been there all along. I presume you were also responsible for that?'

He made a little gesture of despair. 'None of that had been the plan at all. I was simply going to let him drink the wine and die and leave him lying in the forest where he fell. He rather surprised me by staggering around for what seemed ages before it took effect. I should have guessed, I suppose, from what had happened to Ulpius earlier – but I began to think I hadn't given him enough. I'd only taken what would fit into a little flask, which I could carry hanging from my belt. But in the end the poison did its work. The trouble was, there was deep snow about and he'd left a lot of footprints while he was stumbling around – and there were my tracks and the marks of both the horses too. I couldn't leave him there – there was so little traffic on the road that anyone could trace where we had been – and the ground was far too hard to bury anything.'

I remembered how I'd followed tracks like those myself today. 'So you put him on your horse and brought him home again?'

He shook his head. 'I did not dare do that. I had no means of covering him up. I went back to the corner where the wood yard was – they supply the warehouse sometimes, and I'd planned to call in with an order anyway, as a reason for being in the area if anyone had noticed I was there. I know they have sacks of sawdust which they sell to inns and I thought I might be able to obtain an empty one. But the owners were not there – they have an ancient mother further down the lane and I suppose that in the snow they'd gone to care for her. So I looked around to see if I could find a hessian bag – but as I did so a rider came along and, of all things, stopped to talk to me. In fact he scared me half to death by asking if I'd seen a purple-striper on the road, riding to Glevum on his own without a slave.'

'Great gods!' I murmured. 'The messenger from Dorn.'

'Exactly, citizen,' Lucius said. 'Though of course I only learned that afterwards. He'd called at the villa and had been told that Genialis had just left. But to his surprise he hadn't caught him up, and the sentry at Glevum reported that he hadn't passed the gate. So he was riding back again the way he'd come, asking anyone he met, in case he'd missed him somewhere on the road. Fortunately he took me for the owner of the yard.'

'And of course you told him you'd seen nobody at all.'

He made a face at this. 'In fact I said that I'd been to and fro all day, collecting wood from down the lane, hoping that would account for all the tracks. But mercifully he wasn't interested in that, he simply thanked me briefly and rode on again. But it was doubly important that I moved the body now – if it was later found in that vicinity he'd certainly remember that he'd seen me there.'

311

'So you went on looking and found yourself a sack?'

He nodded glumly. 'Two sacks. Genialis was too big to fit into a single one. I had to use an axe I borrowed from the yard and chop him into two.'

'You did it very cleanly – I observed that at the time – though I suppose that for you, it wasn't difficult. I'd forgotten that you'd been a woodman in your youth.'

He took the comment as a kind of compliment. 'I tried to do it as neatly as I could. It wasn't desecration I was aiming at. I even moved his clothes to stop them getting stained, but he'd been dead some time by then, and lying in the snow, so he didn't bleed as much as I had feared. I covered up the bloodstains as much as possible, by scraping snow and leaves together with the axe – it even helped to clean the blade before I took it back. Then I cut his horse's bridle and let it wander free and brought my grisly burden home with me.'

'Pretending it was venison, if anyone enquired?'

He almost smiled. 'It did look rather similar – and it's a commodity we've handled once or twice. I didn't mean to take it into store. I thought that I'd be able to drop it in the dock, but I found I couldn't do it straight away because the slaves were always there, stirring the ice to keep it from the quay. So I brought the sacks in here and packed them round with snow, then told Vesperion that it was venison.

312

He didn't question it – he just wrote it in the records as he always did. I tell you, citizen, most of what happened wasn't planned at all. I just did the first thing that came into my head.'

I nodded. 'And you might have got away with it,' I said. 'If you hadn't tried to be too clever at the very last and put half the body out there to be found.'

That rueful smile again. 'I agree it was unfortunate. Especially when Adonisius accidentally betrayed the fact that we'd discussed the details, before I was supposed to know the corpse was found. But when you told me what had happened to the priest...'

'You thought that you could replicate the circumstance, and I would think that there was some connection between the two events?'

'Of course.' He made a noise which was a bitter ghost of his old hearty laugh. 'After all, I had already cut the wretched thing in half. And nothing legal could be sorted out, till Genialis was officially recognized as dead. It almost seemed a kind of augury.'

'So you sent Adonisius out to hide it in the snow, today, after you had sent your other slave to me?'

A nod. 'He had a good horse, so he could carry it, and I knew he would get there much sooner than the searchers in the cart. And since Alfredus Allius was to be here with me, I would have a—' Lucius began, but he got no further. There was a sudden hammering at the door and a flustered Allius put his head round it.

'Citizen Libertus, your patron has arrived. And he has brought the lady Silvia to see Lucius as well. What should I do with them? And what about that slave that they're holding for you on the ship? Silvia says that he belongs to her. Do you still want him, to talk about that sack, or should I do as she requests and let him go?'

I glanced at Lucius. 'I think I have all the information that I need – at least for the present,' I said carefully. 'In the meantime, you may let the Syrian go. Assure the lady that the slave is free to leave with her, but I may wish to talk to him another time. In the meantime, tell my patron that we are on our way.'

Alfredus nodded and went away again.

Lucius was breathing rather heavily. He put his hand into his belt and in the dimness of the lamps, for a moment I thought that he was going to draw a knife, but it was just the rabbit mittens that he'd lent me earlier. 'Have these, citizen, with my thanks,' he said. 'I am more grateful than I can express. I could not bear to think of Silvia in the dock and poor Adonisius only did what I had told him to. I'm happy to take all responsibility myself – I hope you will tell them that I confessed the truth, though I know I can expect the cruellest punishment. What is it that you plan to do with me?'

I looked at the offering he was holding out. He was not an evil man at heart, I thought – his attempt to shield his two accomplices had rather touched my heart. And the penalty for carving up a citizen would be a dreadful one – however much the victim had deserved his fate. All the same...

'You have some gold, I think?' I asked him urgently. 'Genialis had some in his purse. Ten gold pieces, I believe you said?'

He looked surprised and troubled. 'You want me to give you that? I thought you might have seen the offer of money as a bribe. I do have them somewhere – there was no point in leaving gold pieces on the corpse – and Silvia brought the rest to Glevum when she came. I was going to see that Alfredus Allius got them back, somehow.'

'So the search for the money at the villa was a sham?'

He shook his head. 'Well not exactly that. The money had already got to me by then, and we could hardly explain how I had come by it. There was more than forty aureii in all. It isn't really mine. But if it's the price of silence...?' He looked as if I'd rather disappointed him. 'Though perhaps – all things considered – it would be best if you simply hand me over to the authorities. I can't afford to go on paying you for years, as you'd no doubt require.'

I shook my head. 'You mistake my motives, trader. I was thinking, rather, that since you had some gold, then you could start again elsewhere. If, for instance, you chose to sail to Gaul tonight, accompanying that cargo that they were loading when I came? I'm sure the captain would agree to carry you – and your wife and servant – if you arranged to pay.'

He was staring at me in perplexity. 'My wife and serv— Oh, I see! You mean that you'd say nothing until we'd got away?'

'You have satisfied my curiosity and I applaud your honesty – but I have my ethics, too, and in the end I'll have to tell my patron what I know. But not necessarily for a day or two. Genialis was an evil man and you are a kindly one. It serves no purpose to have you put in jail – or worse,' I told him patiently.

I thought he was about to fling himself before my feet, but in the end he simply seized my hand. 'You think she would come with me?' His face was bright with hope. 'Do you know, citizen, I believe she would! She was going to come here after Genialis died, even if it meant forfeiting her status and estate, and by and by she would become my wife in common law – but then your patron came and overruled the scheme...' He stopped abruptly, looking crestfallen. 'Ah! Your patron! I had forgotten him. He is now her legal guardian, of course. He would never permit her to come away with me. And even if she wanted to defy him and elope, it would not be easy to escape his vigilance: every moment when he isn't there himself, she's got that nurse to keep an eye on her.'

I gave an inward sigh. I had not meant to get involved in this. But in for a quadrans, in for a denarius! I dropped one eyelid in a knowing wink. 'Give those lovely mittens to His Excellence,' I said. 'Tell him they're a thank-you present for his wife, and leave the rest to me.'

So saying, I led the way outside, blinking in the sudden brightness of the day.

TWENTY-FIVE

Marcus was standing on the quayside by his horse, clearly impatient at the short delay. It was unusual for him to have to wait for anyone and he'd obviously made no secret of the fact; the captain and Alfredus Allius were fussing round him like a pair of anxious ants. My patron was in his winter finery, a blue fur-lined cape and purple leather boots, and had become the centre of a small admiring crowd: dock slaves, street-hawkers, boat crew, customers, even a Roman soldier in full uniform – presumably sent here to protect the quay in case of any repetition of last night's disturbances – all of them edging closer to get a better look. Normally this sort of thing would flatter him, but today he was tapping his baton on his thigh in a way that I recognized as dangerous.

I made my best obeisance, dropping to one knee despite the uneven kerbstones, which were bitter cold. 'Patron!' I murmured, taking his hand and pressing my lips against his ring. 'Forgive me for not being here to welcome you at once. The news is so distressing; it has taken us some time to come to terms with it. Though you must be pleased that Genialis has been

318

found; it ratifies your role as guardian of Silvia, after all.'

Marcus said 'Humph!' but did not withdraw his hand.

That was a good sign and I scrambled to my feet and greeted the lady in question with a distant bow. She was standing apart on the outskirts of the crowd, where she had just been helped gently to the ground by a rumpled Adonisius and a mounted page. She had clearly been a passenger on the page's horse – although I knew quite well that she could ride herself, at need. She was still dressed in deepest mourning, as she had been throughout, though she had abandoned her attractive Grecian fashion for a more sober black cape and stola now – but as she saw me she pulled aside her veil, and her face was as lively and beautiful as it had always been. There was not the slightest evidence or pretence at grief.

'Citizen Libertus!' She flashed her charming smile. 'I am glad to find you here. And Lucius as well. I am doubly favoured.'

'Madam, I offer you condolences,' I said warningly. 'It must be alarming for you, learning of the state in which your former guardian was found.'

I saw the look that she exchanged with Lucius and realized that she'd already known. I wondered when she'd had the opportunity to talk to him alone – but, since he had accompanied her to Marcus's villa a day or two ago, I decided that he must have told her then.

But my tone had reminded her of the role she had to play. 'It was a shock,' she answered, soberly. 'Though I'm certain that my friends will do the best they can for me, and ensure that his body gets the treatment it deserves.'

That was ambiguous, and she'd intended it to be. I remembered suddenly the first time that we'd met – Lucius had spoken of Genialis then as though he was already certain he was dead, and she'd corrected him. The lady had a considerable wit and intellect. Lucius would have his hands full if he married her.

But my patron was addressing me. 'Bernadus is arranging the funeral, I believe. He was the one who told us that we would find you here. He said you'd come for hyssop to purify the corpse – though apparently the funeral women have arrived and they said to tell you they have all the herbs they need.'

Lucius bustled forward. 'Then I'll let my steward know. He is searching the warehouse records for it, as we speak.' He turned to Marcus. 'Mine is a humble household, Excellence, but what there is I place at your command. Would you care to enter and take some wine perhaps?'

'You are courteous, trader, but we won't impose on you.' Marcus contrived to sound at once polite and yet appalled. 'I came to find Libertus and tell him of my plans – and to bring Silvia back to my apartment in the town, since I understand the funeral will be held in Glevum now. I'm sure that she will want to oversee things for herself. I'll make arrangements for her to stay here for a while – her attendant nurse is already on the way. I myself propose to go to Rome within a day or two. It will mean a journey in ill-starred Februarius, but that's unavoidable.' He gave me a proud smile. 'I presume, Libertus, you've heard the news that my old friend and patron is confirmed as Emperor?'

There was a ragged cry from somewhere in the crowd – 'Hail Pertinax!' – and it was taken up by others instantly until the quayside echoed with the chant. I had almost forgotten that there were people listening in. 'I don't think you need worry that he lacks support. The town is full of banners and garlands praising him,' I said to Marcus under cover of the din. 'And images of Commodus have been torn down and burned.'

He shook his head and frowned. 'Honour is due to the title of Emperor itself, irrespective of the person holding it,' he said. 'This kind of thing is actually dangerous. Mobs are volatile and can change their minds. This makes it still more urgent that I get to Rome.'

I was likely to lose him as my patron very soon, I thought. He was already talking like a chief advisor to the Imperial throne – a role in which he doubtless saw himself. But I had seen an opening and I seized it with both hands. 'And your lady wife? She will accompany you? Because Gwellia thinks...' I moved a little closer and whispered in his ear.

He gazed at me in genuine surprise. 'Julia!

But surely...' His face was flushed with sudden joy. 'It's true, she has wanted to talk to me in private for some days, but with Silvia there and Lucius it has not been practical – and I've not disturbed her in the evening because she's not been well ... Oh, great gods! I do see what you mean. Why by great Olympus did I not think of it?' He reached out and took my arm – a friendly gesture I had almost never known him make before. 'Libertus, my old friend, I have misjudged you, I'm afraid. I thought you'd grown too old for solving mysteries – this one appears to have defeated you. But I see that you're still your old observant self. Remind me to reward you for your perspicacity.'

I was about to protest that it was not my perspicacity at all, and that I was only guessing even now, but some instinct for self-preservation stopped me just in time. In any case Marcus would not have heeded me. 'But that makes things very difficult,' he was exclaiming now. 'If she's in that condition, what am I to do? I can't take her with me all the way to Rome, especially at this season of the year – and I don't like to leave her on her own. And yet I am convinced that it's imperative I go. Just listen to this crowd.' There was still sporadic cheering and much waving of wool caps. 'If this sort of thing is also happening in Rome, you mark my words there will be riots very soon.'

I did not point out that there had been riots here already. Instead I murmured gently, 'What you need is the services of an experienced nurse and midwife to stay with Julia. You still have that Nutricia, haven't you? She attended Julia last time, at Marcellinus's birth. I know that you've given her on loan to Silvia – but I imagine any handmaiden would serve as well for that. Come to think of it, I know Bernadus has a girl slave at his house in town. He might be persuaded to part with her, I think.'

Marcus clapped me on the back. 'Well thought of, my old friend. I'll go and talk to him. If you don't think that Silvia would mind such an exchange.'

'I'm certain that she won't.' In fact, she'd be delighted, I thought privately. No one else would keep so close an eye on her. 'And meanwhile I'll accompany Silvia to your flat. Or let Lucius do that – he'll look after her and she'll have Adonisius to attend her, too. I will go and speak to Bernadus about the slave. That way you can get straight back to Julia – and maybe intercept Nutricia on the way. Don't concern yourself about the funeral here – there are other people to take care of it, and you can pay them later out of Genialis's estate.'

Marcus was hardly listening to all this. His mind was entirely set on Julia and Rome. 'Very well!' he told me. 'I'll leave it up to you. In the meantime, I don't like this mob. Things could very easily get out of hand. Fetch me that soldier and we'll try to quiet them.'

I looked around and saw that he was right. The rhythmic chanting was much louder now and everybody on the quay was joining in: dock slaves had put their burdens down, despite their masters' protests by the look of it, and were stamping to the beat. A pie seller was jumping up and down, waving his empty tray above his head, and even the more respectable were swaying to and fro, clapping their hands and shouting with the rest. No one was any longer thinking what the chant was for.

Only our little party seemed to be aloof. Alfredus Allius was at the warehouse door, talking to Adonisius and Vesperion who appeared to be staggering beneath a load of scrolls. Lucius had taken Silvia aside and was murmuring something to her, under cover of the noise, and when she saw me looking she raised a hand to me in what was very clearly a gesture of salute. Lucius, I realized, was nodding happily – it was not difficult to guess what conversation had passed between the two.

However, I had my patron's errand to perform. I went up to the soldier – who was joining in the chant, banging his baton cheerfully against his shield – but he broke off when I came to speak to him. I gestured to Marcus and explained what he had said.

Instantly the soldier became a different man. He put the baton in his belt and drew his sword instead, rapped that on the ground and held it overhead. 'Enough! Disperse now! In the name of Pertinax!'

For a moment this did not seem to have very much effect. A few of the nearer chanters broke off uncertainly – nudging their neighbours and pointing out the blade. Slowly, one by one the others stopped as well and there was an uneasy shuffling. Then one dock slave picked up his burden and took it up the plank towards the ship, and a moment later everyone was back at work again, doing whatever had brought them to the dock. Only the pie seller was shouting now, calling down every deity in the pantheon, as he scrabbled on the paving tiles to retrieve his scattered wares – but even the gods could hardly help him now; most of his pies had been trodden on and squashed and all of them were broken into bits.

The soldier put his sword back in his sheath and marched across the dock to where my patron was standing. 'In the name of his most Imperial majesty, the Caesar Com— I mean Pertinax...'

Marcus held up a held to silence him. 'That was well-managed, soldier. May I know your name?'

The soldier gave it, together with his rank.

'I will mention this to your superiors! Now you may dismiss and go back to your duties.'

The man saluted and marched proudly off. I noticed that when he took up his post again, he stood more upright, and looked a lot more military than he'd done before.

Marcus turned to me. 'Then I'll take the horses and go back to Julia and the villa straight away. Though, perhaps I should take my wife a little gift?'

I beckoned Lucius across. 'I think that this

trader has a little something for her anyway. A present for your hostess, is that not the case?'

Lucius looked surprised, but he produced the gloves. 'A thank you for your household's hospitality,' he murmured, making a low bow. 'Finest rabbit, from Iberia. We import...'

But Marcus had no interest in the warehouse now. 'Very fine. And thank you for the thought. Though they're generous in size. If I am to travel all the way to Rome...' He slipped a mitten on his hand – it fitted perfectly. 'I'll ask her what she thinks.' He slipped the gloves between his toga folds and underneath his belt. 'Now, I'll leave you to Libertus. He knows what I have planned.' He raised his voice. 'Farewell, Alfredus! And you, slave, bring the horses over here.'

The boy obeyed, assisted Marcus to his mount, and the pair of them went cantering away.

Alfredus and Vesperion came hurrying across, accompanied at a distance by Adonisius, who was still clearly keeping space between himself and me. The captain hastened over at that moment too.

'Trader Lucius, if there is more to take aboard, we need to load at once. We must leave by sunset if we're to catch the tide.'

Lucius didn't answer. Instead he looked at me. 'Citizen, your patron spoke about a plan. What did he mean by that?'

I outlined what I had suggested to my patron earlier. I didn't mention ships, of course –

326

Lucius would have to work out for himself that there was now an opportunity. 'So if you take charge of Silvia and the Syrian slave,' I finished, silkily, 'Alfredus and I will go back into town. He can talk to Bernadus about the funeral – and tell him that expenses will be paid from the estate: I'll just call in briefly to enquire about that slave girl Marcus wants. And – though I doubt that they'll be wanted now – I'll take those scrolls with me. I am anxious to get back to Minimus and my wife as soon as possible. Fortunately I have a mule to get me there.'

In fact I was especially anxious to have witnesses to this, and proof of my movements for an hour or two. If Lucius and the lady were about to disappear, I wanted it known that I was somewhere else.

Alfredus nodded. 'Let's be on our way. If you are hoping to get back home tonight, you had better hurry – even with a mule. In an hour or less it will be getting dark.'

I was about to turn away, but Lucius grasped my arm. 'Thank you, citizen. We will not forget.'

'I doubt that I will, either,' I told him with a smile, then – together with my witness – I turned and left him there.

TWENTY-SIX

When I reached the workshop a little later on, Minimus was positively hopping with concern.

'Master,' he greeted me, throwing himself with unaccustomed fervour at my feet. I thought for a moment he was going to kiss my boots. 'I had begun to wonder what had become of you. If there are really crazed murderers about – as the commander of the town watch seems to think – when you were late I was not sure if I would see you back alive.'

'Well, here I am alive and well.' I put down the pile of scrolls that I was carrying. 'But, unlike the commander of the watch, I don't think there's any danger of this happening again, though I'm glad you managed to deliver your messages successfully.'

'So you've solved the mysteries?'

'Not exactly that. But I understand at least a little better now. And I think I can promise that, after yesterday, it isn't going to happen again.'

Minimus was busy packing scrolls into our linen bag. He screwed his nose up, like a rodent sniffing cheese. 'You mean because the new Emperor has been confirmed? Everyone at the garrison is saying that Commodus was cursed, but now that Pertinax is Emperor instead, the gods will be appeased. No more dark omens; everything is going to be much better from now on.'

I patted his small head, indulgently. 'If the army says so, then perhaps it's true. I do think that omens may have been involved. But get your cloak on and let's be on our way. And don't cram any more scrolls in that bag – you'll damage them. You'll have to carry the others in your arms while we ride home.'

It wasn't easy either. Arlina seemed to know that she was losing me as master very soon. She ambled so slowly it would almost have been quicker to have gone on foot – despite the switch I was deploying on her rump. Minimus was too busy clutching scrolls to help and I was not sorry when at last my roundhouse came into sight.

I stopped at the enclosure entrance and let Minimus get down.

'You go inside and let your mistress know you're here. I'll take this creature to its owner, and then I'll come myself. And make sure that you take care of those records while I'm gone. I'm going to need to read them overnight so I can report to Marcus before he leaves for Rome.'

I was serious in this. Of course, I knew that there would be no question of investment now – half the warehouse and its contents would be forfeit to the state, once Lucius was legally a fugitive, especially if a charge of *raptus* –

abduction – was entered against him in the courts. And that was possible. The fact that Silvia was a willing victim did not change the case. Alternatively, Marcus as her guardian could decide to let her go without entering a formal plea of rape – and in so doing ratify the match.

But whether Marcus chose to recognize their union as a legal one or not, it would be a year before a *usus* marriage would apply. In the meantime he would still have governance over her estate (one reason why I doubted that he'd try to bring her back) so my business information might be useful in the end. He might yet want to find a buyer for her share of everything – even if Lucius's portion had been forfeited.

Minimus had dropped a number of the scrolls in getting off the mule and he was busily engaged in gathering them up when there was a cry of 'Master!' from behind the palisade and Maximus came running out into the lane. I allowed him to greet me and then I sent him on to help pick up the scrolls. 'Tell your mistress that I shall be hungry by and by,' I called, and leaving them to it, I rode off down the lane.

Arlina seemed a lot livelier with a smaller load and it was not long before we reached the farm. Once at the gate I slipped down from my seat – or more accurately, I lumbered down, keeping my balance by leaning on the wall – and was about to enter when I heard a voice.

'Citizen? You have returned more quickly than I thought.' It was Cantalarius, who was

330

raking hay into the enclosure where the mules were kept. I noticed that the second mule was looking better fed. I was about to say so, when he put away the rake (a sorry object made of iron nails, hammered roughly through a piece of wood and attached to a handle, though it seemed to serve) and came across to meet me at the gate. He wiped both grubby hands on the sacking round his waist and held one out to me. 'I hope Arlina has been satisfactory? Did you succeed in finding that missing councillor?'

'Half of him at any rate,' I said, and was interested to notice that he turned deathly pale. Encouraged by that visible response I said remorselessly, 'Rather like that ancient priest who promised to come here.' I was suddenly convinced that Cantalarius knew more about that incident than he'd been telling me.

I had been rather hoping to surprise him into speech but, though he was clearly shaken, he said nothing more, except, 'Well I'm glad you found the mule to be of use.'

He took the halter from me and led Arlina into the enclosure with the other animal, where – while murmuring endearments in her ear – he removed the harness and put it in the stone hut as before. Then he smacked her on the rump to urge her off towards the hay. By the time he had joined me and shut the gate again, she had already shouldered her companion to one side and was munching happily.

'Was there something else that I can do to help you, citizen?'

I was startled at the question, although – of course, since I had already paid him for the hire – there was really nothing further that should detain me here. However, I was unwilling to leave him without one more attempt to find out what he knew about the body in the pond. Besides, I'd grown unreasonably fond of his stupid, plucky, self-willed animal.

So I said slowly, 'Well, I shall come to you again, if I require a mule.' I was struck by inspiration. 'Could we come to some more permanent arrangement, possibly? I couldn't continue to pay you at that rate all the time – but if I were to have her, say, once or twice a month? Could some sort of deal be arrived at, do you think?'

He looked at me suspiciously, but then seemed to conclude that I was serious. He heaved a heavy sigh. 'Well, I use the mules a lot myself, but I can't pretend I'd not be glad of a bit of regular income of that kind. Perhaps you'd better come into the house. Though give me a moment to prepare my wife. She's busy cooking dinner and plucking a dead goose – since we lost the slaves she has to do that sort of work herself – so she'll be all covered in feathers, and not prepared for visitors.'

I nodded. My own wife, Gwellia, would have felt the same. 'I'll follow at a distance,' I told him, and I did. It was only yesterday that I'd been here last, but already the farm was looking less forlorn. The milder weather had allowed the stock to come outside and I could see half a dozen hungry-looking sheep cropping the thin grass in the nearer field, and there was a thin goat tied up in the corner of the yard, while a few bedraggled geese and chickens pecked among the flags. The barn door was half-open as I passed, and when I looked inside I could see the slave mute inside, forking straw about, and there was feed stuff in the manger baskets on the wall. Cantalarius had clearly put my aureus to use.

The slave looked up and saw me and waved a clumsy hand, making a sort of formless roar I took to mean, 'Hello.'

I shouted 'Greetings!' and went on to the house, though the mean-faced mongrel bared its ugly teeth at me and growled. It was tied up to a post beside the empty shrine and it could not reach me, so I did not greatly care.

Cantalarius came bustling out as I approached, bearing two stools and a pitcher full of wine. 'Sit down for a moment. My wife will soon be here. She says she has some flatbread baking on the fire and we have some soft-curd cheese that we can offer you.'

'You are very kind,' I muttered, though I was not keen. I have eaten that kind of home-made cheese before – thin and sour, like scarcely curdled whey. I'd come to prefer the firmer kind the Romans liked – Gwellia had learned to make it when she was a slave. It involved a lot of arcane processes – straining, rinsing, pressing, drying and the gods know what – but it was well worth the effort and she was proud of it. I couldn't imagine that Gitta would make a cheese like that.

I was right. When a moment later she came hurrying out, in a clean green tunic which she'd clearly just put on, she was carrying a pan with runny curds in it, and a bowl containing a steaming hunk of bread. She too was looking better than she had done yesterday: her face was more composed, the wild hair drawn back in a tidy plait, and the simple cut and colour of her robe showed off her tall form and her shapely legs. I could see why Cantalarius was so attached to her.

She set the foodstuffs down beside us on the ground. 'I'll fetch a knife and bowls for you,' she said. 'And a pair of goblets so you can drink the wine.' She gave me a doubtful smile. 'Cantalarius tells me that you have a proposition to discuss and that you want to hire the mule again? I gather it was useful to you yesterday.'

'Indispensable,' I told her heartily. 'You knew that I was searching for a missing councillor? Well he was found this morning, or half of him was at least.'

I had said it in the hope of provoking some response, but I could have not guessed how effective it would be. She dropped the spoon that she was holding and made a dash at me, pummelling my chest and arms with both her fists. 'How dare you, citizen! You can't come blaming Cantalarius for that one, too! He hasn't left the farm since you came here yesterday – except to buy some hay and foodstuffs from a trader at the gate. He's been here with me and Sordinus all the time.' Every syllable was punctuated by a blow, each strong enough to bruise.

I caught her hands and held them, though she tried to struggle free. She was quite athletic and I had to hold her hard, putting one arm around her waist to pinion her, while she attempted to continue her attack. I was quite breathless with the effort, but I contrived to say over my shoulder, to Cantalarius, 'So after all you did not pay the money-lender back?'

Gitta stopped struggling suddenly, and whirled her head around to glower at her spouse. 'What money-lender, husband? You didn't mention that! Dear gods, don't tell me that we are still in debt!'

He shook his head. 'Gitta, be silent. It is not what it sounds. I will explain it later.'

I had a sudden surge of confidence. 'You will explain it now! I don't believe you got that money from a lender after all. I think you may have got it from the body of the priest. What did Gitta mean by what she said just now – that I couldn't come here blaming you for the other death "as well"? You know more about that sacerdos than you are telling me. What happened? Did you go back to the temple after dusk? I hear they found a ladder by the sacred grove – was that because you'd used it to climb across the wall?'

Gitta had started struggling again. 'You can't prove anything!' she spat through gritted teeth.

'There was nobody about. They were all at the evening sacrifice by then – he told me that no one could possibly have seen him climbing in.'

'Gitta!' Cantalarius's voice was hollow with despair. 'When will you ever learn to hold your tongue? Don't you realize what your foolish words have done? You might as well have told him outright that I went back to see the priest!'

I forced her hands a little further up her back and she let out a squeal. 'To kill him?' I enquired. 'Tell me, or you can see what I will do!' In fact I think he guessed that I would never injure her – and if anybody was in danger, it was very likely me. I said quickly, 'And I shouldn't plan to murder me as well, if I were you. My patron knows I came here, to return the mule, so if I go missing he'll know who to blame – and you know what kind of penalty you'd be facing then. Bad enough that you have killed a priest. That is what you went back for, that evening, I presume?'

The farmer let out a helpless little moan. 'Of course I didn't, citizen. What help would that have been? I didn't want a dead priest, but a living one. I went back to confront him for a final time, that's all – one last attempt at persuading him to come.'

'But I thought he had agreed...' I began, then shook my head. 'But of course he hadn't really. Go on with your tale. Your wife – as you say – has implicated you, and you have acknowledged the truth of what she said. That is quite enough for me to call the guard and have you formally arraigned before the courts, but I'm prepared to hear your version of events.' It was mere bravado. From where I was at present, I'd be lucky to escape if I made the least attempt to go and summon the authorities.

But Cantalarius seemed quite willing to go on. 'When I went to talk to him that afternoon – took him that image of the god and everything – I thought that he was ready to agree to come. But at the last moment he seemed to change his mind. He said that I would need to bring him twice as much in gold, and then perhaps he would consider it. He was actually laughing when he said the words. I was so furious that I tried to take my offerings back – but he prevented me. Said they were donations to the gods and if I tried to take them, he would call the guard. I don't know if you've seen the temple-slaves at all, but some of them are huge.'

I nodded. 'And immensely strong, as I have cause to know.'

He shrugged. 'In that case you can see how hopeless it would be for a hunchback like myself to try to tackle one, if they came to throw me out. I tried to reason with him, but he only laughed at me and in the end I had to give it up. I went back to the market where I had left the mules – and found there was a little hay and straw for sale, enough to save my livestock, if I only had the money with which to purchase it. But of course I hadn't; I had given it away to that confounded priest. Well, I was determined that I would get it back. I told the vendor to await me at the southern gate and keep some hay for me. He promised that he would. That left me with the problem of getting to the priest. I knew that the temple would be closed by then – they would all be busy with the evening sacrifice, except the slaves on duty at the portico – so I tried to find some other way of getting in.'

'The sacred grove, of course! Outside the temple proper, but still inside the grounds. And there was a building site not far away,' I said. 'With a convenient ladder as I said before? And you used that to go across the wall?'

'Don't tell him, husband!' Gitta twisted round and tried to dig her teeth into my arm, and I had to restrain more vigorously again.

Cantalarius heaved a heavy sigh. 'He seems to know about it anyway! And he is right, of course. One of those simple ladders – just a single piece of wood with steps lashed across it, but it was perfect for the task, because it had a weighted rope attached. I could throw it up and make it safe against the wall, then pull the ladder over after me and climb down safely on the other side. My first intention was to try and find his private room – where I had gone to see him earlier in the day – and wait for him to come back from the sacrifice. But then I saw him standing at the window of his cell, or at least I thought I did – praying to Fortuna and the moon.'

I nodded. 'One of the temple-slaves observed him too.'

338

This caused a bitter laugh from Cantalarius. 'Only, of course, it wasn't him at all. That was the thing that made me angriest. I recognized the right room when I got inside, and managed to reach it without being seen. In fact, I was surprised that there was nobody about. No one expects intruders in a temple complex, I suppose – especially not in the dormitory area. In any case, I found the door with ease. I even tiptoed in – I did not want to disturb him at his prayers. And what did I discover? He was sitting on the bed, counting money into little piles. He had put that image in the window space, put his cloak and hood on it and stood it where only the outline would be seen – so that people would think that he was worshipping the moon. He was worshipping the money! That's what angered me. He'd cheated me of everything, and he was a fraud!'

'So that is why you killed him!' I prompted, helpfully.

'I tell you that I didn't!' He half-rose and bellowed, and for a frightened moment I thought he'd lunge for me, but he sat down again and added ruefully: 'I admit that for a moment I was afraid I had. When he looked up and saw me, it gave him such a fright that he gave a gasp and clutched his chest, rolled his eyes back and tumbled off the bed. I was convinced that I had frightened him to death.'

'And had you?'

'Of course he hadn't!' Gitta's voice was shrill. 'He'd fainted, that was all. If my precious husband only had the wit to leave him there and run away, that would probably have been the end of it. But that was too simple! Once he found the man was breathing, he had a new idea. He would bring him to the farm and make him perform the atoning sacrifice before we let him go. After all, we'd more than paid for it, he said.'

I looked at her husband, who was sitting with his head between his hands. 'Is that true?' I asked him.

'It's not as idiotic as she makes it sound,' he grumbled. 'The priest knew who I was in any case – if I had run away and left him, you can imagine what he'd do. Claim that I'd come to rob him, at the very least – that would be a charge of sacrilege – and you know the dreadful punishments for that!'

'And you didn't rob him?' I said sarcastically. 'I thought that's where you got that money which I saw in your purse.'

'I only took exactly what I had given him. And I even left the jewels that had been the statue's eyes – can you believe that he'd extracted them? From the image of a god! And he a priest as well! The man had no respect whatever for the deities. And I couldn't bear to see it standing where he should have stood himself – I took it down and laid it on the floor beside the bed. I expect they'll find it, if they look for it.'

I nodded. I was beginning to have some sympathy with this unhappy tale. 'So then what happened? You took him to the ladder and across the wall? And no one saw you? That sounds difficult.'

He shook his head. 'He was so thin and frail that he was feather-light. Less than a full-grown ram in any case, and he wasn't struggling. I could have carried him one-handed, if I'd tried. I put him round my shoulders as if he were a sheep, climbed over and pulled the ladder after me. I didn't even stop to put it back, just went to where I'd left the mules tied up, put the priest's body on the frame that I'd used to bring the image into town, covered him with the blanket that I'd wrapped it in and rode back to the farm. Several people saw me, but it occasioned no remark – no one thinks twice about a farmer with a loaded mule, and in any case it was getting dark by then. I even found the trader at the southern gate and managed to buy a little hay from him – just a sheaf or two that I could tie on top. I suppose it made me even less remarkable.'

'So when you got here, he was still alive?' I said, incredulous.

Gitta let out a long, despairing wail. 'If only that were true! I told him it was stupid. A frail old man like that! And after having given him a dreadful shock as well!' All the struggle had gone out of her, and suddenly her frame was racked with sobs. 'So there you are! You know now! I told you we were cursed!'

I let her hands go, and she raised them to her face, covering her eyes and the tears that flowed from them. 'But I don't know,' I said gently. 'I understand that he was dead when he arrived – but not how he contrived to be discovered in that pond. Nor how half of him was missing by that time. I don't believe in demons. I presume you put him there?'

Cantalarius had lumbered to his feet. 'Citizen, I'll tell you, but first I need a drink.' He picked up the pitcher and brandished it at me. 'Would you care to join me? I will get a beaker each. Stay, wife!' he added, as she broke away from me – but he was too late and she had already wriggled free.

She was flushed and weeping and utterly distraught – what I have heard physicians call 'hysterical', though I am not convinced it is an affliction of the womb. At all events she was disturbed enough to stamp her feet and shout. 'I'll tell him, husband! What does it matter now! We shall both be executed anyway, for the illegal abduction of a priest! They can't do any more to us for bleeding him and trying to use his blood as sacrifice.'

I looked at Cantalarius. He put the pitcher down and came across to take her in his arms. She was red-faced and ugly with distress, but he looked at her as tenderly as if she were his bride. 'It was my fault, citizen. She thought of the idea – what blood could be more pleasing to the gods than priestly blood? – but she'd never have put it into practice but for me. And we did try to give him a decent funeral – in fact you almost interrupted it...'

'The pyre!' I said. 'How simple! Why, of course! And then, of course, you said it was a slave!'

He nodded. 'I wondered if you'd notice that our last slave was still alive, but you did not question it. We had lost several others and we had kept the pyre alight – so adding him to it seemed an obvious thing to do, a kind of burnt offering even, to appease the deities. We even washed the body and treated it with herbs – and that's when we discovered the final insult to the gods! You know the fellow should not have been a priest at all? A priest must be physically perfect in all respects, of course – is that not always a prerequisite?'

'No limp; no impediment of hearing, speech or sight; and no physical or mental deformity,' I quoted, in assent.

'Only he had a birthmark, across both his upper thighs. A great big purple birthmark, bigger than my hand. Someone must have bribed the temple priests when he was young, for them to have accepted him at all.'

'Surely it is possible that it developed afterwards?' I said. 'These things do happen sometimes, I believe. And priests can go on acting when they are frail and old – after all, apart from the Servirs of the Imperial cult, a priesthood of the Roman deities is generally for life.'

He shook his head. 'I know a birthmark when I see one. I should do; I was born with one myself. And it was always held to be a sign of judgement from the gods – an indication that I

343

was born unworthy and unclean – like this crooked shoulder that I bear. How could I offer that to purify my land? I cut off the offending limbs, and wrapped them in his priestly robes and took him to the pond next morning before light. I knew the place where the other corpse was found – perhaps that's what gave me the idea – and we put him where the ice had already been disturbed. I knew that someone would soon discover him – I thought perhaps that would prevent a further search and people would simply think that he'd been gnawed by wolves. The last one had been, so I understand. But I reckoned without your involvement, citizen.'

There was nothing much that I could say to that. 'So that is why the temple was so sure that it was him! They must have known about the birthmark too – but of course they couldn't say so publicly. No doubt that's also why they held the funeral so soon and privately. And, judging by the fact that you had put him on the pyre – or the part of him that you were offering to the gods – very shortly before I got here with my slave, both halves were cremated not very far apart. I see now why your wife was so upset when we interrupted that – especially when we talked about a missing man. Where have you put the ashes?'

He let go of sobbing Gitta to wave a hairy hand. 'You are looking at them, citizen. We put them on the land. Isn't that the way to use a cleansing sacrifice? But there you are. We

344

meant no disrespect. For one wild moment, we thought you might be right – the sacrifice we'd offered had removed the curse – but of course I realize now that it was quite the opposite. Though I have to tell you, citizen, this has been a relief. I have not slept a moment since I found that he was dead. In fact I tried to tell you once before – but you misinterpreted. I'd said that I'd been tempted in the marketplace...'

'I thought you meant the money-lenders!' I said, remembering.

He nodded. 'Precisely, citizen. But now you know the truth. So what, exactly, do you mean to do with us? I am unimportant – I am ruined anyway. But after all, perhaps you could contrive to save my wife? She was going to leave me, because she thought me cursed – poor creature, it turns out that she was right. Could you let her get away and go back to her home? Then it doesn't matter what becomes of me.'

Perhaps it was that plea that made up my mind for me. Or perhaps it was Gitta sobbing as she clung to him. 'Husband, don't say that. It's my foolish tongue again. I should not have threatened that I was going to leave. How could I know that you would take it so to heart? You're old and you're ugly, but you've been good to me. How could I let you make a sacrifice like that?'

It was not entirely clear what sacrifice she meant, but Cantalarius looked as thrilled as if he'd found the golden fleece. 'You hear that, citizen?' he said to me. 'Perhaps she would not have left me after all.'

I did not have the heart to point out what this meant – that all his bargaining and worry was in vain and that he need not have troubled with the priest at all. But I had come to a conclusion. Earlier I had let Lucius and Silvia escape, on the grounds that they were honest and that no purpose would be served by handing them over to the authorities. I could not in fairness do any different now. These people were not wealthy – they had neither charm nor beauty or much intelligence – but they deserved no less.

'Listen,' I said. 'I have a proposition for you. Pour me a cup of wine, and I will tell you what it is.'

EPILOGUE

Marcus was in a jovial and expansive mood when I arrived with my report, and from the way that he was leading Julia by the arm and looking at her in that doting way, it was clear that Gwellia's assumptions had been right.

'Well, Libertus!' he said heartily, seating her on the most comfortable folding chair and taking the less ornate one for himself. 'Have you heard the news? Peculiar, isn't it, the way these things turn out?'

'News, Excellence?' I murmured.

He patted the stool beside him, inviting me to sit. 'Of course, it's disappointing, from your point of view. Usually you're clever at unravelling mysteries. But not even you could have worked this out, I think! It turns out that Ulpius was murdered after all – and Silvia and Lucius suspected all along.'

I had the wit to feign surprise at this.

'And you'll never guess who did it,' he went on gleefully. 'That guardian of hers. Lucius has actually demonstrated that – though he had to kill the culprit in the course of proving it. I don't quite understand what happened to the corpse. I think he hid it somewhere, but of course they've found it now, and Bernadus has arranged a funeral for it. Just as well, since Lucius and Silvia have fled. Silly people, they feared I'd prosecute – of course I would never do anything like that. Such a charming lady. I wouldn't wish her harm.'

'She's declared a usus marriage and gone to Gaul with him!' That was Julia, blooming, as she plumped her cushions up. 'I'm glad to think she's happy, and has found a man she likes.' And glad it wasn't Marcus, her expression said, though of course she did not voice the thought aloud. 'They wrote us a letter, confessing everything. I don't suppose you knew?'

I shook my head. I had been ready to disclose the truth myself by now – but better, probably, to leave things as they were.

'Well, never mind, Libertus. No one can be clever all the time!' Marcus seemed amused to think that I had failed. 'I'm glad to say that you were right on other counts. I've spoken to Nutricia and she's agreed to stay – though I fear that I shall still have to go to Rome. However, I'll be back before the baby comes – perhaps we'll be able to go back again, a little later, as a family. Pertinax may want me to be close at hand.' He beamed at me. 'And what would you do, if I were not here? I could commend you as a client to Alfredus Allius. He seems to think highly of your talents, as it is. Or would you rather I proposed you for some office in the town? They'll be wanting another aedile very soon – and they're short of a candidate, with Genialis dead.'

I shook my head. 'Patron, it is far too soon to think of things like that. Who knows what the Emperor will have in mind for you? You may end up as Governor of Britannia, yet.'

He preened a little. Flattery always pleased him, though what I said was true. 'Well, we shall see. Perhaps if this child turns out to be a girl, we might even leave her in Glevum to be nursed. We could name you as my proxy, to be her guardian. In the meantime, you have something to report?'

'It concerns that list of names that you consulted me about.' I produced it from the leather pocket at my belt. 'I have made a note of everything I've learned about each person, underneath the name. I think you'll find your questions answered, Excellence.' I handed him the little scroll of bark paper.

I did so proudly. It was a labour which had taken many hours, but he scarcely looked at it. 'Excellent, Libertus. Though I may not need it now. Lucius has forfeited his rights, of course, and I think I shall let Alfredus Allius have the warehouse after all. He's prepared to pay a handsome price for it – says he'll keep that steward on to run the place for him – and I don't think I really have an eye for common trade. So if there's nothing else...?' He stood up, smiling, and clapped his hands to summon in a slave. 'We'll order some refreshments and then we'll let you go.'

'There is just one thing, Excellence,' I said. 'I've learned there is a chance that you could add to your estate. There is a little farm nearby which has come up for sale – the farmer has been ruined by this recent snow and he's compelled to leave it and move on elsewhere. He's commissioned me to find a buyer, and I thought of you. It's not in good condition – he has not had the labour to make the most of it – but with your land slaves it could soon be turned to useful fields. I know that you were thinking about trying out some vines – and if you had some money from Silvia's estate...?'

Marcus looked at me. 'I take it that there's something in this deal for you?'

I nodded. 'A little something, Excellence. And he also has some information that he's promised me – something about that ancient priest who died and some peculiar kind of sacrifice he once helped to make. He's written it all down. It might be relevant. I'm sure the temple would be grateful if you passed it on to them. But that's dependent on my managing to find a purchaser for him. Though I don't expect it will be difficult. He's forced to sell, and quickly, so it's a bargain at the price.'

Marcus grunted, but it was not an angry sound. 'Oh, very well. I think I know the place, and it might be suitable. What is he asking?'

I named a price – a little more than I'd suggested to Cantalarius.

My patron shook his head. 'It's far too much! I don't know why I'm thinking of extra land at all. There is no advantage if I am leaving anyway.'

'On the contrary, husband!' Julia had been listening to all this. 'The bigger the estate, the more you'll get for it. And if this is the farmstead that I think it is – it will make a perfect package with the land you've got. Besides, I'm sure Libertus would not give you poor advice.'

'I think I could persuade him to reduce the price a bit,' I said, nominating the proper sum this time.

Marcus said, 'Hmmm!' and stroked a thoughtful chin. My little subterfuge was having an effect.

'And, husband, there's another thing you haven't thought about,' his wife put in. 'If you have more children, you need more land to leave.'

He looked at her, his handsome face dissolving in a smile. If this deal succeeded, I'd have Julia to thank. 'Oh, very well, Libertus. Draw up a bond and find some witnesses. I'll put my seal to it. How soon can we have the ownership conveyed?'

'As soon as possible,' I said. 'He has vacated it. I'm to convey the money to her parents' home, which they have retired to for the present. I think they hope to find a smaller place elsewhere. Across the northern border with the Picts, perhaps – they have acquaintances there. She has some scheme for keeping ewes and making cheese for sale.'

'Talking of cheese,' his wife said, plucking at her husband's sleeve. 'Your slave's been waiting in the doorway for several moments now.

Don't you want him to fetch some refreshments for us all?'

Marcus gave his orders – 'Figs and cheese and wine!' – and the servant went trotting off again.

Julia turned to me. 'Well, I'm glad to have solved the problem of the farm. And you say that you have made a little profit too? I hope so – you deserve it. You must have worked for hours to provide my husband with that information on the list. But you earn a little something from this, I believe?'

I nodded. 'A little something called Arlina,' I told her with a smile. 'A stubborn little creature with four legs and a tail. I just hope my wife is pleased. Gwellia has been telling me all year that I should get a mule.'